Praise for *Giraffe*

"By any standard an ambitious and remarkable first novel. . . . I was continually reminded of Harold Bloom's remark about all great books being strange." —*The New York Times*

"Mournful yet lovely . . . A bravura debut, a rich composition with suggestions of steelier Scottish organizational rigor below its mazy surface. . . . As in an archeological operation, the author uses brushstrokes to lay bare a mood, a state of mind that in its era was all-consuming and now . . . though faded into folkore still evokes an enduring measure of terror." —*San Francisco Chronicle*

"*Giraffe* is a fantastic beast . . . Dreamy and yet gripping, it offers the bravura opening of the year." —*The Guardian* (London)

"A profoundly affecting debut novel that will wake you up and break your heart. . . . A stunning and richly thematic work; highly recommended." —*Library Journal*

"W. G. Sebald meets Milan Kundera in this weird and wonderful tale." —*Esquire* (London)

"Ledgard is no ordinary writer. . . . A potent, disturbing dream, as if Radiohead's 'Idioteque' had mixed with something by the Japanese novelist Haruki Murakami. . . . *Giraffe* is as rich and sinewy as a fairy tale; it stirs up the reader's subconscious. Not a word is wasted." —*The Cleveland Plain Dealer*

"A masterly and poetic novel to be placed alongside writers as prestigious as W. G. Sebald."—*Le Nouvel Observateur* (Paris)

ABOUT THE AUTHOR

J. M. Ledgard was born on the Shetland Islands, Scotland, in 1968, and educated in England, Scotland, and America. He has been a foreign correspondent for *The Economist* since 1995 and is a contributor to *The Atlantic*. He divides his time between Europe and Africa.

Giraffe

J. M. Ledgard

PENGUIN BOOKS

PENGUIN BOOKS

Published by the Penguin Group

Penguin Group (USA) Inc., 375 Hudson Street, New York, New York 10014, U.S.A.

Penguin Group (Canada), 90 Eglinton Avenue East, Suite 700, Toronto,
Ontario, Canada M4P 2Y3 (a division of Pearson Penguin Canada Inc.)

Penguin Books Ltd, 80 Strand, London WC2R 0RL, England

Penguin Ireland, 25 St Stephen's Green, Dublin 2, Ireland (a division of Penguin Books Ltd)

Penguin Group (Australia), 250 Camberwell Road, Camberwell,
Victoria 3124, Australia (a division of Pearson Australia Group Pty Ltd)

Penguin Books India Pvt Ltd, 11 Community Centre,
Panchsheel Park, New Delhi – 110 017, India

Penguin Group (NZ), 67 Apollo Drive, Rosedale, North Shore 0745,
Auckland, New Zealand (a division of Pearson New Zealand Ltd)

Penguin Books (South Africa) (Pty) Ltd, 24 Sturdee Avenue,
Rosebank, Johannesburg 2196, South Africa

Penguin Books Ltd, Registered Offices:
80 Strand, London WC2R 0RL, England

First published in Great Britain by Jonathan Cape,
an imprint of The Random House Group 2006
First published in the United States of America by The Penguin Press,
a member of Penguin Group (USA) Inc. 2006
Published in Penguin Books 2007

10 9 8 7 6 5 4 3 2 1

Excerpt from "Song of the Spirits Over the Water" by Johann Wolfgang von Goethe,
translated by A. S. Kline. Copyright © A. S. Kline, 2004. Used with permission.

Excerpt from Bellini's "La Sonnambula," libretto by Felice Romani,
translated by Avril Bardoni, Decca Records.

PUBLISHER'S NOTE
This is a work of fiction. Names, characters, places, and incidents either are the product
of the author's imagination or are used fictitiously, and any resemblance to actual persons,
living or dead, business establishments, events, or locales is entirely coincidental.

THE LIBRARY OF CONGRESS HAS CATALOGED THE HARDCOVER EDITION AS FOLLOWS:
Ledgard, J. M.
Giraffe / J. M. Ledgard.
p. cm.
ISBN 1-59420-099-8 (hc.)
ISBN 978-0-14-303896-2 (pbk.)
1. Giraffe—Fiction.   2. Czechoslovakia—Fiction.   I. Title.
PR6112.E34G57 2006
813'.6—dc22   2006043784

Printed in the United States of America
Designed by Stephanie Huntwork

FOR MARTA ANNA

In Memoriam
Alexandr Hackenschmied

1907–2004

Democritus, if he were still on earth,
would deride a throng gazing
with open mouth at a beast
half camel, half leopard.

—HORACE

Snĕhurka

A Giraffe

ST. HUBERT'S DAY

NOVEMBER 3, 1971

I KICK NOW IN the darkness and see a coming light, molten, veined through the membrane and fluids of the sac, which contains me. I am squeezed toward the light. Let it be said: I enter this world without volition.

My hooves come first, then my nose, then the whole of my head. I hang halfway out. I swing. I fall. I am found, I am found at this moment, and my coming into being is a head-over-hooves tumble from weightlessness to weight and from the drowning, which has no memory, to what has breath and is yet to be.

It is white-hot out here, thin; it sears. The falling takes the longest time. The first thing I see is my own form, my hooves impossibly far away, slicked with fluid, and my mazed hide, bloodied, flickering in the haze, burning, as though I am not passing from my mother to the ground, but from the constellation Camelopardalis into the Earth's atmosphere.

The ground comes to me from upside down, a flopping view, flopping with my neck. I see a blue-and-cream swallow flying close and away up onto an ash-colored grassland, where forms of other animals and trees are pegged to the soil, not falling into the azure sky below. I hit the ground headfirst, with a thud. Dust rises about me and settles. I lie quite still, among gathering ants, taking the measure of the air and of gravity. I blink back the light of the sun. I feel my lungs swelling. My heart beats on its own account, for me alone. Such a volume of blood passes through my chambers, rises, and rises again, and sinks, circulating within me, creating a buoyancy that will keep me upright for all my living days.

My mother nudges me with a hoof and now with her nose. She licks membrane from my hide in a thoroughgoing manner. I do not stir. I remain motionless in the dust until the shadow of a cloud settles above me and comforts me; I am without understanding and remember nothing of constellations but only that it was darker and thicker where I came from. I slowly lift my neck. I kick out my legs. I try to stand. Several times I climb up and several times I fall back down, so there is a question about my form: How can I be upraised on such slender legs? Now I make it. I quiver here, beside my mother. Instincts and customs of the herd enter me, unbidden. I see the order of my captivity, my searching up, gravity pulling me down, and the resultant journeys across. The sounds of this world, which came at first to me as single and unbroken, break now into songs of the earth, of termites, vultures, armored beasts wallowing, and of my own breath. I run a little, from one cloud shadow to another and back again to my mother, as on stilts.

I know I will grow fast now, as grass after rain, and that the form of my growing shall be upward. This is as it should be, as it was ordained since my earliest embryonic stage, for I am a giraffe and everything about my body is for stretching up. I am a giraffe, I am about that space a little above the blade, and my bodily intent is to be elevated above all other living things, in defiance of gravity.

Sněhurka

I HAVE GROWN INTO the finest young cow in my herd. I move confidently down cuts in the hills of red stone that bound the ash-colored grassland and emerge at other places, among various striped zebras. Most of the giraffes born with me have died of sickness or been killed by predators in their infancy. No lioness has come for me. I am alive under these acacia trees. I browse on my hind legs now, in the upper branches, where bull giraffes most often have claim. I am aware: I see the green metal flying toward me in this white light. I try to move out of its path; I know it is a tranquilizer dart. It deeply pierces my rump. A band of Czechoslovakians resolves out of the thorn trees. I bleat once at them—the first audible sound I have ever made. I run in one direction; my herd runs in another. How I run from these Czechoslovakians! My legs extend, my mane catches in the wind. Faster and faster I go; I reach a full gallop, swifter than any horse. It is no use. The Czechoslovakians keep pace behind me in tan-colored trucks that bounce over dry streambeds and rip through insect trails.

Chemicals rise within me. I slow. My eyes open into hemispheres of panic and then dull from the etorphine. My head falls back, my muzzle rises, my ears flatten. I cannot go on. I have no breath; all the air in my trachea is dead. The trucks circle. Around and around they go, revving, braking, drawing close. I move toward a watering hole, thinking to drink. A Czechoslovakian in a safari hat jumps out of one of the trucks. He makes a hand signal. Two African men rush forward and steal in under me. They draw a short rope around the upper part of my forelegs and my chest. A few Czechoslovakians come close now and sling a noose about my neck. They all of them pull smoothly at the ropes. I reel. I collapse. I feel these men around me, upon me, impossibly above me. I try to kick out at them, to catch them with a hoof, but there is nothing in me, there is no control. The Czechoslovakian in the safari hat kneels down beside me. I feel his hands around my throat, searching for my jugular vein. He finds it. He takes a long needle and drives it through my hide into the vein and injects me with the antidote diprenorphine. I am blindfolded. My ears are packed with cotton wool and muslin. I feel myself hauled upright and walked to one of the trucks.

I am tied to hot planking and driven now on the back of this truck in a silence and blindness that is my own, that is not of the womb, but is instead immediate, fearful, buffeting, hot with the midday sun. I am unbound and unmasked at a makeshift camp under the red hills. The Czechoslovakians stop and stare up at me. They examine me and give me the name *Snĕhurka,* or Snow White, because of the unusual whiteness of my underbelly and legs, which they say reminds them of the snows of Kilimanjaro. From this point on, for as long as I live, the voices of men will call after me, "Snĕhurka!" They will call my name, and I will recognize the sound, as I have long ago learned to distinguish the sound of one insect from another.

There are many other captured giraffes in the camp. We are not divided between our subspecies. I am fenced in with Rothschild and Masai giraffes as well as other reticulated giraffes. We are not so separate. Our height and gaits are similar, our horns are the same iron color. Only the patterns of our hides are distinct: the Rothschild blotched, the Masai drawn in fig leaves of Adam, the reticulated, as mine, in a fine lattice of white. We might mingle and breed, although this sometimes produces blank offspring, free of any marking.

There is one young Rothschild bull placed in a pen by himself. He rushes about in fits. He snorts. He draws back his neck and shoulders in a bow and bares his yellow teeth like a wild ass. He keeps himself drawn tight until this moment, when the Czechoslovakians shrug, open the fencing, and set him free. I watch him buck and skid out past the

tents in the camp onto the grassland, disappearing quickly
out of sight.

"Look at his neck," one of the Czechoslovakians says.
"See how it rolls forward and back with each stride, like the
mast of a sailing ship in a heavy sea."

I STAND LOOSE AND SILENT near the fence. I am aware of
the barefoot African boys who feed me branches and fruit,
moving by me in the darkness. They carry pails of water and
walk with their heads down, watching for sharp stones. I
make out their patterns, the contrast between the pink soles
of their feet and the dusty black of their calves.

Czechoslovakians move between us, making observations,
taking measurements.

"There is socialism in our method," I hear them say. "Capitalists capture one or two giraffes, while we take an entire
herd; because our intention is political, to issue forth a new
subspecies."

Other Czechoslovakians are gathered around the camp-
fire. Their white faces are open to laughter and to drafts of
clear *slivovice,* or plum brandy. Their shadows fall giant-sized
and gaping-mouthed upon me and upon the other giraffes,
who are also silent and sleepless, who also step lightly through
these shadows, watching the lanterns the guards swing at the
edge of the camp to scare away hyenas. We watch through the
night how these guards set down their rifles and drop on their
haunches to contemplate the moon or to smoke a Czechoslovakian cigarette.

· · ·

A Czechosolvakian stops before me now.

"Sněhurka is strong enough for transport," he says to the others. "She will not die at sea."

"True enough," one of the others says. "And see how calm she is. Calm enough certainly to survive in our zoo."

I have no answer to this; I do not even bleat, and so am condemned to further captivity, not only of time and gravity, but in the passage across also. If only I had stood against the Czechoslovakians as the young bull giraffe did, baring my teeth, or stumbled deflated about the back of the enclosure, then perhaps the fence would be opened to me as it is now to the weak and nervous Masai giraffes. They are sorted and set free. They do not buck and skid off as the young bull did, but stand in the camp looking back at the rest of us, the strong and stately giraffes, wondering at our confinement, where food comes easily, without reaching up. Only after shots are fired over their heads do they move off.

The Czechoslovakians are closing down the camp. I am roped again and placed on a truck. I stand tethered here, looking deep into this cool dawn, waiting for them to come with the blindfold. I see a line of other giraffes similarly waiting. I see gray mist shrouding the caps of the red hills; the rains will be here soon. I see a single star low and bright over the grassland. I see the Masai giraffes turning lonely circles on the sunlit horizon, seemingly in flames.

I am driven down rutted tracks through villages I cannot see, to a railhead. My blindfold is removed. I am placed on a cattle car of a train bound for the Indian Ocean. It is crowded with the bodies of thirty-two other giraffes; our necks stretch far out of the car, over the tracks. The train jolts and shunts forward. I bleat once more—the second audible sound I have ever made. It is terrifying to move and yet remain standing still, to feel myself falling but never to strike the ground.

After a day and night, the train passes into a country that is lower and wetter, no longer ash-colored but verdant. African children run alongside when the train slows. They wave and shout up greetings to me and the other giraffes. Some of the children jump up to try to touch me. I look down at them as they rise, or through them. Their small bodies hover for an instant; their fingers stretch out to me. But I am too high, I am out of reach. They fall away again to the blade, which holds them close.

It is night. The train is halted on a cliff above a city. The Indian Ocean stretches out beyond the city, its waters cut up by trade winds. There is a harbor between the city and the ocean where ships are lit like soft glowing embers. The waters of the harbor are motionless, sheltered from the surf by a breakwater of coral. We stand halted on the cliff until the constellations have revolved under the ocean and Camelopardalis is submerged. Now the train starts forward again and I draw breath of the sea. We roll gently down from the cliff to the end of the line, past an old Portuguese fort, striking the buffers on a pier.

DAYS HAVE PASSED, so that I can taste salt on my hide. The sounds of this place have become wearisome, clacking; metal scrapes metal, ropes creak, hooves tear and split on concrete. We stand tall in this quarantine. There is clear water on either side of us, and an East German freighter, the *Eisfeld,* or *Ice Field,* is tied up before us. At some points in the day the ship casts a shadow over our enclosure, cooling and comforting us as the acacia trees have done. Czechoslovakians move on and off the *Eisfeld* with papers and equipment. East German sailors play cards and sunbathe on tarpaulins they roll out on the pier beside us. I have smelled other giraffes in these days, and they have pushed against me. I have stood alone at the edge of the quarantine also, watching movements in the water. I see flashes that I do not fully understand, which are not of an advancing predator, not of a rising hyena, but are the argent tentacles of brand-colored medusas and shoals of red fish advancing forward at great speed and at right angles.

"Sněhurka!"

I lean myself toward the sound, as plants turn toward the light; I have already begun to associate it with food and the offering of myself. I lean down and see a Czechoslovakian staring up at me. He holds a branch. I extend my tongue. I wrap it around the branch and take it. I begin to strip it bare. As I do so, I feel other men moving in behind me with ropes and harnesses. I am hooked once more.

"Now!" the Czechoslovakian shouts.

A crane whirs. I am raised up, off the blade. This is my point of departure. I am no longer in Africa, nor yet set down on the deck of the freighter. I float here, a reticulated giraffe, a camelopard, between shore and ship, sky and ground. My colors are white, dark chocolate, liver-red, russet-rayed in chestnut, yellow, black about my hooves. Saliva drools in strings from my mouth. My eyes are liquid opals, meeting the world enormous. I look down. I see Czechoslovakians and East Germans staring up at me. They shield their eyes. They must see my white belly against the sky.

*And the communication I have
got to make is, that he has
great expectations.*

——ÐICKENS

Emil

A Hemodynamicist

MAY 5, 1973

I AM NOT CONCERNED with the Communist moment, but with some beautiful moment gone before. I am a student of hidden flow. I imagine my own self as blood already passed through the heart and slowed in a distant part of the body, in the foot perhaps, and occupied there in remembrance of the cathedral-arched beauty of the ventricles.

I LIGHT a *Rudá hvězda,* or Red Star cigarette, and get up from the black plastic armchair by the elevators on the top floor of the "shipping company." I go to stand by the window. I look down. I inhale.

Československá Socialistická Republika, or ČSSR, unfurls itself before me in factories, towers, and delicate spires worked through with sump-black cobbled streets on which pass only red trams and white police cars and a very few citizens treading slowly along with a downcast air. It is unseasonably cold. Snowflakes sail horizontally in front of the window, not falling, but sailing to the horizon, as though the Earth has tilted and gravity has lost its will. The clouds are scudding now. They break open. A single beam of sunlight strikes the building and illuminates me. I am suddenly the golden center of my own triptych. An elderly couple look up from the street below. They see me, but only for a moment. The clouds close over. My triptych vanishes. My face cools. The couple drop their heads and walk on. So it is: I am no longer visible, I am already a faint outline of what has been.

The River Vltava flows past this building at cross-purposes with the snow. I cannot say how deep it is. As deep as two people, the one standing on the shoulders of the other? As deep as four people? I try to picture the contours of its bed, to calculate where the current scores it most deeply. I imagine the fish within it, hovering against the flow, their mouths in a bony *O,* their gills opening and clamping. I consider water passing over their scales, the viscosity of their eyeballs. There is a reflection on the water of the snowflakes, wheeling crystalline across, and of the clouds opening and closing, although the surface of the Vltava is smooth, because the wind runs above the ČSSR but hardly ever comes down and touches its face. I catch sight of a furled swan. It speeds away on the current, in the direction of Suchdol. Its whiteness reminds me of an angel, of a painting I have seen of the archangel Michael. I frame the swan, I photograph it with my eye. This is what I do when I see beauty. I take a picture. I shutter it with a blink, keep it in my mind, and turn it this way and that until the Communist moment recedes and beauty is in the ascendant.

The elevator opens. A small man steps out, biting his knuckles. His hands are doll-sized, white as porcelain. He looks at me inquiringly.

"Freymann?" he asks.

"Yes, sir," I say.

"Come with me, will you," he says, in Czech.

His voice is high-pitched, a warble. He is the "shipping director." I follow him down the length of the corridor. It is long and dimly lit. This is another thing I notice about Communism: how it lengthens and darkens the corridors of ČSSR, year by year, into the corridors of nightmares.

He ushers me in.

"Sit down, please," he warbles. "I won't be long."

He picks up the telephone and calls a "port" far away. I light another Red Star and tap it out into an ashtray, which rests on a stand next to my chair.

It is maritime in here. Large maps detail the shipping lanes of the Black Sea and the Baltic. There is an oil painting of an Austro-Hungarian schooner in a gilt frame. A scale model of a new Council for Mutual Economic Assistance, or COMECON, oil tanker sits on a side table. A coil of rope and an anchor are on the floor next to a Murmansk Shipping Company crate marked with the symbol of a pacing polar bear. I am removed from Czechoslovakia in this office: That is its purpose. It is not for me to be intimate with such salt-washed things. I have never seen the sea, and when I imagine it, I envisage only a passage from a children's story in which boys pick yellow starfish from rock pools while gulls sweep and bomb above and waves break somehow polyphonically in caves beyond.

This is a shipping company in my landlocked country, on which no wave has ever broken, where there is not a single vantage point from which to sit and contemplate the turning of a tide; in my Czechoslovakia, which has no memory of the sea and no words for *spume* or *barnacle* or *jetsam*. In our fairy tales the first kings do not arrive windburned in longships from across the sea. They grope blindly from out of the side of breast-shaped hills, caked in peat, as though they are a crop sown by God for this land and no other. Our freshwater streams are narrow, shallow, unpeeled by the moon, are tepid, muddy, and thick-haired with reeds. Only milk-aspected fish, voles, *vodníks,* and *rusalkas* move in them. We have no seals, no mermaids. Brine arrives in tins, from overland. The helical narwhal tusks and dolphin fetuses arranged on the shelves of the Strahov Monastery in Prague were purchased through an intermediary: The monks of Prague have not confessed before the body of any ocean, still less made their stand at the edge of the Atlantic, on wet-black cliffs among the storm petrels, as the Irish monks have done.

The windows in here give and release like a lung. We could be in a cabin of an old airship tethered over the Holešovice district. The tower is poorly constructed, of the Communist moment. It will not last. It is all glass. It will soon be shattered, just as the greenhouses of Czechoslovakian country manors were shattered with the coming of Communism.

The shipping director puts down the phone and lets out an involuntary spasm. "So you're the giraffe man?" he says in Russian.

"Yes," I say in Czech.

"Speak Russian in here."

"If you like," I say in Russian.

"I do like," he says. "What exactly is the nature of your work?"

"I study blood flow in vertical creatures, in men and giraffes. The morphology of the jugular vein and such."

He looks blank.

"Yes?" he says.

"The work has application for cosmonauts and high-altitude fliers," I say. "For instance, the skin of a giraffe is thick to protect it from thorns and is so tightly wrapped as to take on the qualities of an anti-gravity space suit, such as we should like to design, which does not allow blood to settle in the lower extremities of the body."

"I see," he says.

"I am especially interested in the journey blood makes through the brain of a giraffe."

He blinks.

I must also look blank. I am distracted now with the thought of circulation in a cosmonaut who falls down to the desert from space and feels the weight of his own body there in the sand as a mortal pin through the breastplate of his silver suit—as though he were a butterfly pinned to a specimen case.

"Are your giraffes ferocious beasts?" he asks.

"Not at all. Giraffes are timid and tolerant of one another. They share food. They seldom fight. They have few enemies, comrade director, because their territory is up, in the branches of trees, rather than along. Although it is true that a giraffe can kick out in any direction with the force of several horses, and leopards have been found decapitated and lions with their heads caved in from where a giraffe struck them with full force of hoof."

He considers this.

"Are they swift?"

"Giraffes can outrun the fleetest horse," I say.

"A Turkmen horse even?"

"Only for a short distance. They tire easily. Their lungs are not big enough to compensate for their size or for the length of their windpipe."

"Hunting them must be simple."

I nod. "The Omanis used to hunt giraffes by following them on horseback. When the giraffe slowed, they moved in close. They leaned out of their saddle, like this"—I lean out of my chair and indicate the ashtray stand as the leg of the giraffe—"and with a single blow of the sword, severed the hamstrings, popped them, so that the giraffe collapsed forward into the dust, like a falling minaret."

"Very good," he says. "Emil, is it?"

"Yes."

"When I say 'Soviet Union,' what is the first thing you think of?"

"Space rockets."

"And again."

"Desert."

"And again?"

"Forest, endless forest."

"Brother?"

I almost say, *Cain*.

"Yes," I say, flushing. "Of course—fraternal relations."

"The proletariat will be triumphant forever. Yes or no?"
Another bite of his knuckles.

"Excuse me?"

"Yes or no?"

"Yes."

"Good, good. Are you religious?"

I want to say, "Communism is a religion also." I want to
say, "Communism is the religion of a flightless bird, a penguin, which has no imagination of flight."

"I believe, yes," I say.

A small bite on the back of his hand. "Unfortunate."

"For you, comrade?"

"Don't be trite. I've seen a man walking on water." He
looks at me closely. "You don't believe me?"

"I've no reason not to believe you," I say.

"Well, it is true," he says. "A remarkable sight. I visited the
port of Arkhangel'sk and took a fishing boat, which sailed for
some days into the White Sea. It was summertime, but the sea
was cold—ice drifted to us from the forested shore. Have you
ever seen the sea, Freymann?"

"No, sir."

"Can you imagine it?"

"I've seen films, pictures."

"The White Sea is not white, you should understand, but of dark changing colors. On the third day, we hit fish. So many fish! We drew up the net. It was a biblical scene, as you might say. The catch was too large. We could not take it on board. If we had done so, we should have sunk. Yet it was hard to let all those fish go. There was an experienced crew member. A blond Estonian—yes, not unlike you, but older and stronger, with nothing left to prove. While we made plans, he walked off the boat—onto the sea! He walked on water, or rather on the heads and bodies of the fish thrashing there at the surface. When he came to the net, he took his knife, reached in, and cut it open. Fish rushed out. He sank to his knees, as though in melting snow. We thought he would disappear whole into the White Sea and drown. We called out to him. He turned to face us momentarily, then looked up. He smiled and appeared transfixed by a gyrfalcon hovering above in the fierce winds. He contemplated the gyrfalcon for what seemed to us an age, then walked on water calmly back to the boat. Through his labor the net was bled of enough of the fish for us to be able to haul it on board."

He stops. "So there is a miracle for you," he says.

"Remarkable," I say.

"You've never seen the sea—have you ever been out of the country?"

"I once went to Hungary."

"All the more exciting this will be for you, then. What we want from you, Emil, is to travel up to Hamburg and supervise the unloading and passage back to Czechoslovakia of an important shipment."

"You want me to go west?"

He gives me a weary look.

"Yes, Freymann. West Germany."

He asks me if I have heard of a zoo in a certain Czecho-slovakian town.

"Yes," I say.

"It is due a shipment of giraffes. Let's see." He opens a ring binder with his tiny fingers and lifts out a few pages. "Here we are. Thirty-three giraffes. A record number, by all accounts. The zoo director is sailing with them from Mombasa in the next week or so. The giraffes are the property of the Ministry of Agriculture, although the shipping company underwrote some of the costs of their capture and transport."

He puts an index finger in his mouth, nibbles. His expression is pained now. "There are concerns about the sale of sensitive information about your ČSSR—or indeed the sale of the giraffes themselves—to unfriendly foreign elements. You'll travel to Hamburg, keep an eye on things, listen out for what concerns us, and make sure all the property reaches Czechoslovakia in good order." He looks up. "But that's all incidental," he says. "The main point is to establish your cover for future operations. You'll be a scientist sponsored by a shipping concern, nothing more. So how about it, Freymann—can you manage?"

"Why me?"

"You're the giraffe man, aren't you?"

"Just giraffe blood, comrade. I just deal in hemodynamics."

"You've the perfect cover. You'll get us access to foreign laboratories. Write some scientific paper from this trip. Indulge yourself. Yes?"

"I'll do my best."

"I know you will, Emil."

I stand. I push back my hair. He slips the pages back into the ring binder. I take it. I open it and see written inside the cover in a flowing hand:

giraffe!

"Thank you, comrade director."

"We'll make a start on your permissions," he says, addressing a finger to his mouth.

I go out. I flick through the file in the lengthening corridor. There is the sound of discordant typing, both fluent and clumsy. I lean against the wall. Only a single image of a giraffe comes to me at this moment; all my learning has been reduced to a giraffe of indistinct color. I see the height of the beast; its neck is translucent; I see blood shooting up its carotid artery to the rete mirabile, or wonder net, stretched elastic at the base of the cranium. The giraffe does not move; it does not turn toward me.

I WALK AWAY from the glass tower now, down Jankovcova Street to the Vltava. I turn up my collar against the cold. I come to the river. It is a vein, opened to the sky. It pleases me. I am a hemodynamicist and I cannot help seeing rivers as veins, and veins as rivers. I am given over, as I told the shipping director, to the study of cerebral hemodynamics in vertical creatures, in men and giraffes. That is, the flow of blood toward and through the brain, a journey that has no begin-

ning or end save in the last beat of the heart, at which point
the veins collapse—the cosmic catastrophe—along with all
calculations. I do not feel the weight of my skull pushed up,
as if on a stick, from this soot-dusted embankment. If I
could hold it in my hands, here beside the Liben Bridge, I
would be surprised at its heft—most of it blood. My intent is
to model the flow of this blood through the brain. I wish to
map out its sinks and eddies, its oxbows, and the estuarine
channels of the wonder net. I use sound waves to determine
the variable depth of arterial walls. (For a long time, arteries
were not understood. The garroting of specimen animals for
dissection engorged the right ventricle and so emptied the
arteries of blood, so they came to be called *arteria,* or tubes,
and were assigned a pneumatic purpose, of pumping air
around the body.) Blood finds no sea. It courses through narrows and rapids of ligament, flows upward against gravity,
and becomes momentarily weightless in the deep of the
brain, where thoughts shoot like comets through a firmament
of crimson stars that give oxygen but no light. Blood is not
opened to the sky; its journey is a hidden flow, is without
light, save in the dawntide, which works into the thin blood
vessels woven across wrist- and anklebones.

I leave the Vltava and walk now through the warehouses
of Holešovice, under Czechoslovakian flags of red, white,
and blue and Soviet flags of red slotted into the conical hold-
ers the State has decreed must be drilled into the masonry of
every building. The flags hang limply. This is something else I
notice about the Communist moment: how it celebrates itself
in a windless land with a display of flags. I quicken my pace. I
am drawn now, like a moth, toward an electric sign blinking

on and off over the main gates of a brick-making factory. A
space rocket bearing the initials čSSR bursts moon-ward from
the slogan

GLORY TO THE EPOCH OF SOCIALIST
AND COMMUNIST CONSTRUCTION!

The initials čSSR and the space rocket blink on and off.
The slogan is ever lit. I look at the potholed street. I walk
under the sign. I do not look up, but see fairground reflections in the puddles of an epoch blinking on, then off.

I catch a tram and walk and come to a pub overlooking
Stromovka Park. I step inside. It is yellow in here. The lights
are yellow, the tablecloths are stained yellow, the walls and air
are yellow with cigarette smoke; there is a jaundiced man
propping up the bar, there are maple-yellow ice-hockey sticks
lined up by the door. I take a beer and sit in a corner. I pull
from my bag a copy of *Great Expectations* by Charles Dickens.
It is a Czechoslovakian edition from before the war. This volume means something to me. It belonged to my uncle. Inside
the front cover there is an admonition he scrawled in large
letters as a child:

Learn from Pip

I flick through it at random, as the pious do with their Bibles.
The paper is yellow.

Death is a confirmed habit into which we have fallen.

is scrawled on the margin of one page. A few phrases are underlined throughout:

What larks!

*And the communication I have got to make is,
that he has great expectations.*

I see an exclamation mark in the margin where Wemmick, the law clerk, carries a fishing rod on his shoulder through London, not with any intent of fishing in the River Thames, but simply because he likes to walk with one:

*I thought this odd; however, I said nothing,
and we set off.*

I shut the book and open it once more and put a finger to a page.

"That was a memorable day to me," I read, "for it made great changes in me. But, it is the same with any life. Imagine one selected day struck out of it, and think how different its course would have been. Pause you who read this, and think for a moment of the long chain of iron or gold, of thorns or flowers, that would never have bound you, but for the formation of the first link on one memorable day."

I know this passage well. The book often opens to this page. This is where Pip returns home from Miss Havisham's for the first time. He has come to understand his position in the world. He sees himself anew, as a common boy with coarse manners and laborer's boots. I read the passage once more. I try to make the words fit my situation.

I cannot. I am an adult, Pip is a child. West Germany is not Miss Havisham's. My education has been limited by the Communist moment, not by poverty, as Pip's has been. My manners are not particularly coarse, my shoes are foreign, well soled, not those of a laborer. It is true this has been a memorable day for me. I am bound by a long chain of iron, after Pip's description. But the links are not of my making; they were formed in the year of my birth, 1948, the year in which the Communists took Czechoslovakia by the neck and wrung it. I close my *Great Expectations.* I look around this pub. The faces I see, one after the other, are yellow, indistinct, banal. They are bound also. They outwardly conform. There is no solidarity here. Solidarity is as likely, the expression goes, as a fire under a waterfall.

Emil

MAY 7, 1973

The sky over Prague is dashed, flashing. A sudden warm rainstorm washes down in sweet hyphens over Antonín Dvořák's grave in Vyšehrad, where I kneel now and lay down flowers. Standing, with Slavonic dances in my head, I see the rain passing over the Soviet military barracks in Smichov and wetting the bronze horses rearing up on the roof of the Národní Divadlo, or national theater, and causing Morse code in the sky over Letná Park, toward the apartment blocks of Obráncu miru.

I am named Emil for Emil Tischbein, the hero in Erich Kästner's children's stories, who famously led a band of child detectives through Berlin in pursuit of a thief. I bear an uncanny likeness to the illustrations in those books, as if I am an adult version of Kästner's boy, grown up in 1960s ČSSR. I have the same mop of golden hair, which falls across my face in the same diagonal way and is pushed back between the fingers of my right hand in just the same manner. I have the same slate-colored eyes, the same button nose. I thrust my hands in my pockets, rock back on my heels, and smile shyly after friends and strangers alike, just as fictional Emil does, in a manner meant to suggest good nature and honesty. I am Czechoslovakian—of course I am; I am bound. But cycling down from Vyšehrad now through Prague in the blushing light of this spring shower, I look more Danish or Pomeranian: The whole of me bears the flaxen mark of the Baltic Sea, which I do not imagine as a dark sea on which a man might walk, indeed not as a sea at all, but as a marine light falling through the unstained windows of a Kaliningrad cathedral flensed of ornament onto the whitewashed grave of Immanuel Kant, while outside, Soviet battleships ride at anchor on vaguely realized swells.

The rain stops. The sun rolls largely over shining roofs. I freewheel on my bicycle down into Dejvice, around the circle, past the tram stop at Zelená Street, past the Hotel International, and on up Baba Hill. This is my hill: I live atop it. I cycle or walk it daily and barely notice its incline. My feet dig into the pedals now, my body rises without instruction from the saddle. I pass the red-clay tennis courts. The coach waves to me. I wave back. My bicycle rolls from right to left. I physically loosen and lighten as I ascend, as though my calculations and deceptions weigh something and can be cast off as I near home, although I know this is not so, that gravity is more insistent among those we love.

I step off my bicycle outside the Freymann villa at the end of Nad Pat'ankou Street: my home. The air here is sifted with sulfur smoke drifting in from high chimneys far away. The large windows of the villa glint in the afternoon light. My grandfather commissioned the villa in 1929 to resemble the prow of a big American train running sunlit through the desert down to Los Angeles. Other functionalist villas were built on Baba Hill then to break the pull of Hapsburg Prague, which hovered planetary on the horizon in black and gold. But the Czechoslovakia these villas were erected to celebrate has long since been plowed under. There have been so many departures from this hillside—to death camps, hard-labor camps, internal exile in villages or industrial towns, to New York, London, Munich, and Tel Aviv. Baba stumbles on as Prague stumbles on, as a wasted body in a fine suit.

I open the front door. I call out. There is no answer. I walk on into silence, into cream and mercury. I feel myself to have boarded some train in a desert, for this is a home of passage, in which there is hardly anything of the Communist moment. My father was raised here. My brothers and my sister and I have been raised here. I descend the stairs now by spare walls, untouched but for a few art photographs. I open the windows of my room onto the garden, lined with dark pine trees, which slopes down to the Dukla soccer stadium below. In summer, the shadows of my parents and the trowels and forks they carry about the garden play on the walls of my room, comforting me and keeping alive within me a sense of childhood.

My father read *Emil and the Detectives* aloud to me as a child. He read tenderly, because he understood the horrors awaiting fictional Emil. If that boy, also with slate-colored eyes, grew into a man and left the pages of the book, he would die fighting in the siege of Stalingrad or drown soundlessly in a U-boat far out in the Barents Sea. If he remained a boy like Peter Pan and lived the same adventure over and over, there would come a time when he was delivered into a Berlin that was burning. And who would care about the money stolen from him—those few notes removed from his jacket while he slept on the train, which made for the adventure—if he had alighted at Berlin Zoo station not in 1930, as the book has it, but in 1944, when the bombs were falling? How many child detectives would fictional Emil have been able to rally to his cause then, when real boys yet smaller than him wore uniforms, carried guns, and died in large numbers?

"Emil Tischbein is free in the way I wish you to be free," my father said.

This was at a family celebration in a country orchard. There were striped deck chairs, Chinese lanterns, beer and sausages cooking on an open fire. Blossoms drifted among the elderly relatives, who sat as they had as children, with their feet in a stream.

"I want you to listen to me now, Emil," my father said.

"I'm listening."

"This other Emil wants to show us it is possible for a child to be upstanding without the authority of a uniform."

"A child such as me?"

"Such as you. *Tischbein* means table leg in German. You can depend on a *tischbein*. Just as there is no question the Tischbeins, mother and son, despised all the Nazis stood for. That's why the Nazis burned *Emil and the Detectives*. They thought it subversive. They threw *Emil* on the pyre."

"They burned him, really?"

"Yes, imagine that," my father said. "As if he were a pestilence."

I DO IMAGINE IT. Fictional Emil going up in flames, page by page, hands in pockets, rocking back on his heels, his shy smile not changing, his innocence intact. There is no more book-burning. *Emil and the Detectives* simply goes unpublished. A few copies of the book are locked away in the cellars of my country's libraries, secured there behind heavy doors so that no one can hear fictional Emil's cries of "Stop, thief!" as he races through the streets of Berlin.

There are other signs of burning in this ČSSR of 1973. We run here and there through the woods in fear of mass incineration during nuclear drills, remembering as we run in suits and masks students who doused themselves in gasoline and made human torches of themselves in protest at our captivity. Pinned to the breast of every child during sessions of Communist indoctrination, there are enamel badges showing three flames, the largest for Party members, the smallest for little children learning to march and sing workers' songs, and the other for teenagers asked to stand at attention beside the grave of a revolutionary martyr, on which flickers an eternal flame. This is another thing I notice about Communism: how its youthful symbol is a book of knowledge set alight and no one comments on it.

THE LIGHT IS ALCHEMICAL in the kitchen now, on the clear fluted jars of dried mushrooms and forest honey. I pick up a paper airplane from a chair and float it across the room. An old postcard rests against a jug of wildflowers on the long table. Only objects with utility or resonance remain apparent in our house: The card must have been left out for a purpose. I pick it up. It was sent from Munich in 1899 to a long-dead Freymann, living then in the Hradčany district of Prague. The address marks out Bohemia as a province of Austria. The message is written in a florid hand but conveys only that the sender will return to Prague by the Thursday morning train. I turn it over. A self-portrait by Albrecht Dürer stares out at me. It dates from 1500. I study the braided hair, the trimmed beard, the expensive fur coat of martens and mink. I note the long fingers scandalously set in mock benediction: This is Dürer as Christ. I hold the postcard up to this strange light. Art can puncture time, so that what has passed can become what is yet to be. The note on the card was written in expectation of a journey to a Bohemia that is no more, while Dürer's self-portrait is futuristic, pushed far out beyond this ČSSR. And this is the way it is with the photographs on the walls of the villa. They were taken by avant-garde Czechoslovakian photographers before the Second World War, before the exterminations, the clearances, the departures and silences, but they are openings, windows speaking to me of some moment not yet arrived.

. . . .

I VENTURE ONTO the observation deck on the roof terrace, which juts out over the garden like a diving board or a gangplank. My grandfather had it built: He owned a small airline and wished to see his planes taking off from a nearby grass runway. The pilots dipped low over Nad Pat'ankou Street in those hopeful days, and my grandfather leaned back against the deck railings and waved his hat at them as they set off for Dresden and Vienna and sometimes as far as Bucharest, which was all glamour then, with a Columbia Records shop near Palatul Telefoanelor selling all the new tunes and Dragomir Niculescu's delicatessen on the corner of Calea Victoriei supplying the fine breads and cheeses, champagnes, beers, and chocolates. "A Dacian King Kong Manhattan," my grandfather said of the oil barons and Transylvanian industrialists, from whom he made plenty of money. It is my habit to stand on the observation deck on clear mornings and evenings in search of beauty. The photographs in the house have done this to me. They have given me an eye that does not sweep as a human eye should sweep, as a cinematographer sweeps, but one which is always stopped photographic in search of beauty.

I look about me and frame and shutter some beauty now. I stare at the *paneláks,* which are tower blocks made of thin concrete panels, rising gray from Bohnice Hill. I keep a few of their windows that are flecked with twilight, like gemstones. I keep the portion of the sky that is spangled with coming stars. I keep the kit of pigeons flying in an arrowhead formation down the River Vltava, which flows black and brown, silent, at the base of Baba Hill. I stop the pigeons as they touch the Vltava with their wings. I watch the kit rise now toward the red-starred fighter jets patrolling far above. I keep the white contrails the fighter jets let out, that join one emerging star to another as children join dots to form a picture. I watch these contrails dissolve into the finest tissue lines, like the scars on my wrist where I cut myself with a pencil-sharpener blade as a boy, letting out droplets of blood. I most often frame the way light strikes objects or landscapes. People are harder to frame. They meet my eye when I stare at them and cause me to turn away. If I frame a person, it is fleeting, when he or she is unaware, caught at a strange angle, or in repose. Animals are easier. They move more predictably. I know this because the Prague Zoo is just down there, on the far bank of the Vltava. I can see the cages strung along the riverbank (when the floods came, they carried off a Persian leopard, which miraculously made it, bedraggled, to the shore downstream, where it prowled the flooded meadows for months afterward). On clear mornings I can frame the sea lions parting the waters of their kidney-shaped pool, but it is too dark now to make out the sea lions or to discern the whiteness of the polar bear; it is too dark even to see the tiger burning bright.

I lean over the railing. I measure the space between the deck and the sloping garden. I feel gravity coming up at me, as if with hands, to pull me underwater. I am drawn to the edge of things, to margins and borders. I stand beside windows. I hike up to escarpments and teeter at the lip of limestone quarries. In 1961 my mother was on a team of

architects who built the noted swimming pool in the Podolí
district of Prague. She designed the high-diving platform. We
venture to Podolí once or twice each summer, as a family. The
point is not to weave a front crawl through the crowds in the
pool, or to sunbathe beside the pool, but to admire the form
of her tower, rising slender, yes, like a giraffe. I climb to the
top of the platform on such outings. I stand at the edge, at
the head of the giraffe, my toes out in space, my hands at my
sides. It is my intention to dive. I look out. There is a fine view
of Prague up there—not planetary black and gold, but green
and blue. I look down at the pool, far below. Invariably, I see a
few faces upturned toward me, looking at me, as did the elderly couple when I appeared to them in the triptych of my
imagination. It is only then that I experience vertigo. Dizzi-
ness overcomes me. I know vertigo has a hemodynamic
explanation: It is nothing more than restricted flow through
my vertebral artery. Still, I cannot let go. Fictional Emil would
dive. He would do a swan dive. Pip would dive. He would be
amazed and humbled, but he would dive. He would carefully
take off his jacket and laborer's boots and set them on the
platform, and he would fall without understanding, grabbing
the air, snatching at it as he fell, in trousers and shirt, calling
out for a blacksmith. I stumble backward from the edge. I
grab railings, inspired by the railings I grip now. I persuade
myself that I am being sensible, that I would drift in my dive
under a gust of wind and strike concrete, ending up with a
broken neck, paralyzed, with nothing to frame but a ceiling,
and not even the cathedral ceiling of Kant. But there is no
wind in our ČSSR. There is not even the faintest zephyr to

stir the flags of the Communist moment. I teeter, I peer down. But in the end I am about safety; I make the safe choice.

I MOVE BACK from the railing and step dizzily to the study at the far end of the roof terrace. I switch on a lamp. I arrange my giraffe papers and the ring binder from the shipping company on the desk and lay out the diagrams of blood flow on the floor: all the capillaries and shunts I have so far traced through the mesh of the giraffe's wonder net.

The study is three walls of glass and one of brick. There are two black-and-white photographs on the brick wall that have never changed position. I know them as openings, other types of windows into past and future moments. The first is of Prague Castle in 1932. It was taken from high up on a south-facing flying buttress of St. Vitus's Cathedral, our national church, looking down into the third courtyard of the castle. The view is vertiginous—a suicidal plunge. My eye is not drawn now to the baroque palaces lining the edge of the courtyard or to the needle obelisk in the center, but to the flagstones of the courtyard arranged in a diagonal grid of black-and-white squares. It is an optical illusion, I know, perhaps induced by blood flow, but I do not see a commonplace pattern. I see something more sinister: The flagstones appear to me as a grid of cages, a captivity into which one might fall.

The second photograph was taken in India. A man falls face-first into the River Ganges, his arms stretched up. He wears a cloth around his waist, but is otherwise naked. His face is touching the sacred waters: The bridge of his nose has not yet broken the skin of the river, while his mouth, chin, chest, and palms are already submerged. Streamers of bandage float about the pilgrim, and flowers and spent pieces of charcoal from funeral pyres. The surface teems with reflections of the quick and the dead, but the crop is such that none of them are in view. It is a lustrous print, black as boot polish. In my mind's eye I place colors of lapis, caramel, and henna in it. I make a comet of it in the deep of my brain. On it is written, by the author, *"Řeka života a smrti,"* or River of life and death. It is dated 1937. That means nothing. This photograph punctures time, as Dürer punctures time. It could be a thousand years in the past, or so far in the future as to make of our ČSSR a forgotten dream.

Emil

THE RED-STARRED FIGHTER JETS have all flown away to their bases in the mountains. The "zoo historian" leans forward on a hard chair and speaks to me of the flood that swept the Persian leopard from its cage, of waters that rose over the Prague Zoo and the gardens of the Troja Chateau by the zoo, where we sit now in his shabby office in inexplicable gloom, so that we are no more than shadows to each other. He tells me of seals swimming up to the steps of the chateau in floodwaters I imagine to be the color of the Ganges, and similarly full of new dead.

"They looked to me like giant newts, coming at the end of

the world," he says. "They swam around the baroque statues depicting virtues and vices, of which only charity remained eerily above water."

We come to the question of captivity.

"I am a historian of captivity," he says.

"The captivity of people also?" I ask.

"A passing knowledge," he says.

"Giraffes?"

He smiles.

"I recently instructed a zookeeper in the history of giraffes," he says. "I will speak to you of gyrfalcons, polar bears, and giraffes."

"Go on," I say unsteadily.

I prepare my pen. I am the giraffe man now and I must know more of these vertical beasts than the viscoelasticity of their arteries.

I smell the soil of the vineyard coming through the open window. I hear the animals in the zoo, beyond the walls of the chateau. He coughs phlegm into a cloth. His office is damp, littered in the corners with mice droppings. I look away, out through the open window, and see candlelight flickering in the chapel above the vineyard.

"The Romans were dazzled by the proportions and colors of the giraffe," he says, quelling his cough, "which they took to be the offspring of a camel and a leopard, so *camelopardalis* or camelopard; others thought better camel-hyena, that a hyena had taken a camel mare and the offspring, the giraffe, was mute on account of the violence of the hyena's entry. In any case, the giraffe was of limited entertainment value to the Romans. It could not easily kill or defend itself from being killed. It could not roar or trumpet. If it appeared in a ring at all, it was only as a curtain-raiser at the beginning of the games. Five thousand wild animals were slaughtered for the inaugural games of the Colosseum. Eleven thousand were put to the sword during the four months of games marking the victory of Trajan over the Dacians."

I consider the cosmic collapse of so many veins. "Rivers of blood," I say.

"Indeed. Rivers such as would further your studies," he says.

Is he looking at me in this gloom? I see his hand movements, but not his expression.

"These beasts arrived in Rome from the corners of the known world in stinking wooden crates, some dead, others sick in the head or in the body."

"What animals," I ask. "From where?"

He is silent, drawing a map in his head.

"Lynxes, brown and black bears, boars, wolves, and wolverines from the north," he says. "Tigers from Armenia. Cheetahs from Judaea. Lions, leopards, hyenas, hippos, elephants, and giraffes from Nubia and the lands beyond the Sahara. Many of these beasts were dispatched by specialized gladiators: *venatores*. Others were set one against another. Still others were released, starving, into an arena that contained nothing but men lashed to metal rings in the sand, as though bound to the earth itself. This was not just in Rome. Other wild animals were killed in smaller games across the empire. Their forms and those of the gladiators and the prisoners were tipped together into pits dug after the games, close to the arena. In some places it must have been that the corpse of a fair-haired barbarian from Czechoslovakia, before there was a Czechoslovakia, fell upon the carcass of a freshly speared giraffe, and the two became entwined and rotted as one."

He catches his breath. I look out and regard a soldier, walking now through the vineyard to the candlelit chapel, a machine gun in his hand.

"When Rome collapsed," he continues, "the pits binding men and giraffes together were filled in and no more giraffes came to Europe."

"The Dark Ages were not illuminated by any giraffe?"

"None: the Roman skills of capturing and transporting wild animals were forgotten. No one knew anymore how to drive a jackal demented with the flashing of metal shields or how to use drums to lure a bear through an oak grove to a clearing in which a lamb runs unhappy circles around a stake."

"Cigarette?" I ask.

He shakes his head.

"In the medieval period, gyrfalcons and other creatures of the north came to be more sought after in Europe than giraffes," he says. "You've heard of these birds?"

"Yes," I say, and inwardly see an Estonian walking on water, looking up.

"Marco Polo believed the gyrfalcon hatched on an island so far north the Pole Star appears behind you. Kublai Khan favored them in his personal caravan while, in a dust cloud trailing to the horizon, several thousand falconers handled lesser birds. Gyrfalcons were valued for their beauty and for the way they had learned to hover in the ceaseless winds of

Iceland and Greenland, on Novaya Zemlya and other islands in the Kara Sea and the White Sea. When gyrfalcons swept back their wings and dived in those places, it was impossible to hear the sound of their fall for the splintering of the ice field. Yet they accommodated the wind, they were not distracted, they kept a straight line, they made their target."

He offers more tea.

"Now we come to polar bears and giraffes," he says. "In 1235, the Holy Roman Emperor Frederick the Second arranged for a line of beasts to parade behind him to Worms in celebration of his marriage to Isabella, the sister of Henry the Third of England. Most of these beasts came from his court in Palermo. They included a column of lynxes and apes of many kinds chained to Muslim slaves, who were themselves chained to one another by metal collars. There is no record of a giraffe having made that wedding journey to Worms, as surely there would have been if one had walked across the Alps at that time. Nor is it possible that the polar bear presented to Frederick by Haakon the Fourth of Norway was among the animals: it had been shipped to Damascus in 1233 as a gift to al-Kāmil, the sultan of Egypt." He pauses.

"I'm following," I say.

"In 1229, al-Kāmil ceded Jerusalem to Frederick in the bloodless Sixth Crusade. Ten years before that, the sultan had stood and listened respectfully as Saint Francis of Assisi preached to him of the rights of animals and on the question of the soul's captivity."

"What of the polar bear?"

"It was likely captured as a cub in Spitsbergen," he says. "No such animal had ever been seen in the Muslim world. It was led out in the cool of early mornings on a long rope to the banks of the River Barada and there encouraged to fish. So also was the polar bear Henry kept in the Tower of London, which was led down to the Thames each day so that it might catch a portion of its daily meat ration in salmon. Henry's polar bear was probably also a gift from Haakon. It was Haakon who had done most to introduce gyrfalcons to the courts of Europe and to the Muslim world. He sent a shipment of gyrfalcons to Henry, and his gyrfalcons flew over Frederick's Palermo. The Frankish city," he says, lost in the damp room, littered with droppings and without illumination, "which the Arabs called Al-Madīnah, had broad avenues, with a turquoise sea before it and yellow wheat plains behind it, through which jackals ran untroubled. Four springs rose in its suburbs, in which Muslims came to mosques at the call of the muezzin. Gardens and fruit trees were abundant. In the churches there were finely worked windows, which shone on altars of colored marble. Christian women of Palermo came to those churches on holy days dressed as Muslim women."

"Which is how?" I ask.

"Veiled," he says. "Garlanded in jewels and perfumed. Painted on the forearms and about the face, here and here, in the patterns of henna, so that, as one Muslim poet had it, 'going to church in Palermo, I came upon antelope and gazelles.' The palaces of Palermo were similarly set above the city as 'pearls encircling a woman's full throat.' Towers rose out of sight from the Qasr al-Qadim fortress. When Frederick's gyrfalcon flew over those towers in 1233 and looked down upon the menagerie arranged on the lawns below, it would no longer have seen a polar bear, but it must have spied a giraffe. For a giraffe had come to Palermo from Egypt in 1215, a gift from al-Kāmil to Frederick, the only giraffe in Europe, the specimen from which comes our word for the animal: *zarâfa,* from the Arabic meaning 'swift-moving.'"

HE CONTINUES ON, in the darkness.

"Around the time the cardinal Hippolyte was creating in Europe his menagerie of exotic human beings," he says, "which included Berbers, Welshmen, and Tartars, Montezuma was further expanding the immense zoo in the grounds of his palace in Tenochtitlán, which is now Mexico City. There were black and golden pumas caged there, together with ocelots, anteaters, and a bison from the North American prairies, a realm the Aztecs called the 'Land Beyond Night.' The Spanish tell us these animals were better cared for than the deformed men and women who made up the rest of the menagerie. Those poor souls were wards of the state. Their tongues were cut out. They limped or crawled about their cages. They were forced to drink pulque, or fermented cactus juice. They were a spectacle. At the solar eclipse, they were the first to be sacrificed to the jaguar, to water, to movement, to the sun and stars, or to the god Quetzalcoatl, with beaked brow, who blew storm clouds in over fields of maize. These men and women, sometimes limbless, or else blind, hydrocephalic, hunchbacked, were dragged up steep-sided pyramids by priests wearing masks of jade and obsidian, so that in their last swirling moments, they saw teeth of coral, eyes of red seashell, and chunks of alabaster, along with ingots of gold, eagles, snakes, and grasshoppers. Their opened bodies were thrown from the pyramids, so the sun shone through where their hearts had been. Their remains were cut into pieces and fed to the pumas. It was long before that, in 1405, that the Ming emperor of China, Cheng Zu, sent out a fleet under the command of Admiral Zheng He to open up new trade routes. Zheng He's sailors saw a giraffe in Bengal that had been sent from Malindi, and mistook it for a *qilin,* or unicorn—spoken of in Chinese prophecy, which was supposed to be the centerpiece of the Sacred Animal Garden of Intelligence laid out between Beijing and Nanjing several thousand years earlier by Wan, an emperor in the Zhou dynasty—because in China the unicorn was still represented with the horns of a giraffe, while in Europe, thanks to the trade in gyrfalcons and polar bears, the horn of the unicorn had come to be represented with the ivory tusk of the Arctic narwhal."

I WALK SWIFTLY HOME NOW, by the statue of charity in the chateau garden, and think of the two keen-eyed creatures brought to Palermo. If the giraffe had looked up, it would have seen the gyrfalcon. It would have been silent, but it would have seen. I try to see the palaces of Palermo as pearls encircling a woman's full throat and I come, in a turning of comets, to how Shakespeare brought Bohemia together with Sicily in *The Winter's Tale* and mistakenly gifted Bohemia a

gravel shore on which the Sicilians landed their ships. I walk
on, through the smoke-filled night of ČSSR, with the sound
of passing trains, and speak the opening line aloud:

> *If you shall chance, Camillo, to visit Bohemia . . .*
> *you shall see, as I have said, great difference betwixt*
> *our Bohemia and your Sicilia.*

Emil

SNOW PEARS AND SILVER LIMES and white elms flick by outside. It is summer now in Czechoslovakia. Wheat has risen in the fields. Mosquitoes dance over the hidden marshes in the forests. It is bright, sunlit, in here, at the window of my compartment. The train speeds toward East Berlin. My father stood, a little while ago, on the platform of the Hlavní Nádraží, or central station, in Prague. He waved me off. He ran alongside the train as it left. I pushed down my window and reached out my hand to his. Our fingertips brushed, as the wings of birds brush in flight. There was a fear in his eyes, that I might break Pip's long chain of iron and never return.

There is a young opera singer in the compartment with me. She has never seen the breast-shaped hills of northern Czechoslovakia before, from which our first kings are said to have emerged, caked in peat. She is moved to tears when I point them out, and name them for her.

"Milešovka and Kletečná are the highest," I say. "Then Lovoš, Oblík, Milá, Deblík, Boreč, and Hazmburk, with its old church."

She looks sickly. Her skin is thin, pale, as translucent to me as the neck of the unmoving giraffe I pictured in the corridor of the shipping company. I am diverted now by her operatic blood. I see it, coursing up. I make my hemodynamic calculations.

"Are you all right?" I ask.

"I'm fine, really I am," she says. "Are they very old? The hills, I mean."

"Oh, yes, epochs old. They're volcanoes. You could journey down through them to the center of the earth."

We can see only a few of the hills now. I frame one. It is seductive from this distance, a mound of soft earth and sweet grass with a nipple thicket of beech trees.

She is going as far as the town of Ústí nad Labem. She has a part in a production of Dvořák's opera *Rusalka* that is playing there.

"Just a small part," she says shyly, "of a nymph rising to the surface of a stream."

"Still," I say.

"Where are you going?" she asks.

I unfold a map for her, which includes parts of West Germany. I put a finger to Hamburg.

"I'm going here," I say.

My eye is drawn to the sea beyond Hamburg. I point also to the town of Cuxhaven.

"Here also."

I draw my finger around the islands of Scharhörn and Neuwerk, which I imagine as two black dots—gull's eyes staring up from a yet-vague swell. "Also here, to these two islands."

I indicate with a sweep the Heligoland Bight beyond Scharhörn and Neuwerk. "I'd also like to sail here."

"You must have seen the sea many times," she says.

I blush. I cannot lie so directly.

"No," I say. "I have only ever read stories of the sea."

I WAKE NOW in Deutsche Demokratische Republik, or DDR. The compartment is empty. That is Saxony out there, so flat and untroubled; those are Trabant 601's, little plastic wonder cars of DDR, putt-putting along moonlit country lanes overhung with elms and goat willows.

East Berlin's train station comes in an electric sign whose lettering, OSTBAHNHOF, brings with it an immediate sense of fictional Emil waiting at a street corner for a signal, and of me somewhere unborn in the Charlottenburg district, in West Berlin, flashing him that signal with a mirror from the window of an apartment. But my stop in divided Berlin is short. There is no thief for me to pursue: My wallet is untouched. I walk from this platform to another and board the night train to Hamburg. I arrange myself by the window. The train pulls out of the station, out past the columns of the great Pergamon Museum, within which I know are the winged bulls of Persepolis. Soldiers come into the compartment. They lower the blinds and secure the window against the dead of night with a padlock, so that I pass through the Iron Curtain unseeing and unseen, with only the stamping of documents to mark my release.

Emil

I HAVE ARRIVED in Hamburg. It is just before dawn. The sky is orange and red. I was blind, but now can see—isn't that what they sing in America? It is a little like that. There is no one watching me. There is no one at my back. I am the watcher now. I take a taxi to the port of Hamburg, where there might be a shore and wind and spume on the wind. I roll down the windows. I let the brightness of the northern dawntide pass in through the veins woven across my wrists. West Germany comes at me in different-shaped buildings and signs, in extraordinary cars and buses and in kiosks

and flower stalls streaming with color. All this new information is painful to me. There is too much here to frame and
stop.

The taxi drops me off by the gates of the port. The East
German freighter is pointed out to me. It is a narrow ax in the
far distance. I walk toward it now in disappointment. The
port is not as I hoped it to be. I want to be made aware of
how far I have come, I want to walk down to a gravel beach. I
want to frame a buoy and a lighthouse. I wish to teeter on a
shore, over seaweed, and be overcome with a different kind
of vertigo, that is not restricted flow through my vertebral
artery, but a vertiginous sense of possibility. But there is no
sea here: The sea is far away. The port is urban. The ships do
not ride at anchor as Soviet battleships do, but bristle against
one another in a hive. They bob on metal-colored water in
narrow channels marked off by granary towers and bounded
with toxic mud, where I see rats scattering now from one
clump of weed and rope to another.

I come under the rusting hull of my freighter. It is called
the *Eisfeld*.

"Who goes there?" a disembodied voice calls down from
the deck in German.

"Comrade Freymann," I call in German. "Representing
the Czechoslovakian Shipping Company."

"Come aboard then," the voice says.

I throw my bag on my shoulder and step up the gangway.
It gives and sways under me. I go up slowly now in the knowledge that this ascent will be my only margin and I shall see no
shore, no Cuxhaven, no islands of Scharhörn and Neuwerk. I

shall not sail across the Heligoland Bight. I look down
between the hull and the quay. I feel nothing: It is not nearly
dizzying enough.

I STEP ABOARD. I see the giraffes and am dumbfounded. I
stop. I stare up. I have worked with one living giraffe, but an
old giraffe, a zoo animal, weary, blind, hunched somehow
under those electric lights. I have seen nothing like this. There
are so many of them, and wild, not of a zoo, and impossibly
stretched. There is no such animal! They scrape this cirrus as
towers of the Qasr al-Qadim. Tarpaulins have been drawn
across the crates, so that only their necks and shoulders are
visible, and this makes them more unthinkable. I run my eye
up and down their necks. They are too tall for me to frame. I
try not to think of blood pressing up inside them, but instead
to consider their muscle and bone. I dwell on their necks, of
the same seven vertebrae that push up my skull, but each one
as thick as a chair leg and grooved, as by a carpentry machine,
the better to hold the slabs of muscle needed to keep the
neck upright. These necks are the greatest natural selection.
The tallest giraffes survived. All others perished—or disappeared into the jungle. I cannot say how I missed these towers
while walking toward the *Eisfeld,* or why I have not thought of
them on my journey, but have instead given myself over to a
chain of flowers and imaginings of a lighthouse set by a cool
green sea. I take a step closer. I place my bag down on the
deck. The smell of the giraffes is pungent, like racehorses
sweating in a paddock after the Pardubice steeplechase. I

count thirty-two animals, reticulated and Rothschild both. They make no sound. When they move, they cease to be towers or minarets, but are instead something flowing underwater, or perhaps a slender tree swaying. There is no urgency in them: They do not in any way resemble the orangutan I passed one winter afternoon in the Prague Zoo, which beat on the Perspex window of its cage to attract the attention of every passerby, as though from the inside of an airless cockpit.

A sailor takes up a bucket of grain and brings it to me—it is his voice I heard from below.

"Hold your hands out—cup them," he says.

I do so. He pours grain into them.

"Now hold them up to a giraffe. That one there. The Czechoslovakians call her Sněhurka."

I see why: Her underbelly is a blizzard.

"I'm Czechoslovakian," I say, still in German. "*Sněhurka* means 'Snow White' in Czech."

The sailor nods and looks up.

Sněhurka slides her tongue out to me. It is the length of my arm, dark as a blood blister. She takes the grain. I feel her lips and teeth against my palm.

The same sailor guides me inside now. He swings open a heavy metal door. I dip my head. The lightbulbs are caged in wire. I breathe in spaceship air, stale, smelling of fuels. We slide down ladders, from one deck to another. The sailor opens and closes steel hatches. There are slogans on the doors. There are hammers and sickles. There are red stars. We pass a galley in which I see pans firing and spitting on a gas cooker. The sailor shows me into a saloon, where the ship's officers are taking breakfast. I recognize the captain of the *Eisfeld* from a picture in the ring binder given me by the shipping director. I introduce myself. I stand here with my hands in my pockets, rocking on my heels.

"Well, sit down then, comrade!"

I sit.

His name is Hans Schmauch. He looks as I have hoped a sea captain would look: elderly, with cropped silver hair and beard, craggy, weathered, with a red nose.

"My father was a sea captain also," he says suddenly. "He plied the Baltic Sea. He brought back iron ore from Sweden and timber from Finland. And here I am bringing back giraffes from Africa."

He tells me of the plans for unloading the giraffes. Each animal will be hoisted up by crane and set down on a Czechoslovakian barge that will draw alongside this morning. I will go with the barge when it departs up the River Labe, tomorrow. The *Eisfeld* will sail home to Rostock.

Over coffee, I make my authority known to Schmauch.

He frowns. He waves me off.

"You have your business and I have mine," he says.

His voice is quieter now, seemingly worn away by typhoons.

"You must understand that the ocean is my only ideology," he says. "Since my passage is across the surface, I am not much interested in the interior of things. Monsters may cruise beneath, but I choose not to speak of them. Where the giraffes are heading and the rest of what you mention is of little interest to me. I am happy to have delivered them. The truth is that the giraffes unsettle me. It is best for me to regard them as not quite alive, like pictures on a postcard."

"That is a strange thing to say."

"I suppose it is. It might be because the giraffes are creatures of the interior, far from any sea. Certainly it upset me when they became agitated in heavy seas and kicked out at their crates, for days, so that all their legs were bleeding and done in with splinters. Or perhaps it is only that they have passed around the Cape of Good Hope on my ship and no longer have a home, but are instead delivered into captivity. We all yearn for a home, don't we, comrade?"

"Yes, comrade captain," I say.

"In dreams I see the parts of the Baltic Sea I sailed as a young man. I dream of approaching a tiny island on my own ship, which is not unlike this ship. There is a little turf on the island and a single birch tree. There is a wooden fisherman's hut fastened to the rock with cables. It is always winter in my dream. The sea is iced over. The rising bow of my ship splits the ice, opening up a channel of black water to usher me home. Even from a distance I see herring drying on a line, candles burning in the windows, and a lit stove."

"Is that dream a comfort to you, comrade?"

We stand.

"Such dreams are the anchor of every sailor," he says.

"The giraffes might dream of a home as you do," I say.

Schmauch looks thoughtful.

"They might, comrade. I'll allow," he says.

He walks away through his saloon. I envy him that his

home is a dream, while mine is a certain place, on a hilltop, which cannot be approached by any ship, but only a propeller plane dipping low.

ALOIS HUS IS on the deck, among the giraffes. He is tanned and clean-shaven. He moves clumsily for an ambitious man—for a zoo director. He trips over a bucket of water he himself has set down. He swears. He is extraordinarily tall. I introduce myself now. I look up at him, as I might look up at a giraffe. We speak formally, in precise Czech. I tell him certain things and hold back others.

"Tell me about the shipment," I say.

"You say shipment, while I prefer the word *migration*," he says.

"Forgive me."

"There are thirty-two giraffes here, the largest group ever transported across the world. This is not a shipment—it is an assisted flight into a new land. For who can say what might happen in the future? The Earth might shift on its axis, so that our ČSSR will become parched and what are now river meadows will become savannah and thorn trees might displace holly trees. If that were to happen, then the descendants of these giraffes might form the basis of a new subspecies."

He swings his arms in embrace of the giraffes. I look up at him in this daylight, which is clearer than the light of our ČSSR. His expression is perfectly serious.

"Our own Czechoslovakian subspecies?" I say. "*Camelopardalis bohemica*?"

He lights up. "Very good, Freymann! I like that. *Camelo-pardalis bohemica.*"

"What plans do you have for them in the zoo?"

"It will be a family," Hus says. "We will build a safari park. The giraffes will walk freely through the parkland."

"To begin with, comrade?" I ask.

I realize we are distant from each other. He looks to the future, to his red-starred giraffes, while I am haunted by the past and engaged in a search for such beauty as will puncture time.

"To begin with," he says, after a long pause, "they will be put in next to the okapi."

The okapi is the closest relative of the giraffe—anti-vertical, of limited hemodynamic interest—which evolved away in the middle Pliocene to live squat and unseen in the depths of the Upper Congo River basin, so well camouflaged that its existence was only confirmed by an expedition in 1900.

"Will the giraffes not be perplexed to see how they are giants next to the okapi?"

"Not at all. They will see only that the okapi is more chocolate and purple in parts than they are," Hus says.

Hus slips and slides away across the wet deck and I stand here among his giraffes and think now of how okapi have been compacted down in the gloom, just as pygmies have been.

CRATES ARE TAKEN UP from the forward hold. Water is given to the ship, and diesel also. West German dockworkers listlessly tie and untie lines. Some of the East German sailors depart for Hamburg. They feed the giraffes before disembarking. They hold apples and pears up to the northern sky. The giraffes take the fruit. I watch the sailors stand for a moment on the quay, looking about them, adjusting the lapels on their jackets, as though they have been made foreign by the sea and no longer know what to expect of the land.

The Czechoslovakian barge ties up alongside. The unloading of the giraffes begins. Each crate is harnessed and lowered to the barge. Some of the giraffes panic at the sensation of flying and dropping down toward water. They kick out at their crates. It is disturbing to watch, as Schmauch said. The crates swing like a pendulum. The giraffes look desperately across the harbor as they swing, across and back, from one granary tower to another, searching for certain trees and animals, but finding no acacias and no hippos moving along the poisonous mud banks. Gulls hover above the crates and squawk, yellow-beaked, at the heads of the giraffes as they descend. A sailor stands beside me and also looks up at the swinging crates.

"Let them walk on air," he says sadly, "for they will never again walk on Africa."

IT IS AFTERNOON. I sit alone now in the ship's library, glancing over documents concerning the estimated value of giraffes, shipping costs, and the waiving of customs duties. In a separate stack are the veterinary reports assembled by the zoo veterinarian on thirty-two giraffes and documentation on the death of one giraffe. I study these more carefully and make notes on the blood pressure recorded in certain giraffes before, during, and after the voyage.

Light sits in porthole circles on the plaster busts of revolutionaries and on the glass cabinet containing the political texts. It is confusing. I am in West Germany, but in the Communist moment also. I am in a port where there is no salt, no waves breaking polyphonically. I set aside my hemodynamic notes. I stand. I browse through the other, open bookshelves and come now across a short history of England, published in Dresden. I flick through it and come, by chance, on this page here, upon a curious detail such as the zoo historian would keep, in place of his own memories. On the orders of Oliver Cromwell, I read, all the dancing and fighting bears in London were shot. The only bear spared was a polar bear that in its white apartness, Cromwell said, would better remind Puritan Englishmen of the majesty and unknowability of God's creation. I close the book and slide it back onto the shelf, and I think now of how that polar bear might have been the descendant of Henry III's polar bear, which was kept in the Tower of London, and in another turning of comets, I come to a flea-bitten black bear I once saw languishing in the dry moat of Konopiště Castle. I stumbled on that animal on an autumn afternoon with wet leaves spiraling downward. It had small eyes and a white streak on its chest below the throat. It did not meet my gaze, but mewed through its narrow snout and opened up its sores with long yellow claws. It was quite willing to stand vertically on its stinking bed, so its blood flowed not along but upward in expectancy of a wonder net, and dance upright for the meanest piece of bread proffered by children, who leaned far out over the spiked railing beside me. When sunshine finally broke on the back of that bear, it also broke through the patterned windows of Konopiště Castle. I walked in the chambers of that place with a sense of incredulity. The walls were nailed floor to ceiling with the heads of deer, bears, wolves— of every living creature that moved in the wilds, down to the tamest otter, all of them bagged by the archduke Franz Ferdinand, the owner of Konopiště, who was himself shot dead in Sarajevo and made into a trophy of a quite different sort.

EVENING LIGHT COMES through the saloon portholes, settling in soft rings on the chests of sailors. I am taking supper. I sit next to a Czechoslovakian tractor salesman, a Slovak, who has returned from Mombasa with crates of machinery in need of repair. He speaks to me of Africa.

"I was summoned to the Czechoslovakian embassy in Nairobi," he says. "An embassy car was waiting for me outside the tractor factory near the coast. I hardly spoke during that long drive to Nairobi. I had only recently arrived in Kenya and I was still greatly affected by its sounds and colors, the way women bang on the roof of your car and try to sell you fruit from baskets, and then the baskets themselves, which they have woven from grass that grows high after the rains. There was not much to do in Nairobi: The officials were happy with the way the tractor enterprise was proceeding. I left for the coast the following afternoon with letters of credit. I took the same road, with the same embassy driver, but the land appeared different to me. Perhaps it was because we set off in the afternoon and were driving into night, or simply that we were heading from the mountains to the coast, and not from the coast to the mountains. There were no crowds of women at the edges of the villages we passed through at that late hour, but instead there were small fires burning outside the huts, and infants being carried inside in the arms of their parents. In one village I saw an elderly man performing a dance around such a fire, holding up a knife in a sheath of monkey leather and a spear tipped with a sharpened hippo tooth. I caught sight of a beautiful young woman in another village, sleepwalking between one grass hut and another. I had the driver stop the car. We got out and watched. Her arms were stretched up, like this, as if she were about to dive upward from a board. She walked and tripped in the dust and rose again, not awake but still sleepwalking. None of the villagers tried to stop her. They ran back from her when she passed them, as though sleepwalking were a kind of contagion.

"We drove on, into the night. It began to rain. The rain became torrential, more violent than any storm I have seen in the hills of my Slovak paradise. The thunder shook the windows of the car, and the lightning came in sheets that lit up the earth, even up to the snow fields of Kilimanjaro, like a camera flash. I could see in those lightning strikes how the soil beside the road was shot up in bolts of mud by force of the rain. It was by that strange light that we saw the giraffes. An entire herd crossed the road in front of us. We saw them in one flash, then darkness, then again in another flash, their heads turned now toward us, then they disappeared into darkness once more. It was only a second, or two. They were moving with the speed of horses, although they seemed to me like creatures from another world, of lesser gravity. We had hardly gone any farther when there was an explosion at the front of the car, a bang, like one of those training grenades they set off in the army to get you used to noise. The driver braked. There was a grinding. He stepped out into the rain. I followed him. The front of the car was smashed in and flowing red with blood and rainwater. A hyena lay on the ground. It was a massive animal. Heavier than me. A rib stuck out from its body. We thought it was dead. It stirred. The driver shouted for me to get back into the car. He jumped in after me. We reversed. Some part of the hyena was still caught in the bumper. It was dragged some distance before twisting free. The driver said it must have belonged to a pack of hyenas tracking the giraffes through the thunderstorm. He said hyenas pick off weak or young giraffes during the rains, just as wolves move after sheep under the cover of summer drizzle in my Slovak paradise. We waited there. We watched the hyena rise from the road. Its shoulders were opened to the bone. One of its forelegs was smashed and dangling. It hopped forward into our headlights. It was lit in the beams. It appeared to be staring at us. It was demonic, like a creature you see at the base of those religious statues on the Charles Bridge, freshly emerged from hell."

I STAND AT THE STERN of the ship. Pennants, neckerchiefs, and other charms have been exchanged. The Czechoslovakians have thanked the East Germans. The East Germans have spoken of giraffes. It is a leaving party now. I am drinking with some of the sailors. I see no lighthouse. I see only silhouettes of the rich buildings of Hamburg lit by neon signs advertising cigarettes, beer, and magazines. The sailors are swapping stories.

"I once glimpsed a mermaid," the ship's mate says. "She was laid out on a floating piece of wood, flotsam, between the ship and the cove of a northern island we were steaming by."

Someone laughs, but uneasily.

"What kind of wood?" someone else asks.

"Oh, I don't know," the ship's mate says. "Planking. A door. A fish box, perhaps. Anyway, she was sunning herself on the wood. It was a hot day. The cove was bright with fish. How to describe her? She had the tail of a harbor porpoise, but speckled orange and black like a mackerel. She was a woman from the waist up, with a navel and breasts, with a green hue to her skin, which appeared from my distance rough to the touch, not scabrous, but prickled, like any skin emerging from cold water. She was small, the size of a child. I could see no gills about her throat, but her nostrils were flattened and appeared to open and close like those of a seal. She had long kelp-colored hair and unnaturally large eyes. She seemed to be singing, or perhaps crying. The sound was anyway closer to a harp than to a human voice. It was the plucking of hairs within the throat. I opened my mouth to call out to the mermaid. I felt a great need for her to look at me, as we all have felt the need for the giraffes to turn to meet our gaze. But the moment my lips parted, even before I made any sound, she slipped from her float and dived down into the cove. The water was clear. I could see her. She dropped right down, faster than any seal. She shimmered between deep rocks, then was gone."

The sailors are quiet.

"Did you report this?" one of them asks.

"To whom would I report it? To our East German navy? To the Party? In what fashion? They would not believe me. If by chance they did, what would happen then? Some expedition out of Leningrad would catch her. There would be a harvest of mermaids. They would be put to production. No. She was wild as the giraffes there were once wild. Let her swim free."

I see now it was the ship's mate who had spoken of the giraffes swinging in the sky—"Let them walk on air," he had said. The sailors around me believe in his mermaid. I am captivated also, but especially by the hemodynamic possibilities of blood flow in mermaids. Might a mermaid have a single circulatory system, beyond the comprehension of Galen? Or does blood pulse through them in a dual system, with womanly veins above and the wonder net of a harbor porpoise cross-hatched in flukes below?

The ship's engineer pours himself more vodka and speaks now in a German coastal dialect.

"Maybe you're right, comrade," he says to the ship's mate. "Maybe you did see this. There is a story of a mermaid from my island of Hiddensee. Just before the Second World War, a local man named Brauhard sailed to the deepest part of our Baltic Sea and there fell in love with a mermaid. He married her and brought her back to Hiddensee in a hold full of water drawn from that deep place, which I suppose to be off the coast of Gotland. The mermaid lived in a tank of that water in the bedroom; on occasion they warmed it and Brauhard stripped off and slept in her arms, her tail wrapped around his legs. The local community was unhappy with the arrangement. Some of them railed against the intermingling of Aryans with mermaids. After some months, when Brauhard was away at sea, bringing back fresh water from the Gotland trench, a mob of Brownshirts broke into his house, led by the postmaster, and dragged his wife by her tail to the strand near Neuendorf. There are photographs of this. It was summer. The sand was hot. They threw her on it and drowned her in air and sunshine within sight of the sea. When Brauhard sailed into the harbor and was told the news, he broke down and wept. He begged his neighbors to tell him why they had done so cruel a thing. They shrugged. The officials sent him a letter stating that relations between a German and a mermaid were illegal."

The engineer takes another swig of vodka.

"My grandmother witnessed all those events," he goes on, "and told me there was no need to feel pity for the mermaid since it was subhuman. I should do better, she said, to contemplate the suffering of a single herring on my breakfast plate. If I must pity anyone, she went on, it should be Brauhard, who remained an upstanding citizen of Hiddensee despite the actions of his neighbors, although he never remarried and left his money to the widows of drowned sailors, some of whom, by our island tradition, were said to have awakened when their bodies settled on the seafloor and taken mermaids as brides until the day of judgment, when the drowned are supposed to rise up from each body of water."

"Did Brauhard give any explanation of how he came

to love a mermaid?" I ask. "Was he himself drowned and wakened?"

The engineer pauses. I frame him now; I keep this moment.

"I cannot say that," he says. "Brauhard said only that the mermaids reminded him of angels he had seen painted on the walls of the whitewashed churches of our Hiddensee."

I HAVE CLIMBED down a rope ladder from the *Eisfeld*. I stand below, on the barge. The leaving party is over. The wind rushes in off the fresh waters, filling my lungs with the fast-coming smell of Danish peat bogs. The wind beats against me and causes my hair to unfurl, as a flag should unfurl.

It is the giraffe called Sněhurka who towers over me at the front of the barge. I recognize her underbelly. I reach inside her crate and place a hand on her. The zoo historian has told me that Egyptians used a hieroglyph of a giraffe to indicate prophecy or foreknowledge. And I wonder why Sněhurka does not kick out at her crate. Can she not see that this Czechoslovakian barge is no ark of Noah, but is instead a vessel charged with delivering her into captivity?

I look up at her. I want her to meet my gaze, just as the ship's mate said. She does not. She stares, unblinking, out toward Hamburg, with eyes large, entire as the Heligoland Bight. She might be sleeping, for giraffes are sleepless beasts, who sleep for only a few minutes each day with their eyes open, unblinking, and move as sleepwalkers in that short sleep, like the African somnambulist the Slovak spoke of, who fell to the dust and rose again still with her arms stretched up. I feel Sněhurka's vein pulsing against my fingertips. I translate the pulse into numbers. I cannot help myself. I am a doubler: I am an agent of the shipping company and of hemodynamics also.

There is a sound. I see Schmauch in the air between his ship and the barge. He lands. He strides down the barge to me, hat in hand.

"I want to see the giraffes one more time," he says.

"I thought they made you uneasy."

"I must take my leave of them all the same. It has been a long voyage," he says. "There have been moments, comrade."

"A mermaid?"

He smiles.

"No, not this time. I was thinking of a day I spent fishing off Zanzibar. A blue day, blue as a flame. The engine of the ship had given out and we anchored there for several days, on a dazzling sea, waiting for the repairs to be made. A Persian motored out from Zanzibar in a dinghy to witness the giraffes. He offered to take me fishing. So I went fishing with that man: He was one of those regal men who devote their lives to hunting one living thing or another. We attached his dinghy to my ship by a long rope, as cosmonauts tether themselves to a space capsule. Or perhaps," Schmauch says, reconsidering, "it was my crew who tied the rope, to prevent me drifting away to Zanzibar, just as a falconer tethers his hawk. In any case, we rowed out as far as the rope would allow and found ourselves sitting upon a dark bloom in the waters, which were sardines come north from the cold southern belt. We took turns casting into the bloom. We were not after the sardines, but the tuna and swordfish we could see parting the bloom. It did not matter to me that landing such a large fish on our small dinghy was unlikely. I was happy watching the sardines swelling and hollowing under us, like bees, or a flock of starlings billowing black at dusk over woods by the seashore. The Persian took it more seriously. He was a fine fisherman. You had only to watch the arc of the line over his shoulder as he cast to understand that. He hooked a swordfish and fought it hard until the line broke and then, without pausing, he tied on a new hook, baited it, and cast into the bloom. 'Watch this, captain,' he said. Sure enough, another swordfish ran straight at the bait and was alarmingly hooked through the top of its mouth. The Persian landed that swordfish in the dinghy. There was hardly enough room for it. It thrashed in the salt water at our feet and gashed my leg here, below the knee. It was only when the swordfish stilled, died, that the Persian pointed out that it was the same creature he had grappled with first, still with that hook in its mouth. The Persian held it up by its sword. 'A swordfish lives by instinct,' he said. 'It has three seconds of memory. No more.' He set down the fish and drew a circle in the air with his hands. 'Here is the moment,' he said. 'It loops, like so, completes, and is gone. That is the mind of a swordfish,' he said. It was a common occurrence to release a swordfish only to have it run straight back at the hook, without remembrance."

Schmauch puts his hand out also and touches Sněhurka.

"I have thought often of that swordfish in the last weeks," he says, "how it has no past and no future, but only the present parting of water before its blade, just as I stand on my ship's bridge parting oceans, without past or future."

SCHMAUCH HAS CLIMBED BACK UP to his ship and I am left alone now among the giraffes and their rising blood. The wind is still blowing hard over the plowed fields about Hamburg, allowing the Communist moment no purchase on this Czechoslovakian barge, and blowing such spirits as linger here away from me. I could speak to the sailors of ghosts, as they spoke to me of mermaids. I see outlines of the dead in ČSSR. Not just my grandfather waving to his planes. I see others also. There is no obvious hemodynamic explanation for my condition: It is more than clinical nostalgia. It is not that the dead step living into this 1973, or that I step into the past; I am not so fanciful. The explanation is more likely meteorological. I say only that it is natural for ghosts to linger in a windless country, where there is not even the faintest zephyr to part the dead from the living, that, in the absence of wind, they leave an outline on ČSSR I am sometimes able to frame and keep.

I glimpse another Czechoslovakia, which I sometimes call Tonakia because the men I see there wear trilbies or bowlers manufactured by the Tonak company. I see in Prague the capital of Tonakia also, which is the Prague of 1933 or some close year. I see quicklime outlines of a vendor hawking ties from a suitcase on Haštalská Street, and an aristocrat running down the center of Národní Street in top hat and tails. I see laundrywomen washing spectral clothes in the rapids of the Vltava before Josef Šejnost's atelier on the Smetana Embankment, and horses stabled in their hundreds under the hill on which the Bohumil Kafka's equestrian statue of the Hussite commander Žižka now stands totalitarian. I see students in heavy overcoats chalking a political manifesto on the steps of a convent on Vyšehradská Street, a tinker singing a Moravian folk song while pushing a cart down Belgická Street, and a blind busker winding his music box outside the Hotel Europa on Wenceslas Square. Coal smoke of the Communist moment mingles with coal smoke of Tonakia and drifts ginger and lime together over the outline of long-dead lovers kissing in the shadows of St. Jakub's church on Malá Štupartská Street and settles in material and immaterial soot on the unfurled spectral wings of geese and swans, nailed like severed angels to the ghostly wooden boards of a butcher's shop that no longer exists.

I CANNOT SLEEP. I lie on this upper bunk in a cabin on the ship. A voyage has ended in which I have played no part. There are signs of departure, in sheets crumpled on the floor, cigarette butts, and reams of DDR newspapers. There are things that have been spoken of in this cabin far from land which cannot be repeated now. The regime, which appeared indistinct in the doldrums, comical even has drawn back into focus. I stare at a photograph pinned to the side of the greasy plywood bunk, forgotten in the rush to disembark. I take it down. It is a black-and-white photo of a woman striding down a concrete pier. She wears a bikini. Over her shoulder is a packed beach. The Cyrillic lettering above the ice-cream stand identifies the beach as Bulgarian. The woman is moving fast by the camera. The lens is turning to meet her. It is a fleeting image, such as I might frame with my eye. It is impossible to say whether the woman is irritated or simply impatient to be gone into the air at the end of the pier and down into the Black Sea. She is no mermaid returning to its element. She is large: Her breasts are barely contained in their flowered cups. Her skin is downy and smooth. There is a scar below her navel, punctured along its edges where the stitches have been recently drawn. She has no tail of a harbor porpoise, no flukes containing wonder nets. Her legs instead end in cheap COMECON plastic sandals.

I pin her back into the plywood. I switch on the transistor radio I have brought with me. I am no longer downhearted: I feel a slight buoyancy of the *Eisfeld* on the harbor waters. This is my first night in West Germany, in the new chain of flowers. I tune the dial. I listen. The songs belong to the West German moment, which is recognizably now the opposite of the Communist moment, in which time is marked out by clocks, loudspeaker announcements, and revolutionary parades no one comprehends; but there is no *now* and it is possible to live without remembering the year, and to have no sense of time passing, save in the changing colors of the seasons. Some of the songs playing are in English. A line in one of them pierces me.

The waters of Hamburg harbor are under this ship and gulls are turning somewhere above. There is a northern sky brightening out there. I cannot see it from in here. There is no porthole in this cabin, no ring of light. I am sunk below the waterline.

Emil

I UNDERSTAND THE RIVER ELBE, or Labe. I have words to describe its course and to detail the life upon and within it. It runs twelve hundred kilometers from the Krkonoše Mountains in Czechoslovakia to the North Sea. It is a river. It wants to show us the sea. If the engines on the barge were cut now, it would carry us on its back through the port and city of Hamburg, by the scarlet poppy fields of Schleswig-Holstein, to its estuarine mouth fourteen kilometers wide in embrace of the world, and with plunging flow might beach us on the island of Scharhörn or Neuwerk, where we might settle, we few Czechoslovakians, with our state-owned giraffes, to breed

a new subspecies under a domed and ever-changing sky, with
feed brought from Cuxhaven. Or perhaps the Labe, with the
last of its strength, would push us out beyond the two islands
altogether, and we should be tossed on this barge across the
Heligoland Bight, deep into the North Sea, and wash up at
last, bleary and bruised, on the salt marshes I can only suppose lie black and tan along the shores of England, perhaps
the same marsh over which Magwitch stumbled in leg irons
before being captured and transported to Australia, there to
provide Pip with his great expectations. We might pull ourselves free from those marshes after some days and drift on
into the harbor of an English seaport, where, under the rule
of Oliver Cromwell, the cubs of dancing and fighting bears
must have been gagged and hidden on small vessels from
Puritans who had orders to shoot them, and voyaged from
that seaport to any land where the bear cubs could grow and
move from town to town.

Ships pass around us in the port. Some of them sound
their horns on sighting the giraffes, who shimmer in the hot
morning light like the granary towers in the port. There is no
drift back to the sea. The engines on the barge are not cut.
They thump us out into the Labe, away from Schmauch, waving his cap on his ship's bridge, just as I see the outline of my
grandfather waving to his propeller planes. We pass under a
bridge. It is thick with early morning traffic. Sunshine catches
on the mirrors and windows of the cars now. I frame a hippie
with long hair sitting in the lotus position on the bridge
before the broken-down engine of his van.

The Labe is poisoned. There are no salmon alive in it. No

polar bear could be led out to fish its portion from these waters. Swimmers emerge with a mustard scum on their skin and a sweet taste in their mouth. Only eels pass upstream with us. They pulse in from the ocean, tapered, like ghostly parts of an atom, working in through smaller and smaller rivers of DDR and ČSSR, until settling at the turn of a stream, or in the stillness of a millpond. I cannot say whether their migration is of their own will or is an act of remembrance, just as some liken flowing water to the subconscious and take the passing through it to be a passing through memory.

Because there is no bunk for me on the barge, I volunteer to sleep out on the deck, among the giraffes. I make a place for myself now at the prow. I sweep the area and lay down a sleeping bag. I tie the tarpaulin to the crate holding Sněhurka. We shall part the Labe together. She is wet with spray coming up off the river and has nostrils that open and clamp like those of a seal or mermaid. But she is not a watery creature. She has never wallowed, but instead cools herself under the shade of acacia trees and is camouflaged there by the markings on her hide, which also serve as open windows dissipating heat, just as the frontoparietal hollows atop her skull cool her brain to a lower temperature than her body.

I sit under the tarpaulin and am lit here by Sněhurka's underbelly. I open my notebook. Inside is a clipping from a Polish art magazine of *Burning Giraffes and Telephones,* a painting by Salvador Dali. I unfold it. Three giraffes walk calmly across the horizon, untroubled by the flames bursting from their backs and necks, while in the foreground a massive eye borne on the muscular legs of a Nubian, with the torso of a boiler or a bank safe, attacks or makes love to a faceless woman whose arms are stretched up somnambulistically. I study the painting as I study passages from *Great Expectations,* or carotid arteries.

Watery meadows appear on either side of us. This is the end of Hamburg. I move up and down the barge now, making notes and sketches of the giraffes for my scientific paper. I am less concerned now with rumination, with the four divisions of the stomach, the Olympic-length intestines, the maneuverability of the tongue, the prehensile and undivided upper lip, the vocal cords that hardly pluck a sound, or even with the laryngeal nerve running from brain to heart and back again, than I am with the viscosity of giraffe blood, five times thicker than water, with a multiplication of crimson stars, in better distribution of oxygen, with the jugular veins several centimeters in diameter, stoppered with one-way valves, in such a way as to regulate flow from the head when it is lifted from the ground. There are thirty-two giraffes here, each with a wonder net hidden from view. When a giraffe splays its legs and sets down its head to drink, the pressure on its cranial vasculature triples. The giraffe's cerebral blood vessels are too thin-walled to constrict against it. But for the wonder net, the giraffe would collapse, as cosmonauts do when certain g-force is applied. It is the wonder net that keeps the living form of giraffes pushed up, even to resemble creatures from a world of lesser gravity. When the head goes down, its endless shunts and meanders spread elastically across the base of the cranium, absorbing the flow that rushes in through the carotid artery.

· · ·

IT IS A HEAT WAVE. I strip off my shirt. I pour a bucket of water over my head, my shoulders, my chest. A man in large mirrored sunglasses drives a cream-colored Mercedes along a country road by the river. I help tend the giraffes. I shovel out dung. I hold up bread to some of the giraffes.

"No!" Hus shouts. "Not bread! Grain, comrade." He comes running up with a bucket of grain. He is also without shirt and shoes. He wears a safari hat and a necklace of African beads made of coral.

"These giraffes will live fifteen years in the wild at the most. They'll manage thirty years in the zoo with my diet."

"Grain?"

"Not just grain. Alfalfa, formulated pellets, fruit, plenty of beets, switches of elm and alder."

"What about the breeding?" I see him now. I see his eyes glint.

"Breeding! That's the thing. It all comes down to procreation in the end. We have a social group here. A perfect mix of healthy males and females. All we need to do is sort them correctly."

"Just like the Komsomol," I say.

He does not hear me.

"We'll see our first pregnancies this winter," he says.

"What makes you so sure?"

"That's what I'm trying to tell you, Freymann. You're a scientist. Look around you. We have a different philosophy. The purpose of a zoo is to breed animals and to entertain the worker. Breeding is the more important. The State recognizes that. And our socialist mind is good for breeding. It wants to know at what temperature, at what angle of entry, between which giraffe bull and which giraffe cow. And the better we breed, the more we entertain. We will build the safari park. Workers will be driven through an open landscape. And we will breed in ever larger groups. We will birth the animals, keeping the best ones, selling the rest, and so continue for generations until we get to our *Camelopardalis bohemica*. It will happen. The climate in our ČSSR is not so bad. The new giraffes will become accustomed to the winters. They'll learn to move on ice."

I throw bread I would have fed to the giraffes into the Labe. Fish come up for it, eels invisibly too, and gulls arriving inland from the sea drop down to it and slash noisomely on the river.

I SIT IN THE WHEELHOUSE with the zoo veterinarian. Hus is at the other end of the barge, filing down giraffe hooves.

"We haven't been formally introduced," he says. "I'm František Vokurka. Call me Franta."

His name means "cucumber," but he is a slight man with stained rodent teeth. He wears a stethoscope. There is an exceptionally long tongue depressor in his shirt pocket.

"Emil Freymann," I say, holding out my hand.

"I know who you are," he says. "No need to worry about the giraffes. No need to worry about any of it. One died on the voyage. The rest are in good shape."

"I read your report."

"I want you to know that what Hus said yesterday was nonsense."

"The new subspecies? The assisted flight?"

He nods. "This idea of his that the giraffes are engaged in some sort of migration."

"They're captive."

"Of course they are."

"The safari park?"

"I'm all against it," he says, turning over the beans on his plate. "The slopes are too steep. They're grassy. The giraffes will fall and break themselves on the ground when it rains. They'll be like girls in high heels coming home from a country dance."

"They might get up again," I say.

"They would be as good as dead," he says. "Their legs would be fractured in many places and could never be put back together."

"Did you tell Hus this?"

"Many times."

"What did he say?"

"He's a careerist. He said the committee has passed the safari park proposal. He said the giraffes had the right to walk free."

"They were free."

"He means they have the right to walk free in ČSSR. He said the giraffes should be allowed to discover where they have migrated to." Vokurka pushes back his plate. He starts playing with his tongue depressor. "Let me tell you of migration," he says.

"Please do."

"Last year, after quite another voyage, I found myself disembarked at the Romanian port of Constanta. I had a day to myself before taking the evening train to Bucharest. I walked from the modern port to the old part of the town, which contained decaying mosques, villas, and a museum displaying Roman antiquities. I walked as far as the marina. Some men were setting up a fairground ride there; it had eight arms, and at the end of each was a carriage that circled, I suppose, at great speed, but would always start and stop at the same point, going nowhere, no matter how many revolutions it made. Turning back toward the port, I came upon a shutdown casino in which swallows were nesting. They were newly returned from Africa. I watched them fall from their wattled nests in the eaves, like cliff divers, and rise vertically again, all the while reflected in the long windows and shadowed on the white and gold rococo plasterwork. I was hardly aware of the sun setting into the land. The swallows gave me a sense of the true meaning of migration."

"Which is?"

"Certitude. The certitude of returning home. Swallows fly with utmost joy, ever so lightly, from Africa to Constanta and on to our ČSSR, over grasslands, deserts, seas, marshes, forests, mountains, all of these. They are joyful because they are forever returning home. ČSSR is home, all places in between are home."

"Unlike the giraffes."

"Who have no home now, but only crates."

"Could you tell me how the one giraffe died on the voyage?" I ask. I look at him blankly, as I have been instructed to by the shipping company, in order to produce uneasiness in the listener, so that they open up.

"Let me first state that giraffes are not meant to stand on the deck of a ship for weeks at a time."

"Granted."

"All went well for the first part of the voyage," he says. "The engine gave out off Zanzibar, but those were pleasant days. We passed around the Cape of Good Hope in calm waters and saw no storm until we were off the coast of Mauritania. Even the storm petrels fell upon our ship that night seeking shelter. I fled to my bunk below the waterline and clung miserably to myself. There was a terrible creaking, as though the hull were being torn open. I was certain we would sink into the Atlantic. I wept. I hoped for nothing more than to be washed up onto a Mauritanian beach. Of course the ship did not come close to sinking. It was only my Czechoslovakian sensibility. The storm subsided. I remembered my duty. With some effort, I made it up to the bridge. The ship's mate was at the wheel. "One of them is down," he said. I realized he was talking about the giraffes. I went with a sailor onto the deck. Waves were still breaking on the tarpaulins. The giraffes were sliding and braking and swallowing salt water. We went to the crate. I pulled back the tarpaulin. There was a young male twisted, broken-necked, on the floor. We jumped in. A wave knocked us off our feet onto the dead giraffe. It looked so much smaller folded together like that in the water. Nothing more than a foal. I did an examination. It is all in the report."

"There's no name in the report."

"That giraffe had no name. We hadn't yet thought of one.

It had no distinguishing features. It was not taller or shorter than the other young giraffes. It was not a leader or a loner. Its hide was forgettable."

"What happened to the body?"

"We decided against an autopsy. We attended to the other giraffes through the day. When the waters calmed, Hus had the Slovak tractor man and a few of the sailors distract the other giraffes with feed. We winched up the carcass. It was heavier than we had supposed. The legs had already stiffened. It swung and cracked against a funnel and fell to the deck. Other giraffes panicked. They started forward in their crates. Some of them began kicking out at the sides of their crates. Captain Schmauch did not like that. He kept calling down for us to calm the animals. Hus came over and we quickly pushed the dead giraffe overboard. It was exceptionally hot and still. The ocean was flat and violet-colored. I remember how we could see the streak of the Mauritanian desert and sharks circling in the violet. The giraffe floated for a time. Its neck and head were the last to go under. Its eyes were closed in such a way as to give the quite wrong impression—of restful sleep."

DRAGONFLIES AND WASPS hover about Sněhurka and are dispersed now by smoke from bonfires West German farmers have lit at the edge of their fields. The smoke causes Sněhurka to shift in her crate. I lean back against her. Her legs push against my back through the slats. We round a bend in the Labe and come upon a nudist beach. Forms and genitals of West Germans sag on the sandy bank like so many walrus runts and milky curds. I do not frame any of them, but wonder at the ease with which I might defect now, as my father feared when our fingers brushed in parting. Hus and Vokurka are playing cards. The bargemen are occupied with the bend. Only the giraffes will see me go, and they are silent. I could do this; I could slip into these sweet-poisoned waters like a merman and swim perpendicularly to the riverbank and reveal myself there, clothed, before the West German nudists. Yet I do not move. I cannot. If I slip into the water now, my home will become something dreamed, and I cannot dream as Schmauch dreams; I am not a sailor—I have no idea of an island in an icebound sea. There is something else. I am weighed down. I can hardly haul myself over to teeter at the edge of the barge. It is as if I have grown a shell on my back to protect myself from the Communist moment and cannot now shed it.

WE PASS THE LAST West German village. We brush against the bulrushes on the bank to make way for oncoming barges and so uncover a young couple lovemaking there. They pull back from each other and give out a little gasp on seeing the giraffes. They stand. They stare after the barge. An old man pedaling a bicycle stops also. He places his feet on the towpath. He leans over the handlebars and stares after the giraffes. This is how it will be for the giraffes. People will stand and stare after them, frame them, and keep them. They will become zoo animals and their form will forever be the cause of exclamation among people and sometimes of reflection.

The Iron Curtain comes suddenly, as a threading between

fallow fields. Floodlights rock across the Labe. American boots strike paths and Soviet jackboots also. There are minefields and trenches dug into the root systems of ash trees, such that badgers can make no progress. Beyond the minefields is a wall of concrete panels, supple, holding to the contours of the land like segments of snake cartilage. An East German flag flutters over a border post in red, orange, and black, struck with a hammer and sickle. I button up a shirt and put on shoes. I speak in Russian to military officials who come to stand and stare after the giraffes. These officials take off their caps and relax their arms and grow visibly more gentle, as though in looking up at the beasts they have recovered a part of their childhood.

We continue a little way up the Labe and tie up for the night by an army barracks. There are no Mercedes here. The air is more sulfurous. Our mood has changed: We walk quietly up and down the barge, and the words we use, and the way we use them, are different from in West Germany. It is as if the world is divided into spheres of thought and we have passed from one sphere into another of lesser possibilities, as through a weather front from clear sky to rain.

I step off the barge into a meadow behind the barracks and stumble through a thicket of yew trees. It is quite dark. It is only now, out in the starlight, that I realize I have passed through the graveyard of a village erased by the Communist moment.

Emil

I AM WOKEN NOW by a breeze billowing under the tarpaulin. I look up. It is the middle of the night. Sněhurka is awake in her crate. She is looking out at a red sack caught in the branches of a weeping willow on the far bank. The sack is torn into strips like the red ribbons that *vodníks,* or watermen, are supposed to hang from willow branches to attract young women. I stare across at the willow. There is always a hope I will see a *vodník* sitting in the branches, playing a violin sadly to himself.

The *vodník* looks after a stretch of a river or stream. He

lives among eels in pools where trout circle. It is the *vodník* who causes a river to burst its banks in spring, carrying off a Persian leopard, and to sink low in summer. It is he who pulls under the unsuspecting fisherman and the drunk ferryman; he is the one who catches and cradles the mortally stricken child who has broken through thin ice. It is so striking, so very Czechoslovakian, that the *vodník* belongs to a single stretch of river, between a linden tree and a bend, or between a weir and a certain copse of crab-apple trees. He is not like the mermaids the East German sailors spoke of, who sink freely down from a cove and sing, with plucking of throat hairs, to whales in the faraway deep. There were *vodníks* before there were Czechoslovakians. In certain Byzantine mosaics you can see over the shoulders of Justinian and Theodora to a *vodník* half risen from a warm lagoon. The *vodník* has been too long exiled in our landlocked Czechoslovakia to move anymore in the sober and athletic way of those mosaics. He has grown thin and is seen most often in the local *hospoda,* or pub, where he fancies his green skin is disguised in the weak electric light of the Communist moment. He keeps his webbed hands deep in his pockets, except when buying rounds, but is nevertheless easily recognized by his ridiculous top hat, which has no place in ČSSR, or even in Tonakia, by the water dripping from the pockets of his jacket, the rank smell of his breath, and the weeds gathered about his ears. He is not a bad creature, not a frightening animal. He is not a potential candidate for any zoo. On the contrary, the *vodník* is a spiritual creature, a caretaker of souls. It is he who preserves all those who come to him. He snatches their descending forms but wants none of them. Those he takes, he takes on higher command. He puts their souls in ceramic jars, which he sets in orderly fashion on the shelves of his home, like the jars of pickled dolphin fetuses neatly arranged in the library of the Strahov Monastery in Prague. There the souls await the final judgment priests used to speak of, in which the drowned will rise from the rivers and the seas, even from the deep of the Baltic, rising straight up through the clouds, shedding lily pads and barnacles, but not before, as scripture has it, the second and third angels have poured vials into the rivers, turning them to blood, and killing all other living things within them, including the *vodník*. If this is so, if this comes to be, then the *vodník* is truly good, and his mournful violin playing from weeping willows hung with red ribbons is not just a declaration of his loneliness, but also of the dreadful end that awaits him and his river.

The red sack beats against the willow and lifts from the tree and is carried away on a wind that will give out long before it reaches ČSSR. I look again and can see no *vodník* in the branches. I look again at Sněhurka. Her eyes remain open, unblinking, and I cannot say whether she is awake now or sleepwalking. I lie back again on my sleeping bag. I close my eyes. I remember at once what my father shouted to me as the train pulled out of the station in Prague: "Remember, Emil, that all the *vodníks* on the Labe, even as far as Hamburg, are Czech-speaking!"

I am woken at first light by the shouting of the bargemen and by ropes being thrown from the riverbank to the barge and by the racing of the barge engines. We continue up, deeper into this sphere of lesser possibility. I go to the wheel-house and drink coffee and smoke Red Stars with Hus. We find common cause in ice hockey. We talk of ČSSR's star players. We share victories. We do not bond; we are too far apart for that, I searching for beauty, he for subspecies, but we come within speaking distance.

The names come easily.

"Then we had Maleček, Zábrodský, Drobný," I say.

"While now we have Nedomanský, Suchý," Hus says. "Not forgetting Černý, Holík, Šťastný, and of course Hlinka."

"Especially Hlinka," I say. "The last victory over the Russians!" I exclaim, forgetting myself.

"That was something," Hus says. "We'll remember that even if the world falls apart and comes back together in a better way."

I am given over to puncturing time and to hemodynamics and doubling, but only in ice hockey do I find myself quickened by the present. I am a fan. I jump on trams throughout Prague with my friends, going from one arena to another. We sit close to the ice in those places, among the factory workers from Kladno. We revel in the Rolbar ice machine polishing the surface before face-off, the players lacing plastic helmets under their chins in a tight bow, the leap from bench to ice. We mark the arc of bodies on blades and the quality of the stick handling—all of it too fast for me to frame. We drink cheap beer and smoke and duck when pucks fly up. We heckle players and whistle at the Soviet troops watching up in the rafters in their soft boots of the steppe. Playing ice hockey is even more pleasurable. I skated through childhood and skate still on winter weekends when the village ponds are frozen. I stand tall on the ice. I push out with my legs. I feel myself falling forward. It is not vertigo-inducing; it can be halted with a square turn of my skates. It is a swordfish moment, a loop on crystal, with no past or future save for a wrist-shot slapped into the goal from a narrow angle.

THESE HOURS ARE DAYS. I sweat here under the tarpaulin. I frame a flying fish breaking up through the skin of the river. I drift to sleep in time with the barge engines. I wake to the smell of giraffes, which is already familiar to me. I sit up against the crate containing Sněhurka. Time is stretched here as it must have been on the *Eisfeld* broken down off Zanzibar. It will snap back when the journey ends and I will no longer be able to remember the details, such as the shape and color of giraffe hooves, just as I can no longer properly remember the details of my army service. I feel Sněhurka's legs behind me, through which veins run like vines, and I perform equations to represent the journey of blood through those veins to the ventricles of her heart, powerful as an elephant's heart, on into thick-walled arteries, up the neck against the hydrostatic pull of gravity to her head, pushed impossibly high on an *f*-shaped stick. I feel her pulse. She cannot wish her heart to stop beating, any more than I can. So much of this life is without choice. I am grateful for that. I know that, were it possible, I might wish my heart would stop for a few seconds on a long afternoon in ČSSR, and I cannot be certain that if I felt that stoppage within me, if I felt crimson stars falling and the coming cosmic collapse, I would have the courage to strike up my heart once more.

IT IS TOO HOT NOW for talk of ice hockey. It seems natural
that Vokurka is combing back his thin hair from his sweaty
scalp and talking of Cuba.

"I spent a year on the island," he says. "This was not long
after their revolution. I was sent to assist with the defense
of Cuba against American biological and chemical weapons.
My job was to examine the ballast of American weather balloons, which had drifted from Florida and fallen to earth
among the cows in the Cuban hills, some shot from the
sky by the Cuban military and others struck down by lightning, in all cases, as I saw once or twice myself, descending like a long mirrored ribbon. The Cubans had an idea that
the sand in the weather balloons, which sifted out over the
farmland as it lost altitude, might have been infected. The
leadership in Havana believed the Americans had impreg-
nated the sand with one contagion or another, designed to
lower the fertility of the chickens, weaken the pigs, or damage
the cows. I drove around the island testing sand samples
and drawing blood from animals in the affected districts.
There were a number of veterinarians looking at different
biological and chemical threats to Cuban livestock. We were
Soviets, East Germans, Hungarians, Bulgarians, and Czechoslovakians. The leadership in Havana took an immediate lik-
ing to us."

"You met the leaders?"

"Several times. We were summoned to a beach villa every
few weeks. We announced our findings and the leaders leaned

forward in their deck chairs and listened. It was quite different from what I expected. There were cigars, but no oratory.
They hardly said anything at all."

"Were the Americans doing that? Did you find any evi-
dence?"

He shrugs. "Americans are capable of many things. We
were careful to make up our own confidential reports in such
a way as to leave open the possibility of contamination. I can
only say that all the sand samples I and others gathered were
sterile. The Cubans had no interest in sending us home
immediately. That would have been to admit paranoia, or that
the intelligence service had given credence to wild rumors. I
was occasionally sent from Havana to the east of the country
to draw blood from animals there. The rest of the time I was
free to do as I pleased. The Cubans asked me if there was
anything I wanted to learn. I told them that I had always
wanted to be a frogman. So they placed me in their military
frogman course."

"You became a merman?" I ask.

"A merman? If you like. I spent all my days in the sea. I
swam with stingrays in the tidal gaps and sometimes with
bottle-nosed dolphins in the reefs. I took up pieces of coral,
shark teeth, and small artifacts from among the timbers of
shipwrecks. I was also taken fishing in the mangrove swamps.
There is a time of year there when the tarpon come inland
and feed on the smaller fish. They are as large as salmon and
colored similarly to precious metals. They are fast, blood-
thirsty, and survive in that stagnant water by coming up to
breathe, like mammals."

"Do you go diving still?" I ask.

"Of course. In the rivers and lakes of our ČSSR."

"In the Labe?"

"Yes."

"Surely you can't see anything."

"Not much," he says. "The water is peat-colored. You can make out the shapes of broken plows and cartwheels in it. It is beautiful only on days like this, when the sun reaches into the water. On these days it is like diving into a glass of beer. You can see trout and pike and the hollows in the riverbank and all the cuts in the bed."

"Are you married, František?" I ask. "Do you have children?"

"Take a look," he says.

He pulls out a photograph from his wallet and hands it to me. He is standing in snorkeling suit, flippers still on his feet, between a girl and a young boy whose hair is bleached by the sun. There is a stone harbor wall behind them.

"That's Daniela and that's little Mirek. She's eight. He's six."

"Where was this?"

"Yugoslavia last summer. My wife took it."

His daughter leans close into him, her hand in his, her head on his elbow. His son stands with arms folded to the right of Vokurka. He has consciously made himself distinct from him. Vokurka looks satisfied.

"Has it been worth it?" I ask.

"Has what?"

"The compromises. Joining in with the Party. Playing along."

"I can't think what you mean."

He is embarrassed, a little frightened. I have crossed a line. My heart beats faster for saying it. My blood roars through narrows of ligament. It is the opposite of being a boy and saying to a girl for the first time, "I want to be with you."

Emil

I T IS THE SECOND night on the barge. We do not tie up but continue, our ascent sleepless through DDR. We have passed the town of Tangermünde and are thumping slowly now through Magdeburg in this early hour, the hour, as Dante has it, "that turneth back desire in those who sail the sea," the hour of lowest blood pressure, when people most often die. I have insomnia. I sit here under this tarpaulin listening to Sněhurka and the other giraffes shifting in their crates and banging their legs against the planking.

There is no movement in Magdeburg save a giraffe-colored fox picking through rubbish on the embankment.

This is the town where the astronomer Tycho Brahe alighted on his journey from Copenhagen to Prague. He had lost the tip of his nose in a duel and replaced it with a metal piece that must have shone as he leaned his head back to regard the heavens with his naked eye. Brahe discovered stars simply by stopping and staring more intently than anyone else. I think now of how many more stars Brahe would have discovered if he had worked with giraffes—had employed giraffe eyes. Perhaps even the modern constellation Camelopardalis, sunk deeply by Perseus and Cassiopeia.

Giraffes are not like insects, who feel the world before them with pubic antennae, or bats shining sonar through the dark, or other vertebrates who smell or hear the world. Giraffes see the world. The giraffe eye is the largest in the animal kingdom, several times larger than the human eye, larger still than the eye of a mermaid. It is almond-shaped, framed by long lashes that in Africa blink away flies and swarming gall-ants, but in Magdeburg now only flutter. The optic nerve of a giraffe is as thick as an index finger, and the celestial view that plays through the nerve on the brain of a giraffe—of stars invisible to the human eye and all the subtle colors denoting the age of the star, which twinkle prehistorically down on us—is more finely grained than any Brahe could have hoped for. The height of the giraffe makes a watchtower of it. With its vision and vantage point, a giraffe can see a man shifting on his haunches a kilometer away. It is not that a giraffe has a mystical power of prophecy or foreknowledge, as the Egyptian hieroglyph had it. It is only that a giraffe sees the present before any other animal: When it shifts on the grassland, all the impalas and gazelles raise their heads in alarm. And if by chance a hyena were to happen upon the riverbank here in Magdeburg, chasing away the fox licking now at the butcher's waste, in this hour that turns back resolve, the giraffes about me, even proud Sněhurka, would see the hyena as demonic and try to take flight. The crates would stop them, and their eyes, if I should frame them, would open wide and whirl in terror about their sockets, so that they should feel the thickness of their own optic nerve.

HERE IS SOMETHING: a Trabant 601 trailing black smoke, rattling over a cobbled square in which Martin Luther preached and Lucas Cranach the Elder painted. I wonder now what these men would have made of the giraffes if they saw them now. I wonder if they'd run up to the riverbank and exclaim, "Giraffe!"

Would they cut and keep an image of these thirty-two beasts for a sermon or a painting? I look up from my calculations and coded notes, down the avenue of giraffe necks, and I see that of course they would exclaim. Of course they would preach and paint, for this is a biblical and painterly scene.

WE PASS THROUGH MEISSEN. The sky here is bone-white porcelain, detailed in purple, like the flanks of an okapi. I walk up and down the barge, under wonder nets. Vokurka is at my side. I do not speak anymore of compromises but instead light a Red Star and talk of giraffe physiology. For instance, the way the thoracic vertebrae slip triangularly from neck to tail. I explain to him some of my theories of cerebral hemodynamics.

"Look," he says, pointing south. "There's our ČSSR!"

He points to the limestone hills separating DDR from ČSSR, like a sailor sighting land. There is a fork of lightning over those hills and another. But I hear no thunder. I see no hyenas tracking us through Meissen.

DRESDEN APPEARS STRANGELY oriental on the southern sky in a silhouette of minarets and domes of the large Yenidze cigarette factory, built fantastically before the First War in the style of Baghdad, or some other city of the *Arabian Nights*. Whole parts of Dresden collapsed under a firestorm brought on by a British bombing raid one St. Valentine's Day. It was said that all the oxygen was sucked up from this point of Saxony that night, so that those not already burned alive or killed by falling masonry were suffocated in heat so intense they experienced no cosmic collapse; their blood boiled away. The view from the Labe is gap-toothed. There is hardly any resemblance here to the paintings made by Canaletto, when the city was known as Florence of the Labe. Zwinger Palace is here, miraculously survived, along with its collection of paintings by Van Dyck, Titian, Vermeer, Rembrandt, and my Lucas Cranach the Elder, as well as Dürer's Dresden altarpiece. But the Frauenkirche, the great Protestant church, is a pile of blackened rubble. I mark a point in the sky where the gold cross rose above the dome of the church. I look for the space in the air where the organ Johann Sebastian Bach once played was, as I mark the spot in the giraffe where its heart is suspended. I frame this emptiness and I frame other spaces around the rubble where streets and squares with common gardens once stood. Grooms led Arabian mares and stallions evacuated from Polish stud farms through the firestorm on those streets. The flames rose up and the Arabian horses rose up also on their hind legs in the orange light. Some survived, others galloped swift and white through the inferno until the *j*-shaped brands on their flanks caught flame. They collapsed without oxygen and boiled also. My grandfather spoke of those Polish Arabian horses. He was brought low by such exterminations. He could not forget and related often the fate of the hundred thousand horses brought to Flanders from Texas during the First World War. They were glossy black and chestnut quarter horses, he said, some broken in by cowboys of Czechoslovakian descent, for there were many in the Texas desert who addressed my grandfather in Czech on his travels there—a Novotný and a Švabinský in the saddle, perhaps, alongside a Gonzalez and a McAllister. The quarter horses were placed on trains at the towns of Marfa and Alpine and sold by auction in San Antonio to British and French government agents, who shipped them on through the port of Corpus Christi to Flanders, there to be drowned in mud, or broken under the weight of guns or injured, or driven to madness and shot by an exasperated officer. That war killed so many horses that the automobile took over and relieved the horse of its burden, and many horses came to be unborn. All suffering is connected. That is the feeling I have now on this barge of giraffes passing through Dresden: One suffering connects to another and binds us, as joy binds us.

We tie up beyond Dresden. I look back through fields of turnip to the skyline of the city. The night is tropical, African. Crickets click and chirrup in long grass. I leap from the barge to the riverbank and sit with the East German anglers, who set their lines at protractor angles into waters where there are no sardines, no salmon, but only eels searching upward and Czech-speaking *vodníks* drifting from one soul jar to another, free of the Communist mediocrity above, which is everywhere, even in the fishing rods about me, poorly made by some East German state monopoly, that threaten to break under the tug of the most inconsequential fish. There is no end in sight to the mediocrity: The socialist epoch would have itself extend, red-starred, into a distant future of centrally planned space colonies, and its desire to understand blood flow in vertical creatures on the moon explains the State's passing interest in my hemodynamics.

Emil

WE PASS INTO the shadow of limestone gorges, shoveling giraffe dung into the waters of the Labe.

"What plans do you have after this, Freymann?" Hus asks, looking down.

"To go to my family country house," I say.

"Where's that?"

"Not so far from the source of the Vltava."

"A large place?"

"Yes."

"Swimming?"

"Yes."

"Swimming, girls, and beer: a Czechoslovakian summer!"
He slaps his thigh. "Coming home!" he says.

THE COUNTRY HOUSE is on a farm built a little before the
Napoleonic wars. It is fenced in with brambles and set on the
rise of a flinty field. There is a pond below. There are no slogans in that place. The Communist moment holds no sway
there, where there is no industry. The only ideology is parent-
ism, of when and how much and how loud. The only regime
is mushroom picking, moonshine, and card games. A photograph hangs on the whitewashed kitchen wall. It does not
puncture time like the man falling into the Ganges. It speaks
to a moment that is gone. My mother stood up to her waist in
the pond. I ran with my sister along a wooden jetty that
extended then into our pond. My mother pressed the shutter
release button. And so my sister and I are captured flying in
the photograph, leaping into the air. We are falling. I am gripping my sister's hand. We are laughing or perhaps screaming.
I remember then falling out through the photograph. I let go
of my sister's hand. We entered the pond separately. I sank
deep into waters such as Vokurka plays a Cuban frogman in. I
looked up to see my sister bobbing near the surface, tucked
together, serene, as if she had never left the womb.

WE ARE IN GOETHE'S GORGE. There are gingerbread villas
on either side, a railway signal box newly built in the shiny
metal of Tarkovsky's Solaris and gardens in which beanstalks
climb high against the limestone face. There are pine trees

and dramatic outcroppings atop the gorge that make me think of a picture I have seen of Quebec. These heights hold in them the suggestion of snow falling softly one Christmas Eve to come. There is a castle among the outcroppings and a sleek Bauhaus mansion of granite and sliding glass, solid, reaching out into space over the gorge, like the observation deck over the sloping garden at Nad Pat'ankou Street.

Goethe moved through this gorge with a hammer. He reflected and scribbled. He took his hammer to the face of the rock and picked out molluscs from the floor of an ocean that once weighed on this place. The thought of Goethe's hammer makes me wish to be a geologist engaged in the study of the flow of time, trekking fit and tanned through the Kola Peninsula bounding the White Sea, picking cloud-berries, concerned only with readings of rock formations that have no cosmic collapse and with fording a fast-flowing stream before nightfall.

The sky is polluted in the south with smoke rising from ČSSR and with gray needles that are *paneláks,* eight units high and four wide. There is a mist on the river and candy cane–colored posts on either bank that constitute the border be-tween DDR and ČSSR. We break through. We pass through no sphere of thought. The bargemen throw out ropes to sol-diers and customs men of our ČSSR. Those on the riverbank stop and stare up at the giraffes. A sergeant takes off his hat and mops his forehead with a handkerchief.

"Emil Freymann?" he asks breathlessly.

"Here," I say.

"Come with me."

I place a telephone call to the shipping company in a customs office. The sergeant fans himself at the door of the office with a copy of the *Rudé Právo,* or *Red Truth,* newspaper. Someone answers the phone now. I wave the sergeant away.

"Take up a pencil," I say down the phone. "I will begin."

THERE IS A BARGE tied up by the customs house in front of our barge. It is packed with horses, dogs, a painted caravan, and a truck with Romanian registration. They are Gypsies. They have no home to return to in joy. They find solace in movement. When they are forcibly settled by the authorities and their caravans are taken from them, they become like a broken people. They dance now on the riverbank before the giraffes. They wail and shout up to the beasts. Naked children and children in ankle-length dresses and white goats in yellow ribbons run in delighted circles. A man with skin as dark as that Indian falling into the Ganges plays a feverish tune on his fiddle. Older girls dance around him. I am not diverted by the blood moving up within them, but frame the necklaces of silver coins beating on their chests. The giraffes sway toward the Gypsies, drawn by the music and the coins. Hus invites an old Gypsy woman, a matriarch, onto the barge. He speaks to her as though she were an exotic. And she is the last of her kind: The journeys she has made have been replaced by other, faster journeys. She has spent many seasons behind horses and has seen the world in the narrows of the caravan's hooped roof in lines of mud, ice, horse manure, verges risen in summer, wasps in autumn feeding on fallen pears, wildcats leaping large across wintry bridle paths, of the sun moving steadily across the sky, changing the light within the caravan,

of the quietude of mornings, matched by the music and arguments of the night, a clip-clop near and through Carpathian
valleys far away, in time with the passing of self. She is almost
blind: She can hardly make out the heads of the giraffes Hus
points out to her. Understanding this, Hus reaches down to
the woman and takes her hands and presses them firmly
against the flank of a Rothschild bull.

"Woman," Hus says. "We call this animal a giraffe."

She runs her fingers down the lines of the hide. Her face
lights up. She speaks in her own Gypsy tongue. She moves
her body closer to the giraffe. She places her head against the
dampness of the animal. She says something more. It
becomes a narrative. A boy is brought forward from the riverbank to translate for her.

"She is saying, 'There was a storm on a bowl of water
circled by sand,' " the boy relates. "She says, 'This animal was
floating on the water when the sky went dark all around. The
wind rose. It was hard for the animal to breathe: It felt it
could not breathe. Sand blew from around the edges of the
bowl into its eyes. The water grew rough. It was hard for this
animal to stand. It was thrown from side to side.' She says,
'This animal did not fall. It was another who fell.' "

The old woman takes her hands away, kisses them, and
presses them again on the giraffe.

My homecoming to this ČSSR of 1973 is not like the
return of Pip from the Orient, or of fictional Emil to his
hometown of Neustadt. When I see gray swans flying by the
castle in the town of Děčín, I feel myself a foreigner. I think

now I should have swum perpendicularly to the West German riverbank and exposed myself to the nudists. I should have had them deliver me to the authorities in that sphere and spoken to them of crimson stars in femoral arteries. I seem to have no understanding of the Communist moment they call *normalizace,* or normalization, whereby hundreds of thousands of Czechoslovakians have lost their jobs for opposing the invasion of 1968, the best replaced with the worst, the patriots with lackeys, the questing with the credulous few. I sit at the front of this barge and the droplets of the Labe wet me and wet Sněhurka behind me and I think that I have not emerged from the side of a hill, but am another soul, windburned and shipwrecked on the shores of Schleswig-Holstein, strayed up the Labe, through Goethe's gorge, into a windless and haunted hinterland.

My bearings come slowly, like a weather balloon's descending onto Cuban hills. I see leviathan gravel-making machines in a quarry on a hillside and rectangles cut into the forests on higher mountains that are pistes I have skied. I have carved those steep slopes on which chairlifts now rock lonesomely in parched summer air. I have stood at their sides over my poles, breathing hard into whiteness. My own sense of captivity comes from a recurring nightmare I have of these pistes. I am a skier—a child. I wear goggles, a ČSSR ski hat, jacket, and racing pants. I am clipped into waxed and sharpened skis. The bindings are tight. I have all my equipment, but no movement. I am caged. I drop into a tuck and clatter into metal bars. I am a caged animal. I call out to those who carve turns around me. They pay me no attention. I call out to the *pisteurs* with their shovels. They glance at me sadly: I am not even a hunger artist to them. I cannot do anything in the cage but ski three or four slalom turns and then herringbone up the slope again, over and over, until the snow melts under me and the grass grows up and I am forced to take off my skis and boots, my hat, jacket, and racing pants, and lie naked on the ground, motionless, waiting for night to come and the stars to show themselves.

We tie up the barge finally in the center of Ústí nad Labem, the town where the opera singer alighted from the train to sing the part of a water nymph. We take our bags and check into a new riverside hotel. Inside the lobby, it is all lacquered plywood and factory-produced tile mosaics describing nothing. I go up and shower and shave. I pack away my giraffe-smelling tracksuit. I dress in a clean white shirt and tie and file with the others into the hotel dining room. A window runs the length of the room, through which we can see the giraffes on the barge in this oily summer light as in a painting by Cranach. Some of the giraffes drop their heads and lift them again, as horses do when trying to loosen their bit. Others remain still and marked above the river in f shapes, just as in that photograph in an East German magazine I have seen, supposedly of the Loch Ness monster in Scotland.

There are ten or twelve of us at the dining table. Hus sits at the center. I am at one end. I pick at my meal of pork and cabbage. We all drink. Hus stands now, before the dessert comes. He supports himself with one hand on the back of a chair.

"Another toast!" he says. "To the tallest of beasts."

We all stand once more.

"Giraffes!" we say.

This is a toast that will not often be repeated. Hus taps his glass with a knife. We grow quiet.

"Not long ago," he says, "a British animal trader was commissioned to bring back a collection of penguins from the South Atlantic. He departed the Falkland Islands with eighty-four penguins. He reached Montevideo with seventy. He arrived in London with eight. Half of the giraffes shipped last year to France and America died in the passage. Capitalists lose most of the animals they capture because they're driven by greed. Greed. They gather indiscriminately. They don't look to sex or character. While we socialists gathered our giraffes carefully, before assisting their passage."

Vokurka interrupts with clapping. He is not drunk. He is one of those who claps like a marionette at Party meetings.

"We watered and fed the giraffes on trucks, trains, on ship and barge," Hus says. "A hundred and fifty buckets of grain each day for forty-four days. Tomorrow we will unload thirty-two of our thirty-three giraffes. We release them onto our ČSSR. They have migrated. They will find a new home in our zoo. They will be happy here."

He pauses. He comes to his Czechoslovakian subspecies.

"Their offspring," he says, unable to help himself, "will come to enjoy our winters."

THE MEAL IS DONE. I am too drunk now to seek out my water nymph at the back door of the opera house. I go instead with the others into the hotel garden. It is windless, but I see no quicklime outlines of the dead; they cannot last in this heat. A bargeman corners me and speaks at me of Hamburg.

"I visited a strange brothel there," he says. "You couldn't imagine. Fancy house on a fancy street—across from a park. I opened the gate. I walked down the path. I thought it must be the wrong place. Still I went on. The house had a square tower covered in ivy. Roses grew alongside the gravel path. I pulled the bell. An old lady opened the door. Refined, you know. I blushed. I held my cap in my hands. 'Please, sorry,' I said. 'Not right,' I said. Well, that was all the German I had. The old lady slowly looked me up and down. She smiled. 'Right,' she said, and waved me in."

The bargeman is going on, up the stairs of the house. I light a Red Star. I smoke and try to pay attention to what he is saying to me. I cannot. I am quite drunk now and swaying also.

I WAKE. IT IS EARLY. I am no longer under a tarpaulin lit snowy by Sněhurka's underbelly. I am on a hotel bed. The sheets under me are soaked in sweat. I step out into the hotel corridor. It extends unlit to a single window far away. I walk down to that window. I stand here. I look down. I teeter. I see swallows diving and rising. I trace them blue and cream through the air. I see their articulated wings. They sail out over Ústí nad Labem, over the opera house they go, through the foundries, to groves of English oak at the base of the ski slopes. I do not frame the swallows. They are almost like ice-

hockey players to me: I could never turn them in such beautiful ways as they turn now. I fancy the swallows speak to one
another in patterns of flight about the thirty-two giraffes on
the barge below, around whose necks they might also have
circled in Africa.

I go back to my room. I sleep and wake again. I fall back
now, remembering my dream, not of Schmauch's island
home in a frozen sea, or my certain home, but the longest
dream of a young giraffe with a broken neck falling from a
great height, from space even, falling and falling in a smudge
of liver red, coming alive as it falls, being somehow oxy-
genated, mended in the neck, then being metamorphosed in
the magic of highest cirrus clouds from a giraffe into a young
woman, an air stewardess tumbling head over heels from a
broken plane, yes, a Czechoslovakian Airlines stewardess, in a
dull uniform, screaming in Czech or perhaps in Slovak, black
hair streaming, falling out of summer into a winter's day, to a
river, no, not a river now, a marsh. It is not the salt marsh on
the English coast where Pip saved Magwitch that comes up
to meet her. It is a lagoon not far from Venice, covered in thin
ice. I am aware in my dream that I have never been to Venice,
that the city floating on eggshell waters is made of paper cut
from the books and magazines I have read. I am in the
lagoon. It is me looking up at the flailing stewardess. I hear
her screaming now. She falls swan-necked and long-legged
through freezing fog: She must see the vaporetto setting out
from the distant islands toward the planar façade of the
Doge's Palace. She is growing larger and larger. I hold my
arms out to her. I catch her! I speak to her in Czech. I take her

fast under the icy water, deep into the lagoon. I am a *vodník* in my dream, not of the Communist-lit *hospoda* but fresh as the *vodník* who appears over the shoulders of Justinian and Theodora in Byzantine mosaics.

I fall back into bed. There is so much falling in life. Falling of the shutter on a camera, or of my eyelid to form an image I may keep and turn. Falling of raindrops to the earth, falling of dead, of newborns, and of the unborn in dreams. Sně-hurka might have seen the nameless young giraffe thrown overboard off the coast of Mauritania. She might have been among those giraffes who panicked in their crates, who would have run out onto the violet ocean without under-standing that only saints and storm petrels and Soviet fisher-men can walk on water, or that even if by some miracle giraffes were added to that number, the dead giraffe would sink before them and their gallop away from the *Eisfeld* would have taken them only onto the shore of Mauritania, to a desert where there are no trees a giraffe might feed on. I have fallen into hands at my birth, just as I will fall again at my death, felled by disease or upended by accident. I will also fall to the earth. My veins will collapse too and all the celestial bodies will fall into a soup of dioxides.

It is raining now outside the hotel. The raindrops are soft on swallow wings and on the seats of the chairlifts rocking on the mountainside. I close my eyes. It is inexplicable how the mind sparks in this state. Inexplicable why the comets in the weightless deep of my brain should light, softly as a beer ad-vertisement over the Hamburg skyline, some lines of Goethe, which once in a summer love meant something to me:

Man's soul
Resembles water:
It comes from Heaven
And must again
Fall to earth
For ever changing.

*If we had a keen vision and feeling
of all ordinary human life, it would
be like hearing the grass grow and
the squirrel's heart beat, and we
should die of that roar which lies
on the other side of silence.*

—GEORGE ELIOT

Amina

A Somnambulist

ST. JOHN'S EVE

JUNE 23, 1973

THIS IS THE MARSH that lies at the end of the Svět, or world. It is larger and wilder and more real to me now in its winter coat. Reeds stand stiff upon it, silvered with frost. The water is thin transparent ice in which filaments of weed have been frozen, fair and glinting, like the hair of a *rusalka* rising from the boggy bottom. The willows stand golden on the island in the marsh, still with their slender leaves, still with their red ribbons. I pass under these willows now in my unlikely canoe, which is not Czechoslovakian but a type I have seen in picture books about American Indians: stretched like a drum skin and curved at both ends. I break the ice and

set a paddle to the water and move past banks of soft earth
on the island that are deep in snow, just as in summer they are
hidden under thorns and poisonous weeds and darkened by
clouds of mosquitoes, which swarm over the dogs set down
each spring by men who cannot bring themselves to drown
the dogs at birth, and instead let them out onto the island to
starve or grow mad on a diet of water vermin.

Some of these dogs appear before me now. They bound
along, not venturing out onto the thin ice, but kicking up
snow at its edge, barking dementedly, stopping, starting,
keeping pace, all the while looking at me. I paddle away from
them at a steady pace until I can no longer hear their barking.
I am overcome with silence. There is no sound but that of an
adder slivering across the ice. I love this marsh, I love it
knowing there are places that are not so still and quiet. I stand
up in my canoe and stretch my arms up for exclamation, as
well as for balance. I am alone in my place at the end of the
Svět, or world, the open waters of which I can make out
beyond the marsh, polished black like a sacramental stone. I
sense in this moment I am more than I expected myself to
be, that I am a character in a fairy tale, a prickless hero, one of
those noble and true characters who find themselves rescued
from a hard life by the intervention of magic, but the magic
has not happened to me yet, or upon me. I am sensible to my
condition: I am a worker in a workers' state.

I stand with my arms stretched up in my unlikely canoe,
balanced in my hard life. The hands I open to the air are cal-
lused and shredded from days of wading out with other
workers into deeper water, to my chest, and harvesting reeds
with a rough blade. It is not the season for cutting reeds. I am

alone in this marsh at the end of the Svět, or world, except
for the mad dogs and the skein of red-breasted geese, which
flies now under the clouds toward me. The geese are newly
arrived from the northern tundra, although this too is impossible; this is the wrong season for geese. They drop lower.
Their honking intrudes on the silence. It is distant and inter-
mittent at first and now clearer. They are fat and ruby-
chested; they shift in space, taking turns to fly at the point;
they pass over me toward the open water of the Svět, beating
music from the air, so close I reach up now and brush their
webbed feet, which are charcoal-colored in the winter light.

It is not the season for cutting reeds. It is not the season
for red-breasted geese. It is the moment for magic. I reach in
my pocket and take out a handful of bright-colored beans. I
examine them and throw them one at a time into the water.
They are large and heavy. They shine as they sink. I watch
them disappear

yellow

blue

green

into blackness. I breathe in, I breathe out. It is enough. There
is a bubbling from below, a stench of disturbed bottom mud,
then a green shooting beanstalk, as fast as a jack-in-the-box,
thick as a tree, high as a tree, two, three, five, eight, thirteen,
and up, eighty-nine trees, one hundred and forty-four, two
hundred and thirty-three, and up, six hundred and ten trees
high, yet remaining a beanstalk with the elastic ladder stems
of a beanstalk.

The air and water are quieted. I paddle over and leap from
my unlikely canoe. There is an instant now in my flight when

I look down and see my reflection and understand myself to be no longer a girl, but a woman. I take hold of the beanstalk and settle myself upon it. I run my fingers across its skin of gooseberry down and bumblebee hair. I set a foot on a stem, pull myself up, and so begin climbing. The magic has happened to me and I climb without fear toward the vaulted heavens, as though in a fairy tale. Far, far up, at the height of two hundred and thirty-three trees, my canvas tennis shoes slip from my feet to the Svět. I climb for many more hours, for a day, even, until the red-breasted geese are no more than motes of dust below me, the town and the castle at the end of the Svět no more than the slightest ' , the forest and the patchwork fields small as a ; , and the Svět itself a black ( ). I pass at last from clear sky into snow clouds. My breathing becomes shallow and rapid in the thin air. I lose my footing many times. I am buffeted by fierce winds, which ride here, but never down on the Czechoslovakian marsh.

I break through into another world, without birds, without clouds, above all precipitation except meteor showers. It is a quite different country, squeezed in between marsh and cosmos, a rolling gray land, not Czechoslovakian gray, not normalized in that way, but a gray that comes with lunar proximity. I step off the beanstalk onto the land, which is made of clouds—is a cloudscape, not a landscape. These clouds have substance; they are to air as ice is to water. My feet make no sound in them. When I twirl like a ballerina, I feel myself to be twirling in powdery snow. I walk across this land. I fall down between clouds. It is a struggle to climb up again. Over and over, I slip back into this crevasse until I find purchase, just here, on a lightning bolt. I walk more carefully, watching my step. I lie down and nap at intervals and when I wake, I look up at the stars, which are so close, and think to find new ones with my naked eye, and I hold out my hands to passing cosmonauts, wishing only to stop one of them and practice my Russian.

I do not ever stray out of sight of the beanstalk: I have no great expectations of the magic. I think I see my parents walking over down a cumular slope toward me, from another plane, but when I approach I see they are only shapes of my mother and father, formed from a collage of remembered photos. My parents have not magically appeared to me; neither have deities, angels, or giants with castles in the sky. There are no oracles or sudden riches of golden eggs. I do not mind: It is enough for me to be suspended on this cloudscape.

I circumambulate the beanstalk until the day is ended and the sun sets. The clouds melt under me a little, just as during the day they gathered moisture from the marsh and thickened. I sink in up to my knees. I wade the last steps to the beanstalk. I take hold of its gooseberry and bumblebee skin. I take one last look at the meteor showers, and my parents blowing flat and tattered in the astral wind. I begin climbing down. I slide from one stem to another. A lightning bolt gashes me. I howl. I slide down through the snow clouds and come again into the enormous sleet-washed space, which is carpeted, I see now, with ČSSR. It is still winter in this space. I see white forests stretching all the way to Prague. I slide down for many hours. I rest on bigger leaves. I continue, until my thighs are rubbed raw, and I reach the thick air where the red-breasted geese fly. They fly beside me, beating off moonbeams. I take a deep breath. Down I go until I am thirteen trees high over the Svět and now three and here, on this broken stem, I slide from the beanstalk to a gravel road outside the front gates of the zoo, which stands near the town at the other end of the Svět.

I stand here on the road, barefoot in the slush. I see the chapel of St. Michael. I see the slogans, the hammer and sickle above the brewery. It is strange to me how I remember all this around me that did not exist on the marsh. I look across the Svět to the town and see the castle, the brewery, the spires, turrets, and chimneys, and my *panelák*. The windows of my room are open. My light is on. I cannot see myself curled on a cot below a picture of the Alps. I cannot see myself and I feel a parting within me, which is the knowledge that I am sleepwalking again.

I open my eyes once. Aha! This is revelation. I am not the same person. It is not the same Svět, or world. It is obvious to me that no one harvests reeds on the marsh at the end of the Svět, or sets dogs down there each spring to starve or grow mad. I have no unlikely canoe. Skeins of red-breasted geese do not ever migrate over our town. There are no bright-colored beans in my pocket and consequently no beanstalk six hundred and ten trees high. I cannot say there is no magic, but it has not visited me; it has not raised me up or papered a cloud with a collage of my mother and father, and I do not ever expect it to, except in sleepwalking.

I walk away from the zoo gates, which are fashioned in metal shapes of giraffes and elephants. I walk toward the castle in the town. I open my eyes a second time. I am awake on the stairwell of my *panelák*. I am curled up. I am shivering on concrete, between floors. It is dark. There are no goose wings beating moonbeams onto me. I get to my feet. I look down. I am shoeless: My feet are bare and wet and covered in blades of summer grass and daisies. I climb the stairs. It is quiet in the building. The door to my flat is open. I step inside. I close it gently behind me. I have opened my eyes twice: Am I awake? I climb into my cot under the poster of the Alps. I close my eyes and I pray now for a dreamless sleep.

I sense you will dissolve into mist.

Emil

T ODAY IS MIDSUMMER'S DAY—the nativity of St. John, whose head was paraded on a salver. I am journeying onward to the zoo in a truck carrying four of the giraffes, including Sněhurka. Other trucks have left before us, packed with the vertical beasts, carrying away Vokurka and Hus also, waving his safari hat. I am dusty with river mud from the quay in Ústí nad Labem and softened by several glasses of beer.

It is more parched today than yesterday. Perhaps Hus is right. Perhaps the world is turning on its axis, hippos will come to wallow in the Labe, and Czechoslovakians will come to believe that it is they who have migrated to ČSSR and the giraffes who were here all along. I slump back in the cab of the truck and let my country come at me. Thistles burst from tall grass and rodents I see swirling and gleaming white-toothed and brown and black in the hedgerows. The woods we pass are as thick and lustrous as the jungles of Zaire, where giraffes are compacted down, day by day, into okapi. We drive carefully along back roads, avoiding bridges and skirting the town of Mělník, where the Vltava meets the Labe, the same Vltava that flows by the shipping office and beneath Baba Hill, on whose waters I saw a swan that in its furled state reminded me of the archangel Michael, a snow-whiteness that now makes me think of Sněhurka's underbelly. I turn to view her and the other giraffes through the window in the back of the cab. The narrowness of the window, a slit in metal, seems to frame their coming captivity. Sněhurka stands off to one side. Her legs are planted for balance, her neck bends, gives as if swaying underwater. She is taller and prouder than the others, or perhaps this is just my imagination, perhaps this is only because I recognize her. They are blind to ČSSR. Their eyes are shut tight. Only when the truck stops do they open. We pass through the center of another town, another broken place, but broken so long ago, by Swedes in the Thirty Years' War, so as to be a necropolis, whose cobbled streets are set with gravestones of colored marble. Lungs are scorched in the chemical plant on its out-skirts; pigs are hitched up on hooks in the meat factory here and cut apart while still conscious: There is hardly a pig in the world who escapes a violent end. The Dresden feeling comes at me again, not precisely of a firestorm, horses, or broken-necked giraffes, or even of this necropolis of marble gravestones, lungs, and twirling pigs, but an understanding only that we are bound together, all of us, by suffering, even more than joy.

I roll down the window. In comes the smell of summer. It is more than rebirth. It is the richest rainy season on the nostrils of the giraffes, of soil, grasses, hops, fruits, of ponds opening and gaining from the bodies of teenagers who swim in them by day and bathe naked in them by night, when there is no one to observe them but a fox silent in the trees. We pass a cement factory in front of which sit workers in stained overalls, smoking, not looking up, not noticing the giraffes that move by them, and the smell of the Communist moment sinks through this sweet summer air in leaded gasoline and black dust.

"We should be heading farther on, to the industrial towns at the foot of the mountains," the truck driver says.

"Why there?" I ask.

"This is not such a high place, where we are going now. These animals need something to look down on them. Some mountain. Like they had in Africa," he says.

"Do you know mountains?"

"I was a mountaineer at one time," he says. "I climbed all the highest peaks of the Soviet Union. I climbed far above the snow leopards in the Pamirs of Tajikistan."

There is a suggestion in him, in his mannerisms and in his interest in giraffes, of where exactly they have come from and what their habits are, of a previous life, different from his present life.

"What were you doing before this?" I ask. "Apart from mountaineering."

"I was an engineer at a factory outside Pardubice. We produced turbines for jet engines and shipped them down the Labe on barges."

"You were fired for political reasons?"

"I caught a worker stealing."

"You reported him?"

"He was stealing a little each day—cables, plugs, copper wire. I had no choice."

"How did he react?"

"The usual. 'You're a bourgeois, picking on a worker.' He reported me to the factory committee for my political views."

"What happened then?"

"I was asked to sign a paper in support of the State. I refused and was fired."

"You do not look so unhappy."

"I spoke out before the committee. I held nothing back. I was punished accordingly. The punishment makes me happy—it is a liberation, even," he says, changing gears. "There's nothing to be compromised by driving a truck between one town and another."

WE IDLE AT A JUNCTION by a pale meadow in which a beekeeper tends his hives. The beekeeper stops and stares through his veiled hood at the giraffes. They lean toward him now in return, like giant flowers his bees might feast on. This is a service the giraffe performs: It moves toward those who stand still before it and offers them a sense of otherness.

It is such a bright Midsummer's Day. The play of light on the concrete granary towers and the military silos we pass on these back roads triggers in me, in a turning of comets, a memory of last summer's Olympic games in Munich, television images of monochromatic tracksuits with bold lettering on the back

CSSR

USSR

USA

ETHIOPIA

of sprinters and pole-vaulters in forward and upward motion, booming Afro haircuts, mustaches on swimmers, light playing on the concrete walls of the Olympic stadium, light playing also on a concrete path on the body of a murdered Israeli athlete.

WE STOP NOW in a village near the town of Žlunice and buy beers in a pub and drink them, leaning back against the radiator of the truck. I am side by side with the driver. Villagers step from their pub. They stare up at the giraffes. They come close. They take in the circus smell. Some of them offer up soup plates of beer. The giraffes lean down and set their tongues to the beer. They lap it up. They are migrants, learning where they have arrived.

We drive still more slowly through the afternoon, by fields and ponds. The sky in the east is slanted with rain, but it has not rained here for weeks. The streams are running low, the *vodníks* are gasping. This is my country, a windless and haunted hinterland of rivers flowing into a flat center and then off to seas that are bordered by other peoples, who did not emerge from hills caked in peat.

This is my Czechoslovakia, which is caught in a spell of normalization, darkened, like an insect colony under the shadow of a stone, so reduced and forgetting that only crows remember the old patterns and lift from the branches of the same trees as crows in the time of the Napoleonic wars, when there were no factories and no roads and the journey to Austerlitz took days going and longer coming back. It is nothing like the icebound island beyond the Pole Star, where the gyrfalcon hatches, or the mountains of Papua New Guinea, such as the shipping director spoke of, where the air is so thin the helicopters bringing the miners to the gem mines below the glaciers gain no purchase and spin a full circle before regaining control. My country does not teeter on any kind of edge, but the edge of self. It knows nothing of Hamburg but what *vodníks* whisper in pubs, nothing of fictional Emil's Berlin now divided, and nothing of the salt marshes of the English coast, where Pip once tended Magwitch and so unknowingly secured for a time his fortune. ČSSR is the middle of things, a middling totalitarian state in the middle of Europe, where deep drops in barometric pressure are not met by the shifting of ocean currents but by a pressing-in of the brain, just here, by the temples, a constriction of blood vessels behind the eyes, a certain sudden melancholy, and a pain in porous molars. It is middling roads over middling streams, in which the fleck of trout grown so-so under middling rains must be visible to the keen eyes of the giraffes. It is middling *vodníks* capturing middling souls and potting them in hollows below middling runs of rushes and reeds. It is middling towns with splendid baroque churches of limited congregations and middle-sized *paneláks* haunted by middling quicklime outlines of the dead, and middling factories that never meet the oversized quotas set for them in the Communist moment, and middling villages encircling the towns, where ambitions are no more than those of the *vodník,* that is, to watch over a stretch of river, to preserve souls, and to drink in the pub. Contemplation of my country is enough to bring on nausea. Not seasickness, but land-sickness: I search the horizon for a sea, as a sailor searches for land. I want the meadows to shift under a light swell and the eels to summon up a hurricane, from the Sargasso Sea of their memory, that might swing the bells in the church towers.

We turn north toward the mountains along the Polish border. Schoolchildren from the cities work the hop fields below the hills. A few of them catch sight of the giraffes. They set down their baskets and wave. A bird of prey, a harrier, is circling above. It spies the giraffes and then some morsel creature in the hop field. It pulls back its wings and drops, just as I saw one of those red-starred fighters drop in another summertime, when I was camping in the Orlické Mountains with a girlfriend. She shouted me awake just after sunrise, from outside. The first light was blue-red through the skin of the tent, as daylight must appear in the veins woven about my wrists and ankles. I climbed out after her into the forest clearing. She pointed up at the fighter jet falling silver from the sky. We saw the pilot eject and drift off, like a seed under a parachute. The jet fell nose-first, silent as the harrier diving now, but with a sense of many tons of unsupported metal, and with a violence of flames ripping back over the wings. It passed under the trees. It was gone in a blink. There was an explosion, a fireball, then a secondary explosion. We put on boots and ran through the forest, into smoke, and at last came upon the wreckage of the jet, in a canyon of the River Zdobnice, which flows into the Labe. We teetered at the edge of the canyon and saw the fighter jet lying red-starred below, smoldering through its metal plates, like a speared dragon through its scales.

"LOOK AT THAT." I point out a shrine at a crossroads. Its window and frame are smashed. The crucifix inside is broken.

"I see it," the driver says.

"People used to put candles and wildflowers before the statues in these shrines," I say. "No one looks after them now. People do not even see them. They pass them unthinking, as they pass under trees unthinking."

"You mourn the crucifixes so very much?" he asks.

"Not only the crucifixes. I mourn the forgetting."

It is getting to be dusk. We stop finally at the edge of the town with the zoo.

"Why are we stopping?" I ask. "It's late. We're almost there."

"I like to reflect for a moment before completing a journey," he says, stretching. "It's a habit of mine."

"Like pausing before a summit?"

He looks at me. "Different," he says.

There is a sadness in his eyes, which is also a registering of a drop in barometric pressure. A thunderstorm is almost upon us. My teeth begin to hurt. We squat down and smoke Red Stars. Insects whir through the smoke rings we blow. We are parked in the yard of a sawmill. There is wood all around, some of it already cut into planking. The smell of wood shavings makes me think of Pinocchio, who was spared because he spoke up. It was a piece of cherrywood, intended for a table leg. It found voice and called out to the carpenter saying that it had no wish to be cut up and made into something dependable, on which a table could stand. So Geppetto got the piece of cherrywood and fashioned his puppet from it. The puppet became a boy, a he, whose face sweated resin under the Tuscan sun.

We cross the Labe. The river is shallow here and contained in a narrow concrete channel; it flows fast with the last snowmelt of summer. We drive past a factory making Christmas decorations and wind through one-way streets to the main square. We pause beside the well-known plague column, of tusk-colored marble, fashioned after Trajan's Column in Rome, corkscrewing similarly up into the clouds, celebrating not a victory over the Dacians, but those who succored the victims of the 1713 plague.

Large raindrops splash from a great height onto the dusty windshield. It becomes a thunderstorm. It is not a hurricane summoned up by eels: It is not enough to swing the bells in the church towers. We drive slowly out by the castle and the town brewery. We edge under a medieval gate onto a gravel road that swings in a *U* shape around a fishpond called the Svět that is some kilometers long and bounded by forest to give it a northern aspect. The driver turns on the headlights. The beams open up a way to the zoo. There are lightning strikes across the sky and out over the fishpond. I turn to look at the giraffes through the narrow window.

"Slower," I say, to the driver. "They're scattering under each lightning strike." We edge along through torrential rain, but I see no hyenas tracking us; the hyenas are farther along, in the zoo.

Through the wipers I make out a white heron lifting from the road. Behind the heron is a young woman. She dissolves and resolves in the rain. She holds a plastic anorak over her head, but her dress is soaked through. She holds a hand up against our beams. The driver dims them. Still she does not move. She stares blindly, or blinded, out at us. The driver stops. He looks at me.

"I'll see what's happening," I say.

I drop from the truck to the road, turning an ankle on the gravel. The rain is like a sheet. Within a few steps I am as wet as the woman.

She calls out, "Why must you transport missiles into the forest?"

She is beautiful: short, light, her hair photographic black, her eyes wide-spaced and large, liquid, opal like a giraffe's. She takes a step back and dissolves once more into the storm. She might have walked up from the Labe or from the fishpond here, yes, like a *rusalka,* or at least a nymph such as the opera singer was playing in Ústí nad Labem; out for love, a ripple that cannot be perceived.

"We're not going to the forest," I call back. "We're heading to the zoo."

She is somewhere there, in the slant of rain and head-lights.

"What's happening?" I call. "What's the matter?"

She steps forward again. "Nothing," she calls in a voice that is sad, not shrill.

"Please, get off the road. We need to pass. We have living animals."

I limp back to the truck. When I turn, she is nowhere to be seen.

"She's by the tree over there," the driver says, pointing a finger.

I see her looking up as we pass. I follow her in the mirror. She steps quickly onto the road after the truck.

The giraffes no longer scatter under the lightning strikes. They remain huddled together, leaning out, looking back at the last stretch of their assisted passage.

We come to the zoo gates. The driver presses hard on the horn. The gates open wide. We enter.

I STEP DOWN from the truck, into the rain once more.

Hus comes running up in his safari hat.

"We thought you would have been here sooner," he says.

"We were careful," I say.

"Do you have enough for your scientific paper?" he asks.

"I think so," I say.

We shake hands. I turn from him. I look finally at Sně-hurka and the other giraffes. I must leave. The zoo is not my place. Snĕhurka's head does not drop now. It is raised even higher, so that her *f* shape becomes an *I,* the better to glimpse that *rusalka* over the walls of the zoo. She is a giraffe, she has two gaits—walking and galloping. Where will she gallop in this place, where the horizon is forever defined for her? I am sad not to have seen her in the wild, not to have been there on the grassland one day in the dry season when she and the other giraffes ran at full tilt, not away from Hus and Vokurka, not that day, but another day, when they were running toward some temporary home under acacia trees, their necks affording them lateral inertia, the legs on one side moving, then the legs on the other, in just the same way as camels and okapis run. I am too late. Snĕhurka will become a zoo animal. Her eyesight will falter. Distances will mean less to her. She will look across less often. Her view will instead be drawn down, to Czechoslovakians stopped and staring up at her.

A lion roars. Snĕhurka and other giraffes start forward and wish to take flight from the wet floor of the truck. Hus laughs. Perhaps he is right; perhaps the giraffes will come to understand that the lion is caged also and can never move on them, but is instead fated to plow, with ruined claws, its own furrow of despair on concrete. Only occasionally, when the light strikes their enclosure in a certain way, as an equinoctial sun struck an Icelandic volcano in Jules Verne's *Journey to the Center of the Earth* and revealed to explorers an opening to the core of the planet, will the pupils of the giraffes dilate in some contrary fashion, betraying in a clinically observable way, even to a hemodynamicist, a memory of something more than the walls that contain them.

Amina

THERE IS NO WINTER wonderland in my waking. It is Midsummer's Day in ČSSR of 1973. It is my birthday. The first light blazes on the walls of my flat, and the ceiling is dappled with the reflected waters of the Svět, which is a fishpond turning with carp, roach, tench, and perch, stretching out of sight from my town and giving out into a small marsh, where a few otters live. My flat is one room of four plastered concrete panels, a few steps one way, fewer steps the other. There is a cupboard with ice-hockey sticks that belong to someone else and a balcony with a view over the Svět. The walls are thin. It is possible to hear the radio playing polkas in the rooms on either side and sometimes shouting and other times lovemaking. I feel trapped in here. It is not a cage, not that, only the sense of inevitability that comes each time I walk out over the frozen Svět in winter, getting just so far, then despite myself, turning, seeing the *panelák,* seeing my room, seeing my return there, again and again, in patterns of footsteps that will hardly ever change.

I am Amina Dvořáková, no relation to the composer. It is I who awake musical, with arias in my head. It is I who open these hemispheric eyes, which my mother said were starlit, as though from within. How I look is mysterious to me. I am shy, bookish, and musical, ill-fitting. I most resemble the romantic suicide in a prewar Czechoslovakian film called *Vzpomúnka na ráj,* or *Memories of Paradise,* which begins with colliers shouldering coal through a Prague of 1935 that is more dense and alive with itself, where coal smoke hangs in a blanket over green domes of old churches, and the shops in the new parts of town are done up with bright lights that promise to blink on and off forever. That suicide whom I resemble stands on the Charles Bridge, looking straight out from paradise into the cinema, at me, and then about her politely making sure there is no beau around who might feel the need to save her. She jumps down into the River Vltava. Her skirt flies up. Splash! She sinks without trace. The film cuts to the surface of the water, breathtakingly oil-black, twinkling with indistinct lights. The effect is of submersion, as though we Czechoslovakian cinemagoers are no longer supposed to be looking from the Charles Bridge to the river, but from the underside of the Vltava at the sky, and to understand by this that the romantic suicide is nothing of the sort, but a *rusalka* returning to her element. My hair is longer than the hair of that *rusalka,* but not so lustrous; it does not twinkle oil-black like that part of the Vltava, as hers did. Our faces are similar in nose and lips, in cheekbones, alabaster skin, and sensitivity of expression. So too our bodies, slender and slight, aerated, unexpectedly strong. She might feel, as I do, of an incorrect density, light enough to one day glance off the face of the world, and to be no longer possessed by it.

I have slept and risen and sleepwalked in the night, and slept once more in my cot under a poster of the Alps. My eyes open first to a scene of Swiss railways, to a red train passing over a tumbling river, up to slopes of Cembra pine and larch, sharpened peaks, and a skier carving a dreamy *S* on hickory skis down pistes to an operatic village of tiled rooftops and seemingly beyond, out of the poster, down my hair, into my narrow place. The arias recede. I throw back my sheets and move about my room. Light plays on my body, settling in the cups of my heels and in warm bars across my flat stomach. I select a record and place it on the turntable. I set down the needle. A Brahms lied for mezzo-soprano sung long ago comes forward respectfully and fills the room.

I go to stand before the sink and sponge under my arms and between my legs. The dress I pull on clings to my skin. I put a kettle on the stove and light a flame under it. I stand still, listening to the music. I look up once more at the faded lithograph on the wall showing John the Baptist standing in the River Jordan, his arms stretched up as though about to lift into the clouds. The piece ends. I pour myself tea. I stand out on the balcony and sip it. It is long before work. The light is

fragrant, the air also—there are two white and ocher butterflies dancing just out of reach.

There is the Svět and the forest. The sky beyond the forest
is yellow. Industrial towns are hidden over there, at the root
of monstrous chimneys. They grow on the proclamation of
the Communist moment. The rain falls acid on them, the
trees in their municipal parks die, and I have seen frogs there
burst in toxic ditch water. My town is older and much smaller
than those industrial towns. It follows the orders handed
down from Prague, but it does not grow in consequence. It
was not created under any red banner. It has its own memories. Here and there it follows its own logic. The chimneys
here are short and few: Our famous town zoo has a chimney, the brewery has a chimney, so also does the Christmas-
decoration factory, where I work. My town is not poisoned. It
is saved from the industrial towns by a ring of forest, where
men march now between secret military bases.

The industrial towns pull men and women from their beds
with tidal force. These workers rattle out of the industrial
towns at dawn, on trams that spark out over fields of beet,
and alight at factories, foundries, and the square mouths of
coal mines. I once took such a journey. It was odd to be moving across fields on a tram, with no buildings in sight. A man
sat across from me, arms folded, in the beret and knee-length
leather coat of 1950s worker fashion.

"I pour steel," he said, out of the silence, "into blocks that
are made into pylons, to hold up power lines."

He stared at my breasts—not in lust, but looking through
me, seemingly occupied by a memory that meant something
to him.

"Please look away," I said.

"What's that?" he said. "Was I looking?"

"I cannot bear your look any longer," I said.

His eyes fell to his boots, but with the same blank expression.

The white and ocher butterflies are gone. I stand here on the balcony and look out over the back of my town. I see the roof of my factory. I see the River Labe flowing in its channel. I see the town walls, the steeples and turrets within, the bright prick of the golden eagle atop the plague column, the castle, the brewery. I see a brewery worker cycling along the gravel road that runs around the end of the Svět to the zoo. I watch him pedal through the parkland, around the fateful bend, dropping out of sight in the fruit trees around the baroque chapel of St. Michael.

THE CASTLE AND THE ZOO are reflected in the Svět, which looks natural, but was man-made centuries ago, when they flooded the flats with marsh water. The men who crisscross the Svět call themselves fishermen because they harvest the carp, but they are more like farmers, sowing seed and fertilizer on the face of the waters, as on a field. The Svět stands a little higher than the streets of my town, so that when they used to cut and drag blocks of ice from the pond in winter, they wore down the banks containing it, and caused the waters to spill out, flooding the deep cellars with thrashing fish. The Svět and the forest have their own rhythms. Winter, spring, summer of storks lifting languidly from their nests on the brewery roof, autumn of short copper days—my autumn of dreamlike afternoons reading in the town library, looking at the departing birds, and the maple leaves swirling up against the boards of the outdoor ice-hockey rink, in which boys play out games in the sand with tennis balls, waiting for winter.

IT IS LONG BEFORE WORK. There are no fishermen or farmers out on the Svět. There is only a corrugated red float drifting from a campsite on the far side. There is a haze over the brown water. I cannot see as far as the marsh at the end of the Svět, or the clearing by the sawmill in which the archangel Raphael is nailed to a tree, where yesterday I went to place wildflowers, as the drovers once did, and saw a couple riding unsteadily on a tandem bicycle, and in the next moment a pair of dragonflies locked together in flight. I sip my tea and listen to Brahms. My dreams are exposed now, in this light. They fade. I was sleepwalking again and awoke shivering on the stairs. I have a memory of ascension, but nothing more.

I walk from my *panelák* to the Svět, to swim before starting work at the Christmas-decoration factory. I come to my secluded place. I slip off my dress—I am that suicide or *rusalka,* made slender and pale from the chemicals of the factory. I wade out. Cattails scratch my skin. Mud stirs about my calves and at the back of my knees. The water comes up to my hips. I push off. It is tepid in here. I swim out and tread water and look back now, at finches and buntings flitting on the shore, and warblers singing tunes from the highest bulrushes. A muskrat slips in with me, from a hole in the bank.

Coots and tufted ducks are about me. Something moves between my toes, some tench's fin. I swim far out to the float. I climb up naked onto it and drift together with it across this brown water without current, whose bottom holds treasure and hollows where cavemen lit fires an age before the Svět was flooded into being.

I am an orphan, a factory girl living alone. I have no telephone. Messages are left for me with neighbors, or at the factory, or written in the margins of postcards sent to me from surviving relatives in other parts of ČSSR. I dip glass decorations in paint to be hung from Christmas trees. I attend to my friends and the small responsibilities of my town. I paddle naked on a corrugated red float across the Svět on this morning of Midsummer's Day. My birthday is of no great consequence. My life will leave no lasting mark. It will be no more than the mark of a cuff button on one's wrist that quickly fades, or these few ripples vanishing as I slip from the float into the water. It is nothing to be sorry about. I am like the swallows around me on the Svět. I touch the world, I rise again.

I backstroke to the shore, watching clouds as I go. I dry myself among irises and take a path to the factory that leads by the statue of a Jesuit standing on the head of a whale or a mighty carp, such as are netted in the Svět once in a generation, and by the Spořitelna Savings Bank, which has above its doorway a stone statue of a fisherman cradling a carp. I step lightly on the bridge over the Labe to the factory. I see my colleague Eva waving to me.

"Amina!" she calls.

We go in arm and arm, into Christmas colors and fumes.

.   .   .

I HAVE WORKED autonomically in the factory all day. I feel awake now in my girlfriend's arms, on a lawn in the parkland sloping away from the chapel of St. Michael. We have drunk some wine. Mosquitoes and horseflies are on our skin. We can hear the evening train passing through the forest. We can smell each other, and the brewery, and the bog and quicksands that circle the old town walls. The trees above us are swollen in the heat. The crickets are loud. My girlfriend rolls off me.

"Did you hear what happened on the Svĕt this morning?" she asks.

"No," I say.

"A brewery worker cycled out there before work with his pockets filled with stones," she says. "He rowed out to the deepest part of the Svĕt. He jumped in. He sank. He thought himself dead. His lungs closed to the world. When his feet touched the bottom, he found his body was not in agreement with his mind. His legs began walking with a will of their own—all the way to the shallows! His head became exposed. Despite himself, he began breathing. A boat laying down fish feed spotted him thrashing in chest-high water, ducking himself, then up again. They weren't sure what they were looking at. He was dazed, they said, with a bloody nose. They drew close. He lashed out at them. His mind was quite made up against living."

"What happened next?"

"They knocked him out with an oar."

"He wanted to escape."

"He wanted to die, Amina," she says with a sad look.

IT IS GOING TO RAIN. The pressure has dropped. I feel a throbbing in my temples. The castle clock strikes nine.

"Do you remember," my lover asks, "the last time we climbed the clock tower?"

"When my parents died," I say quietly.

"The dial on the clock was almost clear."

"We could see through time," I say, "all the way to the zoo."

"We watched the cogs of the clock. The bells were below us. Remember how we were so amazed the hands on the clock turned in a different direction?"

"Going backward, never stopping," I say.

"We thought if we stood there long enough," she says, rolling back toward me, "your parents would be waiting when we climbed down."

We kiss once and fall silent now. Our conversations often end with a moment that has already gone.

WE GATHER OUR THINGS and run from the tempest in different directions, to other parts of the town. I hold my anorak over my head, like a flightless glider, and dash between the swollen trees, over silenced crickets, and stop breathlessly at the concrete tanks by the Svět, into which carp are sluiced at harvest time. The tanks are empty now, gathering only rainwater in their deeps. I have seen them full in the Christmas season, when ČSSR demands carp gills for supper. I have seen how those fish beat themselves into the air with the desperation of something that knows it will soon be knifed anyway. They hold themselves up from the crowd below, eyes popping in the air, then fall down onto the backs of other carp.

I leave the concrete tanks and come out onto the gravel road, which curves inevitably around to the *panelák* where I live.

Lightning forks and strikes out on the Svět. A white heron is ahead of me on the road. I make it out before it rotates its speared head, sees me, and lifts away. I see a truck coming slowly up behind the heron. Its headlights blind me. I am paralyzed. The truck stops. A man jumps down from the passenger side. I see him through the rain. He has golden hair. He is about my age.

"What's the matter?" he calls.

I realize now he is calling to me.

"Nothing," I call.

"Please, get off the road. We need to pass."

He climbs back into the truck.

I feel suddenly weak. I stagger to the side of the road. I lean against the trunk of an oak tree, breathing hard. The truck goes past me. I look again. It is not, after all, a military truck heading to the forest. I see the man in the passenger seat staring down at me. I have dropped my anorak and my bag at the base of the tree. I am standing a little out from it with my hands at my sides. The rain seems to pass through me, washing through the paint-spattered rubber clogs I wear.

I see something moving behind the cab of the truck, some high load, which is not missiles or logging machinery.

"Giraffes!" I call out, then put a hand to my mouth.

Four giraffes blink and gather in the storm light. The sky pours wet down their necks. Without thinking, I run out behind the truck. I stare up at the giraffes. I am captivated by them. Looking at them, I feel awakened. They are as slender as I am, with sensitivity of expression. They are also of an incorrect density, reached up, as on tiptoe, off the face of the world, aimed for that place I would like to be. I see their necks and chests, but not their bodies. I run a little farther behind the truck. The giraffes move toward me. They see me. They lean down. I wish to jump up and touch them, but they are gathering speed away from me. Lightning forks. I see the giraffes in silver, as nacre jigsaw puzzles that are in need of no solution.

It is just a few soundless seconds. They are gone now, around the bend into the zoo.

I walk slowly back to the oak. I pick up my anorak and bag. I close my eyes. I see giraffes precisely welted on the back of my eyelids. I open my eyes. I follow my footsteps in the gravel away from the zoo, toward the *panelák*. I am wet through, as if I have also walked involuntarily from the bottom of the Svět, with stones in my pockets. I must look even more like that *rusalka* or suicide who jumped from the Charles Bridge. That is not so. I am not a *rusalka*. I do not belong to the creatures in the water. I am wet with rain and rain comes from above, where I would like to be. My element is air, not water. I am not so important, I am a voiceless worker. I have this one understanding, that I am slight, aerated, strong with bird ribs, and am not meant to be within, or down. I am meant to reach up, as arias and lieder reach, as these giraffes reach. If it were possible, even in sleepwalking, I would stand on the Charles Bridge, with my hands above my head, and lift off out of the Communist moment, just as John the Baptist appeared, on my lithograph, to be rising from the Jordan, on this, the day of his nativity.

Amina

THE SKY IS PINK, the Svět petaled with fish coming up
for flies, and swimmers making for shore. My town has
slowed and sunk in the heat. The bogs and quicksand circling
the town walls are dried up and cracking open. I stand in the
parking lot of the zoo, getting up the nerve to enter. It is an
hour before closing. The parking lot empties around me,
buses departing to the industrial towns under the mountains.
Each bus carries workers and their children, people like me,
but more alert, as though awakened by the otherness inside
the zoo. I gather myself. I walk to the gates shaped in metal

forms of animals. I have not stepped in here since I was a
child, when my parents were alive. There is no wind to carry
the smell of it across the Svět, but I see it reflected in the
water by day and there are nights when I hear trumpets and
howls through my open windows.

The ticket seller looks up at me from behind metal bars.

"One, please," I say.

"We're almost closing," she says.

"I'll be quick," I say. "I just want to see the giraffes."

I do. All I want is to contemplate their stretch up.

"The giraffes aren't showing, dear," she says, as if talking
of a film, as if the zoo were a cinema. "They've only just
arrived. They'll be showing in a few weeks. Still want in?"

"Yes."

She hands me a ticket stub. The zoo is not expensive. It is
a subsidized workers' entertainment.

I go in. I pick a path at random. I walk swiftly along it,
away from the cheetahs, past ornamental ponds. I pass an ice-
cream vendor, a man I seem to recognize, pushing a cart with
a polar-bear sign. From a cage comes the sound of a radio
comedy. I see a zookeeper scrubbing the floor of the cage
with a long soaped brush. I hear the comedy break off and
the state news broadcast come on. "Now we are switching to
Bratislava," the voice says in state monotone. The news is in
Slovak. This is curious. I do not usually notice such things.
There is a smell of an incinerator and of dumplings coming
from the zoo restaurant, but it is not more powerful than the
smell of the animals. I walk on, up the slope. There is propa-
ganda here also, red banners and old Party members in lilac
uniforms sitting on benches, but it is easier not to notice it

among the wild animals. I look across, but I cannot see any giraffes stretching up, into pink.

I dwell instead on a rhinoceros, such as may have trampled me in my childhood nightmares. It stands enormous and gray in a pit that slopes down to a green stagnant pool. It does not look up, but circles with utmost gravity around piles of beet and mounds of its own dung. Its sides seem like plates of armor, its legs like columns, its ears like feathery cones. It has no neck—the head meets the body directly. Its eyes are small, without color or expression. It better belongs to the dinosaurs, to the rhinos that charged around Czechoslovakia before it was sunk to the bottom of an ocean and raised again molten. I cannot imagine how dimly the world must arrive inside the head of this rhino, whether it sees me through its lanced eyelets, or ever notices the red banner hung over its pit declaring: OUR MORALS ARE FIXED!

I step over a stream of white effluent. I walk on. I come to a cage containing wolves. They also move in gray circles before me. They are large and bony; their lope is springy. And I think of a story told to me in the factory cafeteria of a zoo in the east of ČSSR, in a town that gives out onto wilderness. The zookeeper was walking home at the end of the day, the story went, when he heard his wolves howling as he had never heard them before. He went to investigate and there saw a pack of wild wolves sitting before the cage. The wolf pack had come out from the wilderness and was communicating with the captive wolves, and the emotion between them was deep.

I come next to an aviary. I expect to see an owl. I see nothing. Now comes a flash. And again, like a struck match, lighting the cage. Now I see it. A creature I have never seen before. There is no name on the cage. I have no idea what this creature is or where it is from. I look more closely. It becomes brighter and stranger. I think of the books I have read in the town library. All the sketches I have made. The animals I have dreamed of in my sleepwalking. Still I cannot make sense of it. This creature is the size of a large otter, with an otter's whiskers. It has the coat of muskrat, like the one who swam in the Svět with me, but orange in color. It has the nose of a dog, the eyes of a fox, the teeth and claws of a leopard, the tail of a kangaroo. It leaps predatorily in the aviary, from one branch to another. A siren sounds, a voice comes over the loudspeakers: "Revered comrades. Please pay attention! The zoo is now closed. Revered comrades. Make your way to the exit."

I walk to the gates past a group of sand gazelles. They appear slight enough, with delicate muscles and polished hooves, to one day lift off the face of the world with me. They bleat and cock their heads in such a way as to remind me of some classical civilization I have read of, in which water was poured into the ears of goats outside the temple so that they bleated and shook their heads vigorously when they were brought before the priests and this was taken as a sign they were willing to be sacrificed. I walk more quickly now by groaning beasts and apes with offset teeth, some spending themselves and others rising or bedding down. The gates are locked behind me. I stand again in the parking lot. The sky is a redder shade of pink now. I look up the slope and pick out a barn in the zoo that might hold the giraffes. I look beyond the zoo to the forest, which encloses the Svět.

Sněhurka

I ENTERED THIS ZOO with three other giraffes under the violence of a thunderstorm. We leaned toward a Czechoslovakian woman stilled in the rain in the very last moments before the gates opened to us. We stood inside the zoo in an idling truck and glimpsed forms of other animals in the wet dark. I saw white teeth. I saw the cherry flash of baboon rumps. I saw all of the baboons, a legion, gnashing, careening forward at us, dashing themselves against the bars of their cage, falling back and beating their arms on the concrete floor.

· · ·

No lioness ever came for me. I moved confidently down beetle-enameled riverbeds. I was darted and captured by Czechoslovakians. I was put on a train. I did not move on that train, but the world revolved under me. I was put on a ship. I did not move on that ship, but the ocean swelled under me. There is no movement now. I am stopped and the blade is stopped under me also. I stand in a metal-sided barn. I am near the doors: I am a leader and I wish to be the first into the light. It is crowded in here. I strike the chests of other giraffes in walking. Fear is contagious in this halt, where there are no barefoot boys to call up greetings, but only a keeper.

I feel the roof more keenly than the walls. I wish to see the sky, to set myself up, against gravity. I stand here by the door whispering to a bull my memories of Africa, of a certain light that struck there, which elongated my shadow across the red earth. I whisper to him of galloping on the ash-colored grassland, sundering termite mounds with my hooves, of being graceful in my immensity, like a whale in ether. I whisper to him of plantations that revolved under us on the train, where women moved along corridors planted in dark soil, picking fruit. The bull puts his neck against mine and whispers to me of the Cape of Good Hope, of sandy coves on which waves broke like clouds, of sea lions on those sands and barking in the waters about the ship. I whisper to him of albatrosses gliding at our heads, of dropping into a trough in the ocean and rising again, so that the many chambers of our stomachs lifted up our throats. He whispers of the English Channel, of a fog bank stretching from the low coastline of Belgium to the salt marshes on the English shore, of the ship becoming a barge, the ocean a river. And I remember now the river narrowing, so that some of us feared predators in the trees.

THE DOOR OPENS, to the sky. I am the first out. I push my head back. I stretch myself up, on tiptoe. I feel an updraft within me that is more than rising blood. I move around the small yard. There is no wind here. There are no oxpecker birds to pick the ticks from my back. I look around me. There are materials in the air: It smells of smoke. I see beyond the zoo to shapes of trees and Czechoslovakians laid out in the sunshine. I see a forest encircling a watering hole. I see spires and towers. I hear a lion. I rear back. I drop my head. I feel my blood roaring.

THE KEEPER PRESSES US back into the barn at the end of the day. I do not sleep. None of us sleeps. We are not bats, who hang down for so many hours and then sweep out on sonar to gorge themselves. We are sleepwalking beasts. Our eyelids flutter but remain open. Our teeth grind in fits of bruxism. We push up. We walk with unfocused eyes through the barn. We bump into one another, not waking but galloping inward across ash-colored grassland and stretching up to the highest branches.

Ah! Sweet innocent girl, lovelier for
your suffering.

—FELICE ROMANI

Amina

I AM NAMED AMINA for the heroine of Vincenzo Bellini's opera *La Sonnambula*. They say it is a pastoral tale. Operatic Amina is the prettiest girl in her mountain village, which I picture to be the Swiss village of tiled rooftops on the poster above my bed. She rises at night and sleepwalks. The villagers mistake her for a ghost and think themselves haunted. During one fit of somnambulism, Amina enters the rooms of a count and, dark to the moment, lays herself out on his bed. The count discreetly flees the scene. Amina's lover is less forgiving. He breaks off their engagement, thinking her

unfaithful. The count then publicly defends Amina, in words
that often repeat in my head:

> *There are some, who, though asleep, behave as though they were*
> *awake, speaking, answering when anyone speaks to them, and*
> *they are called "sleepwalkers" because they walk and sleep.*

Amina steps from the window of a water mill in the cli-
mactic scene. She sleepwalks along a plank set precipitously
over the mill wheel. The plank is rotten and gives way, threat-
ening to cast her down into the blades of the wheel. There
are gasps and screams from the villagers below, who now recognize her as a wronged girl, not a specter. They cry out:

> *God in Thy mercy guide her unsteady feet!*

Their prayer is heard. Amina makes it to the grassy bank
on the other side. She awakes there, agitated and bruised, in
the arms of her unworthy lover. Her innocence is proven.
She is wed at once. The villagers sing a joyful chorus and in
the last line of the opera express their true feelings for her:

> *Ah! Sweet innocent girl, lovelier for your suffering.*

This is what my father used to say to me when I mis-
behaved and he was forced to punish me. I have no such
romance. It is strange to be named for an operatic orphan
and then to be orphaned, and stranger still, in this age of cosmonauts, to have grown into a somnambulist in resemblance
of her. I sleepwalk without wishing it. It is a condition. It

comes from too little rest or too much, from being an orphan, and from paint fumes settling under my tongue in the factory or bubbling in a particular way in my chest. The root of all sleepwalking is surely with Adam, who stood with his eyes open and his arms stretched up out of the Garden of Eden, as God reached in and peeled out a rib, from which he fashioned Eve. It began for me as a child with *pavor nocturnus,* or night terrors. The chemicals meant to hold my body in paralysis were not released as they should be, so that my waking and sleeping states became mixed. I was caused to sit upright in bed. I was a little girl, jackknifed in fear. My eyes were wide and rolling. I let out the longest screams, until my parents came and shook me awake and comforted me. It was always impossible for me to explain to them what had so terrified me. It was something more than achluphobia. A charging rhino maybe, or the underside of the world seen slipping away from space, or a childlike understanding of how the finite drifts like the tiniest mustard seed on the winds of the infinite. After I was orphaned and there was no one to wake and comfort me, the night terrors gave way to sleepwalking. I rise at night with dilated pupils. I perform complex tasks in my sleep. I sponge myself at the sink. I cook. I listen to records. I sew. I have vivid recollections in sleepwalking of lifting off. Snatches of the dreams remain with me, as in looking down from a cloud to slicks of goose fat floating on the surface of the Svĕt, and to reeds being fed to a thresher on the deck of a paddle steamer grounded on a dried-up channel in a marsh. I sleepwalk out of my *panelák.* I walk with the eyes of the hypnotized; I am a ghost to the fishermen stumbling home drunk. I sleepwalk along the edge of roofs in the dead of night, naked, on tiptoe, my arms stretched up like John the Baptist's, without chorus or lover to witness my foot reaching out into space. I do not fall but often wake bruised and agitated under linden trees or at the base of the helical plague column. I lower my eyes to the painful daylight and sing quietly to myself parts of *La Sonnambula* and lines my mind has added, such as:

Dear God!
Where am I?
Revered comrade, tell me from what height have I fallen!
What's happening?
Ah, I beg you, comrade, don't wake me up!

The birdsong has quieted outside. I place *La Sonnambula* on the turntable. I set down the needle. I turn the sound low, so as not to disturb my neighbors. I listen. There is scratched silence. The record revolves. Then a first line

Viva! viva! viva! viva! Amina!

My parents were struck and killed at a bend in the gravel road by the Svět. They were flattened by a military truck headed for a secret base in the forest. I sometimes imagine them to have died in other ways, for instance to have been blown from the clock tower or from a mountain above the industrial towns, for they were not large people. I have grown to love the music they left me. I am light and knitted strong with bird ribs. I will reach up. I will lift off the face of the world, just as the arias in *La Sonnambula* stretch up on tiptoe, swell in eights into bel canto, and lift from the stage. The villagers feared operatic Amina would drop into the mill wheel. They did not notice she was walking the plank on tiptoe, with her arms stretched up. They had no understanding that the intent of sleepwalkers is not to dive down like the suicide or *rusalka* from the Charles Bridge, but to lift off into another place, like John the Baptist, perhaps even beyond that part of the sky the religious speak of that is lined with the pure and holy.

I ENTER THE TOWN NOW from my *panelák,* through the oldest gate. I go under the portcullis and on by the brewery with its sign advertising REGENT BEER, SINCE 1379.

I come to the town square, where the plague column stands. A few high windows on the castle are thrown open at this hour to circling bats. Mosquitoes rise from the puddles. I continue by the courthouse of 1572 faced with a Latin inscription and under the all-seeing eye engraved on the lintel of the former Masonic hall. I go by the fountain of St. George spearing a dragon. I pass a socialist grocery, which sells no butter, only margarine. I line up there for oranges. I do not line up for sausages: They are filled with horse guts. I go under the Gothic stone carving of a winged cow. I pass by the shoe shop, which offers hardly any shoes, but only empty shelves lined with brown and yellow flowered wallpaper. I linger by the civic bulletin boards with their announcements, red and gold graphics, and portraits of the spectacled men who govern the Communist moment. I am hardly aware of the footsteps I take to reach here and to return. I remember them only because I repeat them. I am awake but I see dimly now, as a rhino must see through its lanced openings, because I am a sleepwalker by day as well as by night. I am not often awake to this ČSSR of 1973. That is why men are attracted to me. They like my lack of strategy, the way I fall into their arms at the end of an evening, when invariably they say, *"God! You're like a dancer to me, Amina."*

I feel nothing. If I am in their arms at all it is only because I stumble in sleepwalking when they speak again of carp. It is difficult for me to remember these men or what happens to me from one day to the next. I dry myself among irises on the shore of the Svět and sleepwalk off toward the factory. I am not so different. This is a country of sleepwalkers by day, who drink by night only as a lesser form of sleepwalking. This is a country where the officials say openly they can do whatever they like with it, if they keep the beer flowing. Hardly any of us are ever awake the way operatic Amina is awake, when she asks her friend to lay a hand upon her breast and feel her heart beating up blood within her, and to sing:

That is my heart, which cannot contain the happiness it feels!

The workers in the industrial towns are pulled from their beds with tidal force, but are not woken. They sit glassy-eyed on trams that pass out over fields of beets. The sparking of the wires scatters the geese feeding in the fields, but no one turns from the tram to look at the geese in flight. They hardly acknowledge one another. They stare without awareness at one another's breasts. They go to work. They mine coal. They pour steel without thought into armored plates such as would dress a rhino. They automatically sluice carp from the Svět into concrete tanks.

The sand gazelles cocked their heads at me. They registered the shape I made and then lowered their heads to graze again. I was awake to the gazelles, as I am awake to the giraffes. I am wakeful when I walk the slopes below the forest that encloses the Svět, and harvest mice scatter before me down smooth ovular holes and make for the balks in the field where the yellowhammers and quail are nested. I wake to the hare breaking for cover, the springing deer, and the skylarks turning away from a merlin in the windless heights. I go attentively down narrowing brambles of blackthorn and blackberries, through creeping thistles and nettles, and emerge in a circle of aspen trees. I take an empty bottle from my bag. I fill it from a spring that rises there, percolating up from deep in the rock. I sit beside the shrine over the spring, dedicated to Mary. I am aware of the wild roses laid beside her blue likeness and the candles burned low. I am held rapt by the grains of sand and flakes of fool's gold dancing in the clear waters. The Communist moment cannot dull such a place. Even if it cemented it over and punished all those who have laid flowers there, so that the act of worshiping was forgotten, the waters would only well up somewhere else. The officials show no interest in the bend on the gravel road where my parents were hit by a truck. Their interest is in the secret military base in the forest, in the electrification of its perimeter, so the animals will bounce off it, and in meaningful camouflage, so I will no longer see the tips of the missiles dug in there, glinting between the trees. The same officials paste political flyers onto the plague column, masking the pox-ridden faces spiraling up the column and the seraphim with wings as tiny as a sparrow's supporting those with their heads rolled back. When I am awake and walking by the plague column and see slogans over these mournful sculpted panels, I understand the Communist moment cannot endure; it does not have the imagination. I know Czechoslovakia will awaken in the far future, agitated and bruised, under a spreading linden tree, to a religious revival, or even to a moment without lines in which the customer is always right.

Amina

I SIT ON A bench under the sycamore tree by the giraffe
house. I watch the Egyptian geese waddling with clipped
wings through the legs of the largest herd of captive giraffes
in the world. I am awake. I do not sleepwalk in the zoo. I see
again how the giraffes ignore the geese, even though they
may have stories to tell of nesting in the Nile among *rusalkas*
swum up there from papyrus roots with trinkets of pharaohs,
who never venture along the Nile because the thrum of the
cities is too much for their watery forms.

A man approaches. He is as tall as the zoo director I have
seen striding now and again between the cages.

"Why are you so often here under this sycamore tree?" he asks.

"The giraffes awaken me," I say.

"What is your name?"

"Amina Dvořáková."

"I am the giraffe keeper," he says.

"I've seen you," I say, embarrassed.

He sits down on the bench. We are quiet.

"This is a good angle to watch the giraffes," he says after some time. "You can see better how vertical they are from here."

He turns to me.

"I have to tell you," he says, "we had our first birth last night."

"Were you present?"

"I came in this morning and there she was. Would you like to see her?"

"Yes."

It is warm and dark as a nest in the giraffe house. The keeper points to the newborn giraffe. I move quickly to the wooden railing. I look through the slats. She is still covered in patches of membranes. She totters on the smooth floor. She makes it to the belly of her mother and puts her mouth to a large teat.

"See how she runs!" he says. "More easily than she walks—she has such a low center of gravity in these first days."

I point to bumps on her head, covered with velveteen skin. "Are they horns?"

He nods. "The skin will wear away and the horns will

come in time—three or four ossified outgrowths. Look at the mother's tail."

It is oxblood-colored with afterbirth.

"Now look at those giraffes nuzzling over there by the door," he says. "See anything unusual?"

"One is a Rothschild giraffe and the other a reticulated?"

"Not that," he says. "They only have one ear."

I see that now.

"This calf will only have one ear too. Too much love! See how her mother is licking. She'll lick the ear until all the blood vessels are closed off and it shrivels."

The reticulated cow with the white underbelly comes forward. She leans down over the fence. I put up my hand to her wet face.

"That's Sněhurka," he says. "She's one of the leaders. She is always the first to step out when I open the doors in the morning. She stands quite still in the open with her head pushed back, like this, almost lifting up off the ground. Then she nods and the others venture out."

He looks up at Sněhurka.

"Animals should be stripped of names," he says, "but I cannot bring myself to do so in her case."

The keeper invites me into his room at the back of the giraffe house. He tells me that female giraffes are sociable, except after giving birth, and that males keep to themselves, moving slowly along the fence in the yard to where the okapi live. He brushes aside flies and fruit flies and shows me the feed of apples, pears, carrots, turnips, and beets. He points out the bales of hay and the browse cut from the acacia trees overhanging the fountain of St. George. He speaks of how the lights in the giraffe house come on gradually in the morning to give the impression of the rising sun, of the giraffes who lick the branches painted on the walls, of the tabby cat who goes undisturbed about the bull giraffes in search of mice, and of how the herd ruminates through the night with unblinking and unfocused eyes.

"The single most important thing to understand about a giraffe," he says, "is that they do not graze down to the ground, but are stretched up to the sky."

"That is what so awakens me," I say.

The keeper gives me a searching look. He must also understand Czechoslovakia to be a nation asleep, of workers normalized into sleepwalkers.

He asks me what I have observed of giraffes, coming to the zoo so often in these months and sitting under the sycamore tree. I tell him I have memorized the patterns on the necks of the giraffes so that I can say aloud to myself on the bench, That one is Jánošík and this one is Rudolf, named for the emperor. I tell how the females lower their heads in submission when a male comes sniffing at their root and how some of them raise their tails in fear at the sound of gunfire in the forest.

"Giraffes are not like white rhinos with their hooked and squared lips," I say, gaining confidence. "When a giraffe is scared, it rears away. When a rhino is scared, it runs straight at the object of its fear, its ears flattened back like those of a cat."

The keeper is listening. We are awake to each other.

"The giraffes do not seem sad to me," I say, "like the polar bears in this zoo are."

"Sadness is difficult to see in beasts," he says. "I cannot say a giraffe is more depressed than a polar bear. I can only say that a giraffe does not frown or smile and is not easily transformed by the act of observation into something human, like animals with soft shapes and juvenilized faces, such as koalas, pandas, lemurs, and certain apes."

"Giraffe expressions are unreadable to me," I say. "They often appear to be looking straight through me, as if I am a ghost to them."

He nods. "Early taxidermists," he says, "exaggerated the ferocity of all animals that came to their table. In their hands, even a mole was poised to spring, its two teeth exposed. After the first specimen giraffe skins arrived from Namaqualand, the taxidermists sought to do the same for giraffes. But whatever they tried, they could not make the giraffe look menacing. It looked in death much as it did in life."

"How is that?"

"Lofty, alien; above all blank. If a giraffe performs at all, it is only a tall-man routine."

"I don't follow."

"In an anthropocentric world, the point of a lion is to roar at us. In such a world, the point of a giraffe is to tower over us. The giraffe is the tall man, just as the hippo is the fat man. If a giraffe appears in a children's story at all, it is only on account of its height. A giraffe never converses in a children's story, just as penguins and other vertical animals are also silent in those stories. And in this respect too the giraffe is nothing like the black bear in the London Zoo that became Winnie-the-Pooh."

"Surely their blankness has a purpose," I say. "A giraffe can be a point of reflection. It can bring out of yourself some feeling you did not know was there."

"For you, perhaps, Amina," he says, not unkindly.

"The zoo is a place where you can look deliberately at living things," I say, "which doesn't happen outside. No one out there examines the faces of cows sent for milking."

"The zoo is nothing more than a contrivance," he says, "to make workers forgetful of the monotony of their lives. They arrive here from industrial towns. They move from cage to cage. What do they want? Not to contemplate, as you seem to do, but to make strange animals see them. You've seen how they put their hands through the bars, how they throw in food or litter, and how they wave their arms until the pygmy hippo takes the smallest step in their direction."

I HAVE SEEN VISITORS who do not look at the creatures in the zoo except through the lens of their camera and curse when they run out of film, as though they have been made blind. Even so, I have often been startled at the way other visitors seem to wake up when they step from under the sycamore tree and exclaim, as I did, "Giraffe!"

Amina

A s far as I can see, there are sixteen windows on my factory floor. The light that comes through them is copper-colored with autumn. In winter, the light in here is blue. This is where we dip Christmas decorations in colors. It has few features. There are loudspeakers at either end that give out announcements. There is paint on the floor and the walls and it is splashed thick over the machinery from seasons of Christmas decorations past. There is a pinup of a Czechoslovakian film star, the packaging from a box of English tea, and a red banner draped over one wall that declares in white letters: TRANSCEND FOR THE GLORY OF THE REVOLUTION!

This is where I work. Its fumes are rotting me from within. They break open my skin into sores and cause my organs to burn with a hundred small infections. I take another tray of clear spheres now. I set it on metal rollers. I push it into the mouth of the dipping machine. I open a vat of see-through polish with a base of nitroglycerin. I mix pigment into the polish until I come to the right shade of silver. I heave the vat to a funnel. I pour the resulting paint into the dipping machine. My hands shake. Some of the silver paint splashes on the floor. I press a button. I stand back, eyes streaming. The machine is loud: I can no longer hear what the other women are shouting to one another. It stops. I pull out the tray. The spheres are hot fuming silver. Christmas silver. I inspect the spheres for blemishes and see myself reflected and shortened in them. I see a young woman resembling a suicide or *rusalka,* an orphaned worker in an apron and headscarf, waiting to get out into the autumn air, to walk beside the Svět.

My job is to take spheres and other shapes of glass and dip them in colors. Each piece has a stem, an umbilical cord; the paint flows down it, coloring the glass from the inside. When the piece has been further decorated on the factory floor above, or in the cooperatives in the villages around the town, the stem is snipped, set with a metal cap, and dressed with a ribbon or a wire on which it can be hung from a Christmas tree. It is not easy to mix the pigment into the polish. Consistency changes with the shape and quality of the glass. It is not possible to say, This is white, or This is cobalt. You have to be

a chemist here, as well as a worker. The pieces we color correctly are exported; the pieces we get wrong make up the
domestic quota. So it is that the Christmas trees of ČSSR
shine off-color in shades of mustard. We make shapes of
Santa Claus with a full sack, bells, pine trees, sailing ships,
angels, bears, and reindeer. Some of the spheres we color are
hand-painted with tropical scenes of Vietnam for the American market. We color shapes of Uncle Sam to be dressed with
a cotton-wool beard. We dip shapes of American fighter jets.
The orders are not openly mentioned by the factory committee of Communists demoted to this lowly enterprise
on account of alcoholism or depression. The shapes of the
American fighter jets serve also as planes for the Soviet market. The greatest demand in the domestic market is for red
spheres. We dip them in Christmas red and send them to be
hand-painted with a hammer and sickle so that they might
better crown Communist trees in place of an angel. I have
hardly any memory of the dipping, only of the redness itself,
which is matte, not shiny like Christmas silver, and does not
give out light, but rather sucks it in, offering no reflection, so
that when I pull out a tray of red spheres and bend down to
inspect them, I find myself invisible in them and feel the light
around me diminished.

ONE OF THE WOMEN WAVES a packet of Red Star cigarettes.
We all leave the machines. We go to stand by the open window at the end of the factory floor, where we can see the sky
and the copper leaves falling from the trees. I take a piece of
bread and hold it out in my hands. A blackbird comes now, a

factory bird, and takes the bread with a single gentle peck. We drop the burning ends of our Red Stars into the undergrowth below. The conversation is distant, befitting those who sleep-walk by day. The women speak of the availability of certain foods and of the latest television serial. I do not have a television. It is enough for me to read the schedule of the state channel number one:

Let's Speak Russian!
Hats off! Agricultural Success Stories of the Day
Quiz: How Well Do You Know Your ČSSR?

I listen to my records and to Radio Vltava, the classical-music station. I will skip the stories of our Communist history and listen to Liszt's "Fantasia Quasi Sonata" followed by *Melodies of Our Dear Cuban Friends.*

I AM YOUNGER than the other women. We do not have so much in common. I do not volunteer myself to them, except when they ask me of giraffes. I have told them of how the giraffe keeper approached me in the springtime and asked why I was so often there under the sycamore tree and I said it was because the giraffes awakened me. They know I sit for two or three afternoons each week before the giraffes. To them the zoo is a contrivance, a diversion they rarely bother with, while to me it is a place where I am fully aware, even in these autumn days, when there are few visitors, no wasps in the garbage cans, and no ice-cream vendor pushing his cart. I can say to the other women with certainty that giraffes are silent, mute as a penguin in a children's story. I have related the story the keeper told me of the zoo's vet in the 1950s who took it upon himself to eat a cutlet from every creature then in the zoo, if not from a dead animal then from the ampu-tated limb of a living animal, such as a female chimpanzee whose arm was caught in the bars of her cage. When the women said I was making it up, I described to them how the vet cut off his cutlets with surgical precision, wrapped them in newspaper, and fried them up at home. I told them how he demanded the zookeepers exhume a black panther that had died while the vet was on vacation. He pretended to examine it, discreetly cut off a piece of meat, and made a marinated dish of it, which he served up to the young and unsuspecting zoo director. All of this, I told them, came to light when the vet died and his diary surfaced, along with a recipe book.

Andrea asks me about the giraffes and I take another Red Star and tell her of how one of the Rothschild cows stood on her hind legs and tried to eat from an overhanging branch of the sycamore tree.

"What else?" Hana says.

"The zoo director ordered an okapi be put in with the giraffes. It cowered in the corner and the giraffes treated it unpleasantly, as though there was some long-standing dis-agreement between them."

"What's an okapi?" Eva says, from the windowsill.

"A giraffe without neck or legs," I say, "which lives in a jungle, where there is no need for it to stretch up for food."

We go back to the machines. There is another order for white. Not polar bears, but snowmen. I mix the pigment into the nitroglycerin base in the copper-colored light. I see dimly.

This kind of sleepwalking is deeper than a daydream, less than a nightmare. I set the tray of snowmen on rollers and push it into the machine. I pour in the paint. I sleepwalk inward from the factory floor to an evening in a beer garden in which fireflies surround the face of my girlfriend, lighting her up in the darkness. Outwardly, there is the din of whiteness injected into a hundred umbilical cords, of snowmen being born. Inwardly, butterflies are rising from a pool in the bog that circles the old town walls, more subtly colored than any pigment mixed into a polish of nitroglycerin, in apple, olive, Veronese green, lapis lazuli, and lemon marked softly on papery wings.

I pull out the snowmen. A siren sounds, marking the end of the working day. A voice comes over the loudspeakers: "Revered workers, gather please for an educational film in the cafeteria!"

FOG IS DRIFTING OUTSIDE, from the Svět. The concrete tanks by the gravel road are filling with carp. All the apples have fallen and leaves are clumped heavily against the boards of the outdoor ice-hockey rink. I sit here in the cafeteria, next to Eva. The political committee is showing us a short film, for our education.

"Lights out!" someone calls.

The screen lights up. An image is brought into focus. I see soldiers marching by, saluting at a parade. Now soldiers in fatigues are running along a Czechoslovakian riverbank. A missile shoots upward. The film cuts to a meadow in which children are playing. The children wear all the different folk costumes of Czechoslovakia. The title of the film is *The Dress of Our ČSSR!*

The children sing and laugh. Some of them set up easels and paint pictures of sunshine and clowns, but also animals. The narration marks out these children as future workers at play. The sky darkens, sirens sound. The narrator shouts, "Danger! Look out, children! Dive! Dive!"

The children scream. They run about in circles. They tear at one another and fall to the ground. Some of them curl into balls, as insects do under a spray of insecticide. A blinding flash dissolves into a mushroom cloud. The film cuts back to the army, who are protecting us from destruction. The film ends. The People's Militia, sitting uniformed in the front row, breaks into applause. They are a rabble, meant to protect the factory from sabotage during an uprising. Most have joined out of a lack of conviction: They believe in nothing, so there is nothing to hold them back. The rest of us are sleepwalkers by day. We do not remark on the banners draped around the town, such as here in the cafeteria: THE TRUE WORKER OBEYS THE WILL OF THE COLLECTIVE.

The Communist moment does not demand that I love it, or be awake to it. It asks only that I do not question it. What can I question? I am below politics. I do not read the articles in the newspaper that begin: "Strict penalties are not enough . . . ," "Revanchism is a tumor . . ."

The political committee of the factory asked me to join their team for the mass gymnastics exercise in Prague. They said I was slight and sinewy enough to be the one lifted from the field to be the point of a red star formed by forty thousand workers. I refused. I am not a socialist heroine, such as appear in mass displays or as models for Communist statues with their hands stretched across in salute. I am an orphaned sleepwalker, named for the same. I dip shapes of glass on a factory floor whose sixteen windows have never been cleaned and cast a murky light, like the underside of the Vltava.

I sleepwalk from the cafeteria to the showers. I stand now under dribbling hot water and soap myself among older women. I am aerated. Water might course through me. I rise on tiptoe. I stretch my hands to the shower head. I wake in this steam. I am not bent double over the dipping machine, I am not watching a political film, nor am I outside in my crumbling town, whose ramparts are splitting, whose Gothic winged cow is broken and without flight, and whose stylish Hotel Crystal Palace stands infested and boarded up on the main square. The factory roof leaks. It is propped up by trees whose branches grow into the building. There are not enough toilets in here. I squat with the other women at lunchtime in that part of the undergrowth where we drop our cigarettes, and urinate there in yellow arcs.

I DRY MYSELF ON the broken tiles and sit on a wooden bench in the crowded changing room. We are all quiet. Even Hana is quiet. We sit here and we steam, with our palms down on our thighs. We are captive in disappointment. We become dull-eyed and stare without focus at the posters on the wall here: MEAT MEANS HEALTH! and PROTECT US, BORDER GUARDS!

I HAVE A SUDDEN SENSE of the other place I wish to stretch my hands over my head and lift off to. It is more than Prague and the America to which we send our Christmas fighter-jet decorations. It is beyond that part of the sky lined with the pure and holy. I cannot grasp it. I understand it only as a color seen on a butterfly wing, an unseen and unimagined color that lies outside the spectrum, into which glass can never be dipped.

Jiří

A Sharpshooter

ST. HUBERT'S DAY

NOVEMBER 3, 1974

I WAKE WITH A start. I see my breath. There is moonlight on the wooden floor. I hear the sound again. I sit bolt upright in my cot. It is closer. I hear it brushing against the side of the hut. I see a form in the window. A stag. It stares directly in, at the antlers arranged on the wall. I am still. I watch the stag breathe on the frosted windowpane, seemingly contemplating the trophies and skullcaps of its kind. It moves off now. Other deer follow it. By the time I get to the window, they are all gone into the forest.

The iron stove is still warm. I throw more wood in it. I brew a pot of chicory coffee. I drink it barefoot now on the steps outside the forestry hut, which are cold, made of stones set down in the forest by a glacier long ago. I am unsettled. It is the saint day of Hubert, the patron of hunters and butchers, who fell prostrate before a stag, between whose antlers was a figure of Christ, fading in and out as our black-and-white television sets do. I see a badger in the half-light, punching through ferns, deeper into this forest, my forest, which surrounds the Svět. The trees creak. It is autumn. Leaves are falling, falling.

I go back inside the hut. I dress. I tuck in my woolen shirt. I pull up my suspenders. I lace my boots up to my knees. I put on my jacket. I set a feather in my cap. I push back my thick, black-framed spectacles. I throw the bloodstained satchel over my shoulder. I take up my rifle, a Mannlicher-Schoenauer 6.5.

I am a forester and a hunter. My father was too, and his father before him. I shot my first boar in 1941, not far from this hut. I was a boy then. My view on hunting is sentimental. I believe in an unspoken pact between certain men and certain beasts; by hunting animals, I give them purpose. I am a Communist. I do not disguise my intentions: I am Communist because I wish to remain in the forest. If they ask me certain questions, I will set down my ax and rifle and leave. They do not ever ask me. They trust me because I am known to them only in the trees, where there are no politics, just as Hubert was loved as a young man because he was known only in moments of fraternity in the forest, away from the disputatious, where the only quarry was a beast. I do not have the face of a functionary. There are fools in every walk of life, including the Party. I say so openly. When I go to political meetings, I speak to the point. Unlike the careerists, I do not introduce into my written reports incidental characters who might be blamed if a criticism is raised or vanished if praise is forthcoming. I take responsibility for my actions. When I fell a tree, I count the number of its rings.

I check the magazine of my rifle now. I load the five rounds. I lock it. I walk away from the forester's hut. I step quickly into evergreen larches, white firs, silver firs, deodars, Bosnian pines, Austrian pines, Hungarian oaks, downy oaks, sessile oaks, wild service, gray poplars, black walnut, hickory, and full-moon maples. I see the sky through the division of their leaves and the patterns at the base of their cones and in the brightly colored arils about their seeds. I belong to these trees. I wish to leap between them and live in them, in their branches, like some baron. Instead, I move dutifully along the forest floor, daubing trunks with arrows as I go; upward for trimming, downward for felling. I am always in shadow, glimpsing rather than seeing, so that when I emerge from the forest, even into the flat light about the Svět, I am dazzled.

The roots of the firs are sprung tight under me. I would feel myself lifted from the ground if I broke into a run now. I do not understand captivity in the same way as the fishermen who work the Svět. They are unduly exposed, without subtleties, on the water. The forest is not a cage, as they say. It is a shelter. Startled deer bound from the fields to the forest, not from the forest to the fields; their prance into the trees that sustain them is so acute and airborne as to seem the work of an unseen puppeteer, jerking them on wires.

I consider Hubert. He dismounted. He unfurled his hands. His fingers I suppose to be snagged from thorns and

tethered hawks. Christ spoke through the stag in a voice I
cannot conceive, saying:

> *Hubert! How long will you pursue the animals of the forest?*
> *This is a vain and selfish passion. When will you consider*
> *the safety of your soul, the quickness of your fall. If you*
> *do not cease hunting, you will go to hell.*

It is contradictory. Hubert bowed down before a beast. He
renounced slaughter, but became the saint of hunters and of
butchers, who cut up the animals brought out of the forest.

I FIND A HARE KICKING hard in a trap intended for a pine
marten. It is anguished, but uninjured. I pull it free. I hold it
up by the back of the head. It pedals the air. It arches itself
and slowly closes its eyes, awaiting a mortal blow. I let it go.
The hare reminds me of a story told to me of an aristocrat
who walked up from the Svět on a summer evening in 1771
and entered the forest under a large setting sun. He went
deep into the forest. He set his musket up behind a rock in a
clearing. He took out his snuffbox from his embroidered
waistcoat. After some hours he saw the largest owl he had
ever seen, larger than an eagle, carrying a live hare in its
talons. The aristocrat aimed his long barrel at the owl. He
fired. The ball passed through the hare but missed the bird.
The hare fell dead at his feet, twice hunted, and the owl
swooped off, unburdened.

I put a bullet into damp air as I put an ax to a tree. The

bullet drills into the chest of a deer. The deer loosens under the blow; it slumps to the floor. It gives itself out into the fir roots, through the hole I have made in it, and is so pressed down in that moment, with no possibility of rising again, that gravity itself seems to me increased, as if there were a magnet hidden in the foliage and another in the body of the deer and they have met and snapped together at the moment of death. I let my hounds off the leash. I run behind them. The deer is always dead when I lay down my rifle beside it. It is already stiff under my gaze, the throat open like a jug.

I imagine death to come on us, on deer also, like the hand of an anesthesiologist, pulling limbs into cruciform, pushing a needle into a vein. There is a chemical closing over, a kind of drowning. The lungs fill with fluid, as in the womb. The eyes close, or glaze over. I run up to the deer. I drag the hounds off it. I regard it. My first thought is of the space between life and death, the fragment when you are neither living nor dead, which in a deer might be a flickering of a divine stag and in a man the longest purgatory.

I WALK THE RIDGE ABOVE the secret military base. I see other foresters in the distance, sawing spruce trees for Christmas. I call out to them, but they do not hear me. My father believed in Hubert and in the communion of saints. He described it as a piece of engineering, a turbine: Saints gather up prayers, convert them into love and majesty, and so power the present with hope. I do not believe in such a communion. I observe St. Hubert's Day only out of respect for my father. He marked the day with a suspension of deer hunting and by taking his hounds to be blessed in the chapel of St. Michael, which stands between the zoo and the town. I went with him. I stood near the altar, holding the muzzled hounds tightly, while around me the music for the mass was performed on hunting horns.

I reach the edge of the forest. I do not walk out. I take up my binoculars. I look down at the town zoo. I see the giraffes stepping slowly through their enclosure. I see a smaller animal, an okapi. I see a young woman on a bench, looking up at the giraffes as Hubert looked up at the stag.

I know okapi from my childhood. A Congolese priest, whose education my father sponsored, wrote us gentle letters in Latin of glimpsing okapi in the jungle, and of his sadness on accompanying scientists capturing songbirds:

> *We are all of us brightly colored birds, over which the fowler*
> *death casts a net. We are thrown to the earth, and so*
> *our song, our form and colors are gone.*

I turn my binoculars on the okapi. The colors are like decaying leaves, the body and neck purple, the legs barred in bluish oil-brown and white. It stands on concrete. It is not right to see it so revealed. It has no understanding of Czechoslovakian daylight. It belongs to the Upper Congo and is meant to move there through boles, creepers, vines, and large leaves, shedding rivulets of water; the priest wrote to us that it was wet in the jungle, "So that whenever an okapi is sighted, it appears to be weeping."

I raise my binoculars. I see the town. I see turrets and spires. I see the bog and quicksands about the walls. I avoid the town. It is not a place for me. The birds sit there, silent and listless, on broken gutters. The people I pass wear vacant expressions; they have migrated into themselves as I have migrated into the forest. There is giddiness only in the hospital waiting room, where those waiting have hope that their malaise will be given a name.

I see the parkland around the chapel of St. Michael planted with English oaks, scarlet oaks, horse chestnuts, Montpelier maples, Cappadocian maples, and black mulberries. I trace the chapel's fine lines of polychrome sandstone and pink marble, its oval windows raised on the backs of sculpted lions with two tails, the yew trees clumped around its crypt, and the slope of steps from its front doors down to the Svět, the most beautiful, wide steps, set on either side with fruit trees of apple, snow pear, sour cherry, plum, and bullace.

I focus on the golden statue of Michael. He is flying down at speed, with an oval shield marked in Hebrew and a gold spear, his feet just touching the chapel roof, as though scattering invisible demons and hydras, who, when pierced by his spear, are made aware of their own weight, are taken by gravity, and fall in great fear toward an inferno.

There is a grille at the base of a yew tree through which it is possible to see the zinc coffins lying in the crypt and a stack of skulls, which are foresters and fishermen of the Svět, bulbous as babies in that dark blue light, stitched across the crown, with many teeth or none, flaking, honeycombed through the nose, some split between the nose and lip, congenitally, or with an ax: forester's mistake. There is an altar in the center of the crypt set with a silver cross and an ivory tusk, spiraled like the plague column in the town, said to be that of a unicorn, but actually the tusk of the narwhal that swims in icy seas. The thought of those seas disturbs me. There are no trees there, nor any soil. The narwhals are massive, corpse-colored, done through with oil and blubber, nothing like the deer that prance from field to forest, whose antlers and skullcaps I hang on the walls of the forestry hut, who collapse into leaves and twigs, bleed into root systems, are dead but still warm when I arrive at them.

I say that I do not disguise my intentions. Well then, there is a fear in me from catechism. Thinking of these things, of crypts, saints, and Congolese priests, seems to make the forest floor brittle and thin as the ice under which the narwhal plows. I fear the judgment that will cause the ground to open and cast me down, so that I will feel the weight of my own body. I am a Communist because I do not wish to believe. I hold to ČSSR out of fear and am openly relieved at its banality.

I remain in the forest now. I take a long swig of liquor from my hip flask and turn back toward the hut. If I were forced to leave the forest, it would be for the mountains. Alpine heights are the only exposure I favor. I wish the forest had not been ground so low by a glacier long ago. I wish it would rise steeply, far higher than the slope with a single rope tow pulling up skiers, above any treeline. I imagine in idle moments a mountain on which socialism with a human face might be built. It would rise from the Svět tall as Pik Communism in the USSR. There would be no factories or *paneláks* on it; all the humdrum living would happen elsewhere. At its base would be a maternity hospital where babies might be

born with a view of the Svět. A little higher would be nurs-
eries and primary schools, then secondary schools, vocational
colleges, up to universities, military academies, agricultural
and forestry institutes. On the broad slopes of the mountain
would be gymnasiums, stadiums, registry offices where mar-
riages might be recorded, cinemas, theaters, a symphony hall,
tearooms, beer halls. Large chalets serving inventors and
explorers would be scattered in meadows of wildflowers.
Sanatoriums performing lifesaving procedures would be hidden above, in stretches of larch, before a lake of melted snow.
So my ČSSR would go, higher and higher, with all life beneath
it, so the ground would not become brittle or give way, until
reaching the state homes for the elderly in the snowy heights
among the chamois and finally the crematorium a little
higher, on the glacier, outside of which brass bands would
gather and play mournful Czechoslovak tunes as the ashes of
the dead were cast onto a breeze, which might blow at that
altitude.

Amina

I WALK FROM THE ZOO now with the smell of giraffes and strip and step naked into the Svět. This is my last swim of the year. The waters are very cold now about my ankles. The reeds along the shore have all broken. The warblers are gone. A single mosquito bites the back of my knee. It falls swollen under the weight of my blood to the skin of the water and perishes there. I push off. I gasp. I swim quickly out to where rowers stroke a boat in eights.

Afterward, I dry myself onshore and wrap myself in a blanket. I light a cigarette. The first frost will be here soon; it is already thick in the forest. I walk along by the Svět. There is a dead fox here on the path. I turn it over with my foot. Maggots squirm curious out of neat round holes in the flesh. Ants and flies are inside also, carrying off the last jelly of the eyes. I see a seagull flying low over the Svět and settling on the tideless water. I saw in the film *Memories of Paradise* gulls flapping under the Charles Bridge, hovering in hope of bread or cake, hardly looking when the suicide or *rusalka* fell through their flock to the river. I look up at the gray sky now and see a white-tailed eagle and an osprey. I see a rapid shard of aquamarine, which may be a kingfisher. I walk on, toward the marsh at the end of the Svět where the otters live.

The desolation of the marsh affects me. I am drawn to it. There are otter tracks in the mud, the claws cut sharply in, the tail dragging. I go on. I wade through ferns and nettles, which rise to my shoulders and bloom in purple and white. I come to the forest. I do not like it. I feel enclosed there. I walk along the forest floor in the gloom, under woodpeckers. I break into a run now, as if through a thunderstorm. I run until I reach the clearing by the sawmill, where the wood carving of the archangel Raphael is nailed to the trunk of an old beech tree that stands sentinel at the crossing of three paths. Raphael leans forward from the beech, his face covered in the woody husks of beech fruit. His arms are stretched up, in flight above the forest. He is oak and cherrywood painted in white. He is chipped in places, revealing other layers of white. I want him to turn and look down toward me, as a giraffe sometimes does. I want him to see me. I stand under him. I put my hands up above my head; I seek to lift off, to that place of a never-imagined color. My fingers touch the lowest carved feather of his wings.

I walk on. I pick up a pinecone. I trace my finger around its spiral base. I am reminded of the Fibonacci sequence we recited in mathematics class:

one

two

three

five

eight

thirteen

twenty-one

thirty-four

fifty-five

eighty-nine

I see the sequence in the petals of the last surviving wild roses and in the coil of seeds in a flower head, and I hear it now in some piano concerto in my head that goes with an eight-tone white scale and a five-tone black to give an octave of thirteen notes. The relation between two and three or between thirty-four and fifty-five is the golden ratio. I go on. I keep to the shore, out of the forest. If I were a priest, humble enough, I would search for the golden ratio between the wings of the Raphael, and if I were a scientist I would look for it in the distance between the eyes of a giraffe and in the arrangement of its neck vertebrae.

Amina

THERE IS A STORY of an orphan girl from my town who was under the care of an imperial gardener at a palace in Vienna. One of the girl's responsibilities was to feed the lion kept in the dungeon of the palace. She had a way with the beast. It was familiar with her and allowed her to approach with food and to pet it. The girl would even open the door of the stone cell and allow it to come up the steps from the dungeon and pace the courtyard in the sunlight. In 1669, the gardener arranged for the girl to be married. She came to the lion on her wedding day one last time to bid it farewell. To avoid bloodying her bridal gown, she held out the meat she had

brought at arm's length. Startled by the way the girl held the
meat across and not high over its head, as it was used to, and
also by the whiteness of the orphan in that gloom, the lion
grew jealous, leapt on her, and snapped her neck.

It is Christmas Eve, long before dawn. I awake, bruised,
under a maple tree in the parkland. It is snowing soundlessly.
The Svět is frozen over. Skate marks catch in the starlight; an
ice-hockey net shimmers far out from the shore. I pause at
the bend in the gravel road where my parents were struck
down. I walk on, to the zoo. I pass the chapel of St. Michael,
where all the countesses lie shrunken in coffins of double
oak inside caskets of zinc. I turn and see my *panelák,* my
room, and the pattern of my footsteps, where I tiptoed in
sleepwalking, over the frozen Svět.

I climb up over the zoo gates, knocking icicles off the
metal shapes of animals. I walk through the zoo. I am no
longer sleepwalking, but I feel faint. My hands and feet are
frozen numb. I tremble. I fall again and again into snowdrifts.
The paths are hard as iron under the snow. I pass cages.
Beasts clear their throats and pay me no heed. I see chamois
run up to the summit of their rocky enclosure and down
again. I see a shrewdness of apes asleep in one another's
arms. I linger before the otter-sized predator in the aviary, a
fossa, which also trembles from the cold, and leaps from one
Czechoslovakian branch to another, with no hope of ever
catching a lemur. A tiger pads beside me, or I beside it. I come
to the giraffe house, an inadequate barn. I have helped
arrange the Christmas tree in front of it. I have dressed the

tree with red spheres and with a rejected shape of Uncle Sam. The lights on the tree twinkle across the snow, lighting up the political banner hung over the giraffe house by the zoo director, which reads: WE ARE THE VANGUARD OF A NEW LIFE!

I make it inside. My head spins in the warmth. I see giraffe legs through slats, rising sheer. I see unfocused and unblinking eyes.

"Amina!"

The giraffe keeper, running out of his room, catches me falling.

"Jesus and Mary! You look half dead."

"I fell asleep in the snow," I say, looking up at him.

He lays me down on a bed in the corner of his room. He dries my hair. He wraps me in swaddling clothes. I sleep a little.

I wake to see him arranging a Nativity scene on a table.

"Merry Christmas," I say.

He looks up. "Amina!"

His face is etched in the strip lighting. He is an intelligent man, not unlike my father, except in giraffe-stained overalls. I have never sleepwalked in his presence. I have never before stumbled and fallen into his arms. He holds the figure of a shepherd in his hand. He places it down among the animals near the manger. He is himself a sort of shepherd to the giraffes. He is the one who pulls them free from the fence, who lances their swellings, and sponges the afterbirth from them. I am happy to be with him now and to put on gloves and help him shovel out what he calls the socialist's Augean stable.

The pattern of my footsteps extends as far as the giraffe

house but no farther. I do not venture into the forest, nor do I often go anymore into the part of town where my lover lives. If I could travel, I would not know where to go. On a tram out from an industrial town, to jump clear into a field of beets? On a train to Prague, to lie on a bunk in a workers' hostel, to sleepwalk the long corridors of our capital? Or on a bus to Bratislava, to pass from the wrong side the metal signs of giraffes placed along the road every so often as advertisement for the zoo?

"I've been thinking about Egypt," the keeper says, sitting beside me. "I've been thinking of the flight into Egypt. Maybe it is our Egyptian geese, or this postcard I've received from the giraffe keeper in the Moscow Zoo."

He holds up the card.

"It's a painting on silt stone," he says, "from a Soviet museum of Egyptology, showing geese lifting from the Nile."

The geese are single brushstrokes of blue and gray, rising from green and yellow papyrus and lily pads.

Radio Vltava is playing Jan Jakub Ryba's *Česká mše vánoční,* or *Czech Christmas Mass.* I drink tea that the keeper brings me now. I say nothing, but think of the harvest mice in their snowed-up balks in the fields and of how strange Christmas is in the town after a year dipping decorations into Christmas colors and harvesting carp for Christmas dinners. The last carp are swimming in tanks beside the plague column. People come for them, not sleepwalking but awake. The carp are chosen, weighed, paid for, and laid on the cutting board. Their skulls of thin bone are heard to pop under the hammer like fingernails.

"I've been thinking again of the history of beasts in

Czechoslovakia," the keeper says. He puts a thermometer in my mouth. "Polar bears first," he says, reading the temperature. "The first polar bear came through our town in 1799, on a cart headed for Austria. The next polar bears passed by in 1874, on a train with the return of the Austro-Hungarian expedition to the North Pole. That expedition failed to reach the Pole, just as other Austro-Hungarian explorers failed in their attempts to reach the source of the River Congo. Instead they discovered an archipelago north of Novaya Zemlya and named it Franz Josef Land and named a bay on one of the islands for the Czechoslovakian town where our composer Mahler was raised. There were twenty-four in the crew, most of them Austrian and Croatian. The only Czechoslovak came from a village that stood then at the other end of the Svět, near the sawmill. He was responsible for feeding the polar-bear cubs, whose kennels slid and rolled on the open deck in the Barents Sea."

"Just as you said our giraffes were tossed around on the ocean on their journey here."

"I was coming to giraffes," he says, smiling.

He pulls out a newspaper-wrapped parcel tied with string. "Merry Christmas, Amina."

I sit up. I open it. It is a framed engraving of a young giraffe proceeding through an Alpine village, such as operatic Amina might have sleepwalked through. The giraffe is flanked by two keepers: an Austrian in a cadet-blue jacket and a Muslim in a white robe and sandals. Villagers move beside the giraffe, their mouths open in operatic chorus. Children throw their hats into the air and weave ecstatically between the infantrymen following behind.

"This is the first documented giraffe in the Austrian empire, crossing the Julian Alps," he says. "It was one of only three giraffes in Europe then. It landed in Trieste in 1828 and walked from the Adriatic Sea all the way to Vienna, having already been carried across deserts on the back of a camel and by boat down the Nile. It caused a sensation. Ladies in Prague and Brno had giraffes embroidered into their gloves and danced 'Galop à la Girafe' at balls. Crowds flocked to Vienna. They clamored at its cage in the Schoenbrunn Zoo."

"What became of it?" I ask.

"It was dead within a year. When they cut it open they found that its pelvis had been fractured when it was tied to the camel."

"It must have walked all that way in pain."

"It must have limped," he says. "No one could have known from that animal how a giraffe galloped."

THE GIRAFFE KEEPER HAS told me a little of zoos. I now know the Schoenbrunn to be the oldest. I know a cage is something that admits air and light, but no escape. I know the zoo evolved from a place of reflection into one of entertainment, in whose confines giant sloths were poked to death with the tips of walking canes and parasols, armadillos were stoned by curious youths, elephants died from eating the copper coins thrown at them, and giraffes slipped on unwashed floors and could not get up. I know the body of a Czech-speaking zookeeper was stuffed by a Venetian taxidermist and paraded, with glass eyes, on the back of a living camel through the towns of Austria for years afterward. I know the zoos of that time were no worse than the mental asylums, such as existed here in the town castle, where humans were chained to walls, or paced stone floors, goggle-eyed, smeared in their own excrement. I know visitors went by the fountain of St. George and paid an entrance fee into the asylum to watch and jab at lunatics, depressives, boneless women, and fireproof men, as if they were no better than sloths.

I sleep a few fitful minutes. I wake with a memory that does not belong to Christmas, except that it is another kind of nativity. I am thinking of the octagonal room in the castle. It is a rite of passage in the town to be pushed into that place, which is not so much a room as an eight-sided corridor, lined from floor to ceiling on all sides with specimen cases. The door is one such case, hidden on the inside. Each glass case is filled with fetuses, stillborn babies, and deformed children who have died in infancy. All the curious dead were brought here, along with limbs, eyes, tongues, organs, tumors, and strange growths cut out by surgeons and sunk whole, like the children, in jars of preservative. There are all forms of Siamese twins, unburied, floating across. There are triplets with a single face, and a child of perhaps five years, floating too, with no legs but with perfectly formed toes protruding from the buttocks, and a girl a little younger, bearing three legs. There are adult arms, double-length, bent like spaghetti. There are wax masks of various plagues and venereal diseases, of a cheek done through with many fine holes, as of a needle pushed in and out. I could not bear that place. I wailed to be let out. I wish I had never been pushed in and made aware of such suffering.

·   ·   ·

"ARE YOU FEELING BETTER?" he asks. "Your temperature is down."

"Shall we let the giraffes out?"

"For a few minutes only," he says. "It's too cold even for Czechoslovakian giraffes."

It is still dark and silver outside. The snow squeaks under my boots. I go around with the keeper as he opens the barn doors. The reticulated cow Sněhurka steps out. She gives no sign of recognition. She glides out, up to her ankles in the deep snow, not turning down to us. Steam rises off her in jigsaws and her breath comes in rivers of smoke from her nostrils.

"Look at her," the keeper says, clapping his hands together in the cold. "Like a dragon in Franz Josef Land."

The giraffes are desperately important to him in the way actors are important to a stage manager, seen always from behind or at side angles.

Sněhurka pushes her head back. She nods. She snorts and walks back in. No other giraffe ventures out. We close the doors and return to the keeper's room. He pours me a brandy but does not lift my mood. He instead speaks of another Czechoslovakian zoo, on which bombs fell during the Second World War.

"There were SS bunkers in the woods behind the zoo, just as we have a secret military base in the forest behind our zoo," he says. "When the bombs landed in the zoo, most of the animals were cut to ribbons. Those who survived, starved;

there was hardly anything to eat at that time in the war. Millions of people were on the move. All the rare ducks were killed for food and the antelope roasted. Some soldiers shot at the polar bear, hoping for his meal, but found he was surviving on a crow, fallen dead from a tree. The director of the zoo had the soldiers arrested. He was a Sudeten German. He did the most to improve living conditions for zoo animals in Czechoslovakia. It was he who insisted cages be hosed down, the animals studied, and a proper diet observed."

"A pioneer," I say.

"No," he says, "an ardent Nazi. When the town was liberated, he went with his wife to the zoo gates. A British officer approached them. A Scotsman. His kilt swung from side to side. He called out to them. They gave him a Nazi salute. The director put a pistol to his wife's temple and blew her brains out, then shot himself. It was never clear whether the couple had killed themselves in grief for the fallen Reich or for the destroyed animals."

"They will drop only a single bomb on us now," I say, thinking of the film I saw in which children lay curled on the ground while the sky was ablaze.

"The Svět will boil," he says.

It is strange to contemplate this. The Communist moment makes so much of nuclear war, of mushroom-shaped clouds, after which there will be no more *rusalkas,* all my operatic arias will be melted away, the hollows under the Svět where the cavemen lit fires will be buried in ash, and there will be no trace of giraffes, and of the town only a panel of the plague column.

"There is a happy ending to my story," he says. "The

giraffes were not killed in the bombing raid, as they were when the bombs fell through the ceiling of the giraffe house in the Berlin Zoo. They ran from one crater to another and so avoided being hit. A Soviet colonel intervened on their behalf when the zoo came under the control of the Red Army. He protected the giraffes. He made sure they were properly fed and cared for, even as he spent his days executing men."

IT IS AFTER DAWN on Christmas Eve and grim, ever so grim. Ryba's Christmas mass has long ago played out. The giraffes are shut in.

"I must go," I say.

"Wait," he says.

He hands me the engraving. He wraps his scarf tight around me. I stand on tiptoe and kiss him on the cheek.

THE SUN HAS CLEARED the forest. They are playing Christmas games of ice hockey out on the Svět. I watch the puck skipping away. I stop myself. My footsteps are snowed under. I cannot follow them back over the Svět to my *panelák*. I walk into the town, not sleepwalking, still awake to myself. I come to the town square. It is crowded here. I do not look to where the fishermen take the carp from tanks. I buy roasted chestnuts from a brazier. I listen to the carolers.

Tadeáš

A Virologist

APRIL 29, 1975

I HAVE NEVER SEEN a giraffe. I have not given them a thought. But there is a randomness to every contagion. It touches one creature and spares another. One child gets a black swelling under the armpit, hard like an apple, another sings about it.

I HEAR THE OFFICIAL speaking quietly to my secretary: They have called ahead to warn me I should expect him.

He walks directly in without knocking. He is young,

almost boyish. Blond hair falls diagonally across his face. He sweeps it back.

"Tadeáš Tůma?" he asks with a shy smile.

He wears foreign shoes and a foreign suit. He puts his hands in his pockets and rocks back on his heels. He exudes Prague. There is something familiar about him, removed from the Communist moment, as though he has stepped from a breezy Czechoslovakian film from before the war.

"You're late," I say. "I didn't catch your name."

He flushes. "I am without a name for the moment."

"No matter. Take a seat, please. I have the results to the tests the ministry requested."

He remains standing, rocking on his heels.

"Please do sit," I say.

It is spring in the secret laboratory I direct, which stands on the banks of the little River Ohře, close to where it meets the Labe. The Communist moment continues here. Outside, a boy in a gas mask is cutting the grass with a scythe. Far away, the city of Saigon is falling. The laboratory is also without name. It is not marked on any map. We deal with animal diseases here. We test blood and tissue samples from beasts eaten away with one pestilence or another, which come to us under cover of night in locked-down trucks. We develop vaccines only; we have no business here with weapons. The plagues and contagion we handle are not generally harmful to human beings. They kill animals or ruin them as a unit of production, which is much the same to the State. The laboratory is an island of loneliness. No train runs to Prague from here, but instead there is a single carriage running once each day through a forest to the industrial towns under the mountains. Aside from the laboratory there is an old fortress of sloping red brick, the size of a town, green-moated and planted with lilacs.

"Would you care to be shown around?" I ask.

"Why not," he says.

My secretary gives him a white lab coat and slippers. He pulls off his suit jacket and shoes. He folds the jacket with the silk lining out, on the back of a chair.

"What's your field?"

"Hemodynamics," he says. "Hence the giraffes."

We shuffle in the slippers down corridors, from one disinfected room to another. Slippers are the style of ČSSR; we are meant to feel cozy in our isolation.

I stop in front of a vault door of dark gray metal. There is a wheel in the center that you turn counterclockwise to open the door. It makes me think of the hatch on a submarine tower that is quickly closed in the last moment before diving.

"Behind here are further sealed chambers in which the plagues are suspended at appropriate temperatures."

"What security measures do you follow?"

Taking his elbow, I guide him upstairs, where no one will hear us.

"I can assure you we are very strict," I say, lowering my voice. "We follow the rules set down by facilities in the USSR, such as the laboratory in Tajikistan, or the laboratory on the Baltic island of Hiddensee. As you know, we are under surveillance. We have certain officers assigned here for protection. They gather information from among our hundred and forty employees. They move among the employees regularly, using first one, then another."

I should not have said *using;* I should have used another word.

He looks at me curiously. He is right to look at me in this way. It is unpleasant in here. It is malignant. My secretary watches me, someone else watches my secretary. The technicians are spied upon.

"Go on," he says.

"There are rules for any laboratory of this kind. The civilian rules, if you like. We change our clothes in an outer building. We strip. We shower. We pass naked through a sealed room. We put on our work clothes on the other side. We follow a strict hygiene. No coming to work with a sickness. No raising of laboratory-sensitive animals at home—no cows or pigs. No visiting relatives who live near a collective farm."

"Impressive," he says flatly.

It is not. There is a fear of saboteurs. All plagues and blights, even those found in trees and root vegetables, are tested for a weapons signature. We shuffle around the laboratory from alarm to alarm, in rubber suits and masks with narrow plates of glass; but for our slippers we would appear like insects to one another. The surveillance is always in search of that one agent, or double agent, who might spread a contagion, man-made or natural, through the livestock of ČSSR, just as in 1950 American spies stole into Czechoslovakia and blighted the potato crop with what came to be known as the American bug. All things here are seen through the prism of contagion, yet the security measures are halfhearted. The windows are barred, but they open from the inside. I could let spores out into the sky. I could cast a vial into the waters of the Ohře, as they talk about in the Bible, and poison the Labe. The blood we test, we also pour into the Ohře. It blooms in a pool where the trout circle, like some prophecy of Libuše. Trout come up to the bloom, gulp blood, and move away. No one searches me coming or going, no one monitors the number of vials I place in the vault. I could cycle away past the fortress of sloping red brick to a cowshed and there spread pestilence. This young man, without name, was not fingerprinted or photographed at the entrance. He did not strip and shower. He did not pass through a sealed room. He offered a code word in Russian and walked straight in.

"CIGARETTE, PROFESSOR?"

He offers me a Red Star.

"No, thank you."

"Do you mind if I do?"

"Not at all."

He bows his head. He strikes a match and lights his cigarette with a flourish.

I open a window.

"What, no danger?" he asks lightly.

SUNLIGHT FLOODS THROUGH the metal bars and stands in grids on the wall of the corridor; it is a cage in here. The Ohře is running fast with melted snow from the fields. It courses around the gravel bar I sometimes wade out to with my fly rod. I point out to the young man the cannon positions in the fortress on the other side of the Ohře.

"The fortress looks like a starburst from above," I say.

"How about those tests," he says. "What's the verdict?"

"Guilty," I say weakly.

He pales. He looks suddenly vulnerable, as though his thoughts have been elsewhere and this news has jolted him back.

"Run me through it, please," he says. "I'll have to report everything."

He leans with his back against the metal bars. He smokes and listens intently but writes nothing down.

"We were given a tissue sample from the tongue of one of the giraffes. We tested it to determine the strain," I say. "You should know there is not one single contagion in this case, but five or six related strains, which cause the same sickness. We have a vaccine against some of these strains but they are specific and have no effect on related strains."

"You're quite sure the giraffes have the contagion?" he says.

"Without question," I say. "We repeated the test. They have the African strain, number two."

"Do you have the vaccine for that strain?"

"No."

"How long would it take to obtain and administer such a vaccine to livestock in a radius of twenty kilometers?"

"Months."

"Sooner?"

"Impossible," I say.

I TELL HIM NOW of the process of testing, of serologic and isolation testing, of catalysts suspended in petri dishes, corpuscles of sheep's blood, injections, of blisters on the soft footpads of guinea pigs.

He nods slowly.

"Which animals are vulnerable?"

"All the even-toed ungulates," I say. "Giraffes and camels, cows, sheep. Not horses, dogs, or people."

"How dangerous is it?"

"That depends on how it manifested itself. If it was recently introduced, it is contagious in the extreme. If it was dormant for some years, for instance in a cyst under a hoof, and triggered by stress, then less so. Dormant strains take several passages, from one animal to another, to reach full strength."

"Is there any way of knowing?" he asks.

"Not for sure."

"What of the giraffes?"

"The policy is clear," I say. "If an exotic animal has the contagion, it must be destroyed. There must be no risk of exposure to livestock."

HE LIGHTS ANOTHER CIGARETTE and turns and stares at a weeping-willow tree across the Ohře, as though taking a photograph of it. I look beyond the willow to the spot where Jewish prisoners were forced at gunpoint to dump barrows of ash into the river. Thousands of Jews died from disease and hunger in the ghetto that existed inside the fortress during the war. They were cremated. Their ash was heavy, white in parts. The wheelbarrows had to be pushed by two people, two pushing the remains of thirty or forty. Those desolate brigades must have gone ever so slowly along the bank, by the trout pool. They must have struggled when they came down to the water. Some of the wheelbarrows must have been tipped in whole and washed out by the flow. A little of the ashes must have floated on the surface, like gruel, and flowed down through the Protectorate and through the Reich also, all the way to Hamburg, while the rest, the grit, sank straight to the bottom and is perhaps still there.

"OBVIOUSLY, THE OUTBREAK will need to be reported to the international authorities," I say.

He flushes again. "That will not be possible."

"The Office International des Épizooties must be told. That is the law."

"This is a matter of national security," he says, hardening. "National security is above the law. The OIE will not be informed. The orders are clear: You will cover up everything, write nothing down, give instructions orally. This is from the top, Tuma. This is from the Politburo."

"I understand the order," I say, after a silence. "They're taking a terrible risk. Suppose the contagion is at full strength. Suppose it spreads from the zoo to a collective farm. Our economy is centrally planned. Our animals live in huge concentrations. There are two million cows and four million other livestock in ČSSR. You know how they grow and live in dark, slopping cities of sheds. The contagion can move between the sheds, like a fire, ravaging all the beasts in them and in the collective farms DDR and the farms of Poland. It can come in through the mouth or through broken skin. It can be carried in breath and saliva, in milk, in piss and shit, in hay, in other feed, by the fork turning the feed, by the worker turning the fork, or else by a bird flying overhead. In the early stages, the animal will run a high fever, the tongue will blister, there will be a massive reproduction of the virus in its circulatory and lymphatic systems. Then pox and sores will break out on the udders and on other parts of the body. The hooves will swell and bleed. The animal will no longer be able to stand. It will topple to the ground. Its gums will also swell and split. It will not be able to eat or drink. Even if it survives, it will be finished as a unit of production. You kill the animal and all of it is infected: the blood, the organs, the flesh, the skin, the eyes. Czechoslovakian animals have no immunity against this strain of the contagion. If it is carried out of the zoo on the air of our ČSSR, it would make preceding outbreaks look incidental."

The young man looks at me steadily. His manner has straightened. He no longer seems to belong in a breezy film.

"Which is why any breach of confidentiality will result in immediate arrest," he says.

"I insist you inform the zoo of these results. It's a mistake not to tell them. It's a question of decency. It will cause them hurt for a long time."

"If we tell the zoo, there will be no secret. The zoo director will go to his friends abroad. There will be a protest. The international authorities will have to be told."

"So what if they are told?"

"Meat and dairy production will be halted. The borders of ČSSR will be closed for months—all of them. There will be no agricultural exports of any kind. We will be marked out as the disease pocket of COMECON."

"Only for a time," I say, "until the contagion is brought under control."

He pushes his hands into his pockets. "The first casualty will be the zoo. The shit of every animal there will be examined under a microscope—your microscope. Whatever you find, even if every test comes up negative, all the animals in the zoo will die and all the animals in the fields and sheds around the zoo will die. All the deer in the forest will be shot, even the stags. The whole land around the fishpond there will be emptied of life. Because that's how it is when national security is brought into question."

I say nothing. I look out to the river.

"This will be done by flame," he says. "The zoo animals and cows and deer will be burned on pyres reaching up to the sky in columns of fatty smoke. The zoo will be plowed under. The staff will be dispersed. There will only be a field, with no memory of a giraffe or of any exotic animal."

He says all this ever so softly, holding on to a cigarette, as though his hold on the present were only through this tiny glowing cylinder.

There is no stand to be made here. I have given over the results. I have protested. That is all. The State has no interest in bad news. Train wrecks do not make it into its papers, much less contagion. It mercilessly enforces silence. I play my part. I enforce the directives of Soviet laboratories. I copy their methods immediately, without question. I put Russian journals on my shelf and keep British journals in my drawer.

"There'll be a further investigation to make sure the laboratory is not responsible for releasing the contagion," he says.

"You have no grounds for suspicion!"

He puts a hand on my shoulder, returning to his former manner. "I know," he says. "That's just the order. The collective farms are to go on producing. The borders of ČSSR are not to be closed, not even for a day."

He turns to look out again at the fortress. "Wasn't Gavrilo Princip imprisoned in there?" he asks.

"The assassin? Yes. You can see the cell, if you like. They've put a plaque on the door. He shot Franz Ferdinand and now he's a martyr for Yugoslavia, an agitator for Slav brotherhood."

"How was it in there?"

"The cell is above ground," I say, "admitting light, but in other respects tubercular."

"I am going directly to the zoo," he says abruptly. "I wish to take some blood samples from the giraffes. I'll need some jars."

"Fine," I say. "How many?"

"Fifty or so," he says.

I pale. "Sorry?" I say, confused.

He smiles. "Didn't they tell you?" he says. "It's the largest herd in the world."

"No," I say. "No one told me."

I lead him downstairs. We pass the vault doors. I see him back into his suit jacket and shoes. We walk wordlessly to the sealed room. I shuffle, he clips. He saunters through the seal, through the showers, to the other side. I see him through the grille of my office window, handing his driver a metal case containing fifty empty jars to be filled with giraffe blood.

*Surely he shall deliver thee from the
snare of the fowler, and from
the noisome pestilence.*

—PSALM 91

Emil

I T IS ČARODĚJNICE—the witching night, the eve of May Day. I try to mark the outlines of witches riding goats and broomsticks on the windless sky. I look for the outlines of demons gliding down on fibrous wings. Demons were meant to be as vertical as men or giraffes. They had the same promising hemodynamics, until gravity got the better of them in the core of the earth and made them inexpressibly hunched, like the hyena a Slovak once spoke to me of. There were witching nights in Czechoslovakia when witches and demons fell from the sky to forest clearings. There were cats gathered on their hind legs around a bubbling pot in these clearings and women who put a hand to the thigh of some malevolent force and were so possessed they could no longer see their own red-faced children, born of previous such unions, trotting around them, shitting maggoty apples as they went. I look again out of the car window. I see no outlines in the sky save a Czechoslovakian Airlines jet. It is witching night in our ČSSR of 1975. The children will dress as witches, the collective farmworkers will drink and throw broomsticks onto bonfires. That is all.

I STILL HAVE NOT STOOD on any shore. There has not been a moment when I might have walked into a graveyard in the salt marshes on the English coast and stumbled upon Magwitch in chains. I have not been swept back into the waters of the Heligoland Bight. I am a doubler. I serve the shipping company with transmissions in code of *The Good Soldier Švejk* and other too-obvious texts, and I serve hemodynamics. I have been sent to Switzerland. I sat cross-legged on a sunny platform at the St. Gotthard junction, tossing a five-franc coin, silver and heavy, over and over. I took the train, as instructed: *Past the Tobler factory to the highest, wind-sheltered valley of the Upper Engadine.*

I came to the village with the secret laboratory. It was autumn. The larch trees were aflame on the mountainsides. I walked through high grass and dandelions to a wooden barn in the center of a meadow. I pushed aside sheep hung with clanging bells. I entered. I found an elevator behind bales of hay. I descended several stories underground. There I examined vials of blood. I gave a talk on cerebral hemodynamics

and was able to gather the information requested by the shipping company. Ascending once more, I saw the meadow
anew as a line of defense. When the sheep collapsed, the
authorities would know a contagion had escaped. There was a
graveyard in the Swiss-Italian village in which were graves of
alpinists. I wandered there and sat on the grass by the old
church. I was in a great amphitheater of mountains. There
was a freshly dug grave near me. I glanced at the new grave-
stone, still not dug in, and was amazed. Buried there was:

EMIL FREYMANN 1901–1974

A man without an epitaph.

I SLEPT THAT NIGHT in the Hotel Saratz, overlooking the
graveyard. A scientist from the laboratory had dinner with
me and later sat with me on the balcony of my room, pointing out the various glaciers and the circling eagles: *What you
say is interesting, Emil. But the motives of animals have always been
under investigation by man. Consider how even here in Switzerland, eels
were put on trial by the church and excommunicated from Lake
Luzern.*

I AM BEING DRIVEN to the town with the zoo, by hop poles
and vineyards. We enter the town now. I give instructions to
pass through the town square. I see the plague column once
again and factory women of good political orientation in
another part of the square in vests and black pumps, huffing

and puffing to a revolutionary tune, practicing a mass gymnastics exercise for the May Day parade. A committee member gives instructions through a megaphone. "Up and down!" he says. "Into the star." He breaks off. "No. Ladies! Ladies. Try to give the impression of being a wave that rises and falls with the anthem." The music starts again. The committee member claps his hands. "Again. Huddle together. Star shape! And up, and down."

We drive on, around the Svět. We come to an armed checkpoint. A notice has been placed here: REVERED COMRADES! THE ZOO IS CLOSED FOR TECHNICAL REASONS. ITS GATES WILL REMAIN SHUT FOR THE COMING HOLIDAYS. THE ZOO DIRECTORATE KINDLY ASKS COMRADES TO POSTPONE THEIR VISITS.

I SIT IN A TRAILER that was set down by crane next to the giraffe house at the beginning of the quarantine. I have replaced a vet from the Ministry of Agriculture. I have been ordered to oversee the liquidation of the giraffes that I ascended the Labe with. I am to shred any written reference here to them. There will be no talk of *Camelopardalis bohemica* because there can be no talk of the contagion. They will be killed without exception, but their absence will not be remarked on. The zoo will receive no explanation. The OIE offices in Paris will not be informed. Inquiries will be directed to nonexistent desks in the Ministry of Agriculture. Complaints will be met with threats of imprisonment. It will be as if the herd never migrated to Czechoslovakia or, having taken assisted passage here and become acclimatized, they simply walked out through open gates, heading north.

The zoo is circled with quicklime. Its administration and switchboard have been taken over by the security services. No outgoing telephone calls are allowed and there is only one incoming call each afternoon, to the giraffe house. Outside the zoo walls are army tents and a disinfection unit. The representative of the Central Infection Committee is there, together with the deputy minister of agriculture, the rectors of the Košice and Brno veterinary colleges, and security officers. Alois Hus has flown back into ČSSR this morning. He will be picked up by the secret police at Prague Ruzyně Airport. He will be escorted here, but he will not be permitted to enter the zoo. František Vokurka is also outside. I walked by him dressed in the chemical warfare suit I have been issued. He did not recognize me but told me to hold up. "You're going too fast, comrade! You need to move like this, languidly, as if you are a frogman underwater."

I do move slowly in this trailer. I sip tea. I pick up the newspapers. I read again of the five-to-two defeat of ČSSR by the USSR in the ice-hockey world championships, quotas and achievements, the opening of the Máj department store on Národní Street in Prague, a new television drama in which an army major proves himself a hero every week, and also in the sports pages of the return to the Communist moment of an eighteen-year-old tennis prodigy called Navrátilová from a world tour that included a string of victories.

There are also veterinary papers. The giraffe keeper looks out of the window, as though expecting a visitor, while I read of placental retention in the giraffes of the Leningrad Zoo, of arterial studies on vivisected dogs, and of the tendency toward pelvic tendon rupture in male zoo giraffes.

I am sober. I understand pyres will be built across ČSSR if the contagion is not contained. They were described to me in Prague. A bed of timbers and railway sleepers, a layer of brown coal, oil, straw, the carcasses laid on top, like some funeral in the time of Libuše. I understand the smoke from these pyres, of chlorine-soaked carcasses, will be more poisonous than arsenic.

I can no longer stop the Communist moment. I find it hard to stop images with my eye in the way I used to, keeping them in my mind and turning them. I stood yesterday in a secret laboratory on the banks of the River Ohře and my eye was drawn to a weeping willow on the far bank, as if in broad daylight I might chance to see a *vodník* sitting in the branches. The professor running the facility was a small man, unfailingly polite, who offered resistance when called upon to do so, conceded gracefully, and had exceptionally thick spectacles from staring so long into microscopes and vials. He showed me the metal doors securing the animal plagues. The doors reminded him, he said, of hatches on a submarine. I was disoriented when he said that. I had a feeling of being upended, as if I were standing on the flat deck of a submarine, cold water rushing about me, and the only escape were into a chamber of pestilence.

WE GO INSIDE THE GIRAFFE house again: *They are impossible. There is no such animal.*

I still regard these beasts in that way. I have forgotten so much in the last two years, but I cannot forget the towers of the Qasr al-Qadim fortress, over which the gyrfalcon sailed and looked down on the only giraffe in Europe. My eyes are watering: There is a high level of ammonia here. It is too crowded. There have been births since I left here in the summer of 1973, just as Hus predicted. There are now forty-seven giraffes; two others have already been shot. I move among them. They have become fully zoo animals. Their eyes have changed in aspect. I do not look at them closely. I do not want to remember the necks I moved under on the barge. I try to regard them only as hemodynamic specimens, pressing blood to the tin roof. I walk away when I catch sight of Sně-hurka's belly in the crowd.

"They're not sick," the keeper says, following me. "It's spring. They salivate with the change of feed. That's all."

He is in denial. The African number-two contagion is in their blood and lymph nodes. I see it here and here, in pox, in blisters, manifested in boils in the inner thigh that are black like the plagues spoken of in Athens, shiny, waiting to break open like rotten fruit.

THERE IS A STORY of a ferryman on the Labe who found himself untouched by a pestilence while his wife and children were struck down. There were the most sorrowful and wretched scenes along the riverbank. Each day the ferryman would leave a parcel of food on the shore and call out to his pox-ridden wife. She would come out of their dwelling with their children. He would, at her heartrending entreaty, row out into the river, within shouting distance only, and so they called to each other loving greetings and he asked after the health of those children not present. When the ferryman could no longer bear it, he rowed his oars hard toward his family, and they took up stones and pieces of wood, even the smallest child, raining them down on him, until he turned back and rowed away, sobbing.

The contagion in the giraffes is not like that. The parting is not man from man, but man from beast. I am vertical, but separate from the giraffes. The contagion is virulent to other hoofed animals but is not dangerous to humans or to animals that are close to humans, such as horses and dogs. I will not develop lumps in the pits of my arms. The contagion will strike down only these creatures tottering in ammonia behind me. It is as Aristotle said—we differ from animals in our ability to speak. We alone can speak of the Communist moment, of justice and injustice. It is our speech that passes judgment on animals, excommunicating eels and condemning giraffes.

"The orders are for complete destruction," I say to the keeper. "Tonight." It is as if I have ordered his destruction.

"They are healthy," he says, but nothing more.

Jiří

ČARODĚJNICE

APRIL 30, 1975

I HAVE A MEMORY from 1941, the year I killed my first boar. I am a little boy, pushing a wheelbarrow from a damp hay barn after a summer rainstorm. I am wearing a raincoat, buttoned to the collar. I cycle across the crest of a meadow. I see a double rainbow and a maypole around which people are dancing on a field below.

Tomorrow is May Day. There will be speeches and parades in the town. They will go around and around the pine tree I have myself cut down and stripped.

. . . .

I AM DRINKING in the sawmill. The windows are open now. There is the smell of cut wood. We're having a party for Luboš, the forester responsible for the Christmas tree harvest. He's moving to a mountainous part of the country, where there still are bears and wolves. Another bottle is uncorked. We cheer Luboš but do not yet break into song.

I go outside with Luboš. We lean against planking sliced from spruce we have grown together in the forest. We smoke Red Stars and drink.

"You're a lucky man," I say, "to be going to such a wild and mountainous place."

"You could move also," he says.

"I can never leave," I say. "I'm too accustomed to seeing the Svět between the trees. I wish only for those heights here."

The comrades have put on the music. We're getting in the mood. I hear someone calling my name.

"Sobotka?"

"Yes," I say.

A Communist official stands before me. I recognize him finally, but I cannot remember his name. He's from one of the industrial towns. His shirt is sweated through.

"Comrade!" I say. "What brings you here?"

"You," he says, unsmiling.

"Have a drink!"

I put an arm around him. He shakes it off.

"No drink," he says. "Listen, we've got foreign guests here to shoot black grouse. We need you to guide them."

"Grouse? This time of year?"

"We need you to accompany us now."

He gestures to two Státní Bezpečnost, or secret policemen, standing by an official car.

"No fuss," he says.

"I'd like to oblige," I say, "but as you can see, I'm occupied."

He puts up a shaking hand.

"Comrade Sobotka, you have no choice in the matter."

WE DRIVE AWAY ON the road by the marsh. There is matter
in the air from the chimneys in the industrial towns, a lumi-
nescence of dust that settles in the sunbeams and on the
petals of the spring blossom.

"I need to go home to change and shave."

He shakes his head and taps his wristwatch. It has a
hammer-and-sickle dial.

"Just bring your biggest-caliber rifle and all the ammunition you can carry."

"I thought we were going to shoot black grouse."

"We are," he says.

I GO IN MY HOUSE NOW. Květa is at the kitchen table, painting faces on snowman decorations from the factory in the
town. I go wordlessly by her. I unbolt the gun locker. I take
out the Mauser 7.92. I fill the satchel with a hundred or so
57 mm cartridges. Květa looks up.

"Back already?"

"Some officials are demanding I guide foreigners after
black grouse," I say.

"At this time of year?" she says.

She glances at the Mauser.

"You're going to hunt grouse with that?" she asks. "Where's your shotgun?"

She has an eye for detail. You see it on these decorations she paints.

"A rifle is what I want," I say, "and a rifle is what I'm taking."

"You're not going dressed like that?"

I stuff the last cartridges into my satchel.

"My wife, my love," I say, "I am in a hurry."

I kiss her on the forehead, and I go to open the front door.

"You could start a revolution with all those bullets," she calls after me.

THE TWO StB MEN STAND in the driveway with hands on their holsters. I climb into the back of the car next to the official. I arrange the rifle between my knees. We drive off fast, skidding around a bend and accelerating toward the town. I am disheartened. I am a Communist in the forest, where I fear the ground might give under me. I feel different out here. I have imagined the Communist moment to have risen higher, to be better and less authoritarian.

I turn to the official. It is hard to see his expression; sunlight is streaming into the car.

"This isn't about black grouse, is it?"

"No," he says. "Prepare yourself for a long night."

"Where are we going?"

"We are going to the zoo."

He speaks to me in the familiar form. It's true—we are

comrades. We are like distant relatives, avoiding each other at a celebration.

"To do what?" I ask.

I feel weighed down by the satchel. The car kicks up dust on the gravel road. The Svět blurs brown beside us. I have heard rumors of contagion, that the zoo has been under quarantine.

"You're aware a contagion has broken out in the zoo?" he asks.

"Yes."

"It is an animal infection. It must be contained."

"That's why you need me," I say.

"You're the sharpshooter. You're the best shot in the district—everyone says so. You're trustworthy, loyal, a Party member. You won't go blabbing the story."

"The story?"

"The story of how you were called on to shoot dead a group of giraffes."

"Show me the order," I say.

The StB men glance at me in the mirror.

"There's nothing on paper," the official says.

"You must have something."

"This is from the top," he says.

I squint into the light.

"I won't do anything without a written order," I say.

WE STOP AT A *PANELÁK* overlooking the Svět and pick up Máslo, the head of the district committee. He squeezes in beside me.

"The comrade is right," Máslo says, nodding to the sweating official. "There are no written orders."

Máslo is neckless, but not gracefully so, like an okapi. He has the face of a functionary. I do not recognize such faces or necks in the forest, where hats are pulled down and collars are turned up against the cold, but they are apparent to me out here, as if they were preordained for it, just as doctors used to say you can tell a thief by the slope of his forehead.

Máslo keeps smiling at me.

"Come on," he says. "The drinks are on me afterward."

I say nothing. Máslo puts a hand on my knee; he keeps it there.

"This is a question of national security. You have to do this for the good of our children, for the health of our ČSSR. As to the written orders, you have my word among witnesses this comes from the top."

WE PASS OUT OF the town into the parkland, not slowing, going by people standing with vacant expressions under a stage that has been set up for the May Day parade. We come to a checkpoint, where the wide steps leading down from the chapel of St. Michael meet the Svĕt. We are ushered through. The road under us is suddenly white, powdery with quicklime. There are Veřejná Bezpečnost, or state security officers, and soldiers guarding the perimeter of the zoo.

"What's going on here?" I ask.

"I told you," Maslo says. "This is a matter of national security."

We get out of the car. I am introduced to the regional director of agriculture, the regional security chief, ranking StB, VB, and army officers, and Interior Ministry officials from Prague.

There are several tents in which army field telephones are connected to zookeepers living with their animals in quarantine inside the zoo. Everyone wears rubber boots and leaves footprints in the powder. It is early evening now. The bonfires marking Čarodějnice have not yet been lit.

The new regional director of the state veterinary service walks over.

"František Vokurka," he says, not extending his hand. "You must be the sharpshooter."

"I'm the forester," I say.

"Thanks for coming. I asked for a sharpshooter. I want to make this as humane as possible. We've tried strangulation. Chemicals are unsatisfactory for this size and number of giraffes. It's too late for arguments or alternatives. Comrade: You are to shoot all the giraffes."

I push my spectacles back. I feel myself falling back, as though shoved.

"How many?" I ask.

"Two have already been shot," he says, avoiding my look.

"How many?"

"This is difficult for me," he says. "I accompanied many of these giraffes from Africa." He pauses, looks down. "Forty-seven," he says. "Including fourteen calves."

I want to walk away, but I do not.

"What about the zoo director? I don't see him here."

"He's been abroad. He's returning as we speak. Look," he says, "the giraffes are done through with contagion. They have the pox. Their hides have opened into sores. There is no time to lose. The collective farms are already bringing complaints, saying their cows are giving no milk and their calves are dying without explanation."

I am taken into a tent. The Mauser is inspected, the leather strap removed. "This cannot be disinfected," a soldier says, holding up the strap. "We'll have to hold it here."

"I want it back."

"Of course."

I am stripped now inside the zoo gates. I hear a leopard or some other cat mewling. I sit naked on a bench with a pack of Red Stars, matches, spectacles, satchel of cartridges, and the rifle. A man comes in with a hooded suit of the kind used in case of nuclear attack. He holds another suit, boots, goggles, and surgeon's rubber gloves.

"Put these on," he says.

I dress. I think of myself as a soldier moving about the secret military base in the forest. I do not put on the goggles.

"I need my spectacles to shoot straight," I say. "You want me to shoot straight, don't you?"

I REPORT BACK TO VOKURKA.

"I am a frogman," Vokurka says, watching me. "I know how it is to wear a suit. The trick is to move slowly and deliberately at all times. Let me see your rifle and ammunition."

I lay them on a table. A VB officer snorts.

"You'll need an elephant gun," the VB officer says.

"What's that?" I say.

"A few days ago," Vokurka says, "the VB were brought in to shoot two giraffes dead. They made a mess of it. They shot into the chests of the animals. They caused real suffering. That's why we called you in."

"Comrade, how much do the giraffes weigh?" I ask Vokurka.

"The adults? Six hundred to nineteen hundred kilos."

"Jesus and Mary!" I rip back my nuclear hood. "Listen," I say, "the heaviest stag I've shot weighed two hundred kilos. At most. What am I going to do with a Mauser? It's a sparkler."

"I've thought about this," Vokurka says coolly. "This isn't a hunt. It's an execution. It's not a matter of sighting an animal running away from you, between trees. The giraffes will be right above you. The giraffe keeper will guide them out. He'll steady them for you. You'll have no problem if you shoot precisely."

"Tell me where I should shoot."

"Not into the chest," he says. "Never into the chest."

He takes paper and a pencil. "Ever seen a giraffe close up?" he asks.

"Only from a distance," I say.

I have never been inside the zoo. I have never seen a beast in a cage. In a trap, but not in a cage.

"Let me draw a giraffe for you."

He sketches a vertical shape.

"You have to aim for the head," he says. "The bullet must pass into the brain. That's not easy. The brain is heavy, tens of kilos, and encased in thick bone."

"Through the eye?"

"No. The best shot is here, just below and behind the ear," he says, marking it with a cross. "The bone is less thick there, between the jaw and skull. It's an aperture into the brain."

"That's a hard shot," I say.

"The ear will cast a shadow," he says. "You can aim for the center of that shadow. If you hit the giraffe here, where X marks the spot, it's *zhasne*—lights out. The giraffe will die instantly, even if the neck cord is not severed."

"How will I shoot them in the dark?" I say.

"Don't worry about that," the VB captain says, intervening once more. "The StB have brought in floodlights."

"One thing," I say.

"What's that?" Vokurka asks.

"I'll need liquor. I can't do this without a drink."

I WALK ALONE THROUGH the zoo, in my nuclear suit. I am out of the forest. I am revealed on concrete. I carry the rifle in one hand, the satchel in the other. I see the floodlights. I follow the footprints in the quicklime toward them. I pass zookeepers who are also in nuclear suits. They move between the cages with shovels and wheelbarrows of feed. I move on slowly, deliberately, as if underwater. I see a swallow, the first of the year. I hear a shotgun: I see pellets in the air like flies and the swallow torn and falling now. A man in a nuclear suit comes running up. He stares at me through goggles.

"We've orders to shoot them down," he says.

I come to the giraffe house. A group of men stand by the wooden fencing. They are also in nuclear suits, but wear aprons over the suits. They are sharpening long knives. They are butchers from a rendering plant. There are two Škoda trucks of a special design, from that rendering plant, parked by the giraffe house.

"They're supposed to be blood-tight," a butcher says. "We'll be here all night. You shoot them and we'll cut them up and drive them off."

A young man steps from a hut and walks toward me. He is not much older than my son. He wears a nuclear suit, but no hood. Blond hair falls diagonally across his face. He looks foreign.

"Comrade Sobotka?"

"Yes."

"I'm Emil."

"Emil what?"

"Just Emil. I'm the scientist."

He folds his arms and unfolds them, as though he does not know where to put his hands. Behind him comes the giraffe keeper.

"I'm sorry," I say to the keeper.

He looks away.

"The okapi?" I ask.

"One of them was shot," he says. "The other is fine."

Now comes an StB officer. He wields a camera with a tele-photo lens, a Zenit PhotoSniper, as though it were also a weapon. He shouts, "Line up!"

We arrange ourselves in a line: secret policemen, butchers, a blond boy, a giraffe keeper.

"ČSSR is in danger," the StB officer says. "Our national security is imperiled. The contagion must be contained."

The butchers turn their knives on the points. I stand with my rifle at my side.

"Orders have been given for the destruction of every one of these giraffes. The zoo is sealed off at gunpoint. No one will be allowed to leave until the liquidation procedure is complete. No one will speak of these events. Anyone who does will be prosecuted and imprisoned. It will be as if this night never happened."

"Who's he kidding?" a butcher says beside me. "Here I am working for twelve crowns and fifty heller an hour and he's going to shoot me after three warnings?"

THE SUN SETS. I see Čarodějnice bonfires burning beside the Svět. I see the puff of other shotgun discharges, and I see new swallows and an unkindness of ravens drop from the sky.

I make a plan now with the scientist Emil and the giraffe keeper. I can see by the way Emil sweeps back his hair over and over, through his surgeon's gloves, and by his confession of nausea, that he fears this night as I do. The keeper seems not to be quite awake. His eyes are dulled from many days living in quarantine. His giraffes will be driven into the yard in groups of three or four. I will climb up on the fencing around the yard and fire off my shots. It will be too messy to shoot the giraffes inside, where they could not be easily separated and would be driven mad by the crashing deaths.

The floodlights the StB have arranged are useless. The light they shed is watery, useless. It is wrong to imagine that ČSSR has held within it some elite; the secret police are only a reflection of what is apparent.

"I have a flashlight," the keeper says. "If you shine the light in their eyes they will be blinded and stayed for a moment. Then you can aim it where you need to shoot."

He looks away and then, after a long pause, back at me.

"Are you the best shot?"

"I'm a fair shot," I say. "No more."

"Do your best," he says. "Concentrate."

I light a Red Star. The StB officer comes over with a paper bag.

"Here's your drink," he says to me. "Two bottles of Cuban rum."

"Don't get drunk," the keeper says.

"To steady my hand," I say.

"You're to fire quickly," Emil says. "One giraffe, two, three. Can you?"

"I'll try," I say.

"If it is not a clean shot, then fire again. I'll run forward when the last of the giraffes falls."

I CLEAN THE LENSES of my spectacles. I measure the yard. Thirty steps by forty. The giraffes will break stride and hit the fencing. I attend to the Mauser. I open and shut its bolt. I oil it.

There are fireworks breaking overhead now, from the outdoor ice-hockey rink in the town. I see my chance.

"Emil!" I call. "Send the first ones out. I'm ready."

THE DOORS OF THE giraffe house open. A bull giraffe stands there. Giant. It makes no sound. It moves slowly out into the yard, clopping on the concrete. I climb up on the fence. I balance. Fireworks continue to burst overhead. It is gloomy, then suddenly white, then suddenly yellow, now bathed in green.

"Giraffe!" I shout, as though calling out, "Timber!" in the forest, as though the giraffe is a silver fir. "Giraffe!"

I level the barrel at the bull. I turn the safety catch to the left. I fire. I put a bullet into green light. It strikes below and behind the ear. It enters into the heavy brain. The giraffe does not slump, but is felled. There is a sound of breaking bone as it hits the ground.

The fireworks burst in red. I put bullets into red light now.

WHEN THE FIREWORK DISPLAY is over and there is no more illumination, the StB officer orders a butcher to hold up a flashlight for me. The keeper drives out three more giraffes. They circle in the yard. I take a long swig of rum.

"Shine the light in their eyes," I say to the butcher. "Then at the back of the head, below the ear."

The butcher does so. He shines a light on the X-marked spot, the aperture. I am quicker. I lift the Mauser. I level it, I fire. I swing, I level, I fire. I swing again, I level, I fire. They are felled.

THE BUTCHER PUTS DOWN the flashlight and climbs down into the yard with the other butchers. They step there among entwined necks. One of the butchers kicks away a crow shot down and fallen on the giraffes. We are comrades also, we hunters and butchers. We are blessed together by Hubert.

The butchers set down knives, clippers, and lengths of rope. I force myself to watch: I have killed these animals. The butchers' touch is rough. A twelve-crowns-and-fifty-heller-an-hour touch. They are not respectful or precise. They plant their knives in haunches while they feel behind the knees, then they pull out the blades and sever the tendons with a single cut. There is the sound of slicing. They fold the giraffes up. They rope them to a winch and drag them across the yard, up a ramp into one of the blood-tight trucks. The necks are stamped on in there and broken, so that other giraffes may be piled on top. The trucks are locked down, sprayed with disinfectant, and driven off into the witching night, gathering powder on their tires as they go.

THE DOORS OPEN AGAIN. Three more giraffes stand there. They do not step out. The keeper moves behind them. He slaps them on their hocks. He claps, he shouts. They do not move. They smell the blood. They sense the violence. I set down the rifle and walk around and talk through the slats to the giraffe keeper and to Emil.

"You're doing this all wrong," I say. "These animals are too strong for you. Try lighting a fire under them."

"What?" Emil says.

"A fire. It's what foresters used to move along bullock carts stuck in the mud on the path around the Svět."

The keeper shakes his head; he can barely speak now.

"Trust me," I say. "It will take their minds off one fear and put it on another."

THE KEEPER BRINGS OUT some old copies of the *Rudé Právo,*
or *Red Truth,* newspaper.

"Tie a few pages to their tails and set them alight," I say.

I go back to the fence. I slide down to the base of it, my
knees to my chest. I swig more rum.

"You've got a nerve, pal," the butcher with the flashlight
says to me, wiping his knives. "You should watch what you've
started."

So I do. I climb up on the fence and I watch the keeper
wrap sheets of red right around the tail of one of the giraffes. I
see Emil lighting the paper with a cigarette. The flames catch.
The tail starts to burn. All three giraffes break forward, like bul-
locks pulling a cart of timber from a slough. The doors close
behind the giraffes. The beasts slide now on blood and urine.
They gallop around the yard, circling an invisible maypole.
There is no sound but their hooves slipping on the wet concrete. One tail swishes, flames. It is another bonfire, another
form of Čarodějnice. I level the barrel, I fire. I miss. I hit the
neck. The giraffe falls. It kicks out on the ground, wounded.

"Hold me!" I shout to the butcher.

I stand atop the fence for a better angle, one leg on either
side. The butcher throws his arms around my nuclear-clad
legs. I load. I fire down at the prone giraffe and kill it.

THERE IS SO MUCH BLOOD. I fire a bullet in the air and cause
a fountain. It is not a flow of blood from a deer into the forest floor. It sprays up to the chest. Whenever all the giraffes

are down, Emil leaps down with glass jars. He squats over the bullet holes. He puts a jar to the fountain and fills it. It takes only a second. There is something of my childhood about it. The blood springs from the giraffes like the pierced side of Christ on the cross in a religious picture, filling grails. Emil seals the jars and wipes the blood from them. He puts a label on each and writes down the name and year of birth of each giraffe I have felled, as the keeper calls them out to him.

"Alenka!" the keeper shouts through tears. "1971."

THE BUTCHERS WINCH UP the giraffes into a truck, but it is not blood-tight; it seeps. The giraffes are removed. The butchers hose the truck down inside and out. They seal it with sheeting and petroleum jelly. They load the broken-necked animals again.

The Čarodějnice bonfires have burned low. Half of the giraffes are dead. They have been different sizes and colors, but always vertical, always up. We take a break. I leave the butchers to climb the fences. I go to the side of the truck and vomit. My mouth tastes of bile. I swig more rum. I go to stand with the others. There is a beautiful girl, somehow materialized here. She is not wearing a nuclear suit. A secret policeman has her by the elbow; he detained her before, during the firework display. She does not struggle.

"How did you get in here?" the StB officer asks.

"Through the zebras," the girl says evenly.

"You're under arrest. You're in serious trouble."

"You'll have to arrest me too then," the keeper says, stepping forward.

"I get it," the StB officer says. "Lovers."

It is such a strange moment. No one has the heart to pursue it. The StB officer does not move the girl on; the keeper does not answer the StB officer. Emil comes forward, soaked in blood. He takes a Red Star from the pack I offer him and wordlessly lights it. We all stand here under the watery floodlights, under the hornets swarming and smacking audibly against the lights. There is no communication with the main gate. Only the trucks move from here, trundling away in leaded fumes. I feel as an okapi must under a Czechoslovian sky. There is a buzzing in my head that is not rum. Too much is revealed. Nothing is glimpsed here; I see everything clearly; I look up and see the shooting stars whole.

The girl seems also alert. Her eyes are large, darting. They fix on me, on the trigger of my rifle, on the doors of the giraffe house. One of the butchers pushes past the floodlights, to the table set with food and drink. He wipes his knife on the apron strung over his suit and puts it in his belt. He does not wipe his hands. They are still dark and sticky as he picks through the salami.

"You disgust me," the girl says to the butcher.

The butcher spits at his feet and reaches for a bread roll.

"What's new?" he says.

I step away. I have lost my appetite. I light another cigarette. The fishermen on the Svět say tobacco takes away the smell of blood. My legs are weak.

The StB officer approaches.

"The girl will hold the flashlight for you now," he says.

I wipe my mouth. I nod.

· · ·

THE GIRL SHINES THE FLASHLIGHT in the eyes of the giraffes. She stills the beasts.

"The back of the head," I say.

She steadies the light.

"Giraffe!" I shout.

I level, I fire.

Emil drops into the yard, into the pit. The drains are blocked with congealed blood and waste. He is up to his knees in blood. He splashes away now through contagion. The fallen crow floats there with spread wings.

The butchers are wading now.

DAWN BREAKS. It is May Day in ČSSR, 1975, and I am quite drunk, as I planned to be.

I can see by this light. I no longer need a flashlight.

"Go to the keeper," I say to the girl.

She moves off into the giraffe house, as voiceless as the beasts I have felled.

There is a delay. The doors open. Three more giraffes stand there. Emil and the girl light a fire under one of them. The keeper is nowhere to be seen. The giraffes splash out. Their heads are rolled back, stretched up. I kill them also.

THERE IS ONE MORE GIRAFFE. They bring her to the door. She is as large as a bull, perhaps eleven hundred kilos. She has

a snow-white belly. The girl beats her with a rope on her fet-
locks. Emil shouts at her. She does not move. She remains
there on the threshold. They light a fire of red right under
her. She bleats just once, like a kid goat, and dashes back into
the giraffe house. They shut the doors. I hear her inside, dashing herself against the fences and walls. I run around the
fence. After some time, we find the keeper.

"She's not going to make it out," he says to me, breaking
his silence. "You'll have to shoot her inside."

I follow the keeper up the stairs in the giraffe house to the
hayloft, where feed is set down at the height of giraffe heads.
The cow runs back and forth below. She kicks out at the
stalls. Her hooves are large and heavy. They leave jagged
marks in the wood and circles in the metal.

"Her name is Sněhurka," the keeper says blankly, "because
of the snow-white of her belly and legs. She was a leader in
the herd."

The keeper slips away. I am without a witness. The girl is
not here. Emil is not here. The StB officer is not aiming his
telephoto lens and photographing me. I am alone in the barn,
which is thick with contagion. I lie down on my belly in the
loft, on hay and branches stripped clean by giraffes. I am
tired. I swig the last of the rum. The stench of the yard is in
here. May Day light slants in through the high windows.

It is harder to shoot across. The point of entry is different.

Giraffe, I say to myself.

I turn the safety catch to the left. I am at eye level with
Sněhurka. She is running away from me on broken legs. I
level the barrel at the aperture. I fire. I miss. The bullet is
lodged in the flesh of her neck. She blinks, she swings on her

broken legs, but she does not collapse. Blood springs from her neck. I slide back the bolt, I load. I level, I fire. The 57 mm bullet is gone from me. The sound of it reverberates.

Sněhurka buckles. She falls. She does not splash into blood, but crumples, enormous, to straw and dung. I stand. I look down. She is still alive. Her eyes level on me; they mark me. I fire once more. Her body tightens into that fragment of existence when you are no longer living and not yet dead. Her eyes close. Her legs kick out finally, as if a puppeteer is pulling her strings one last time. She is dead. Blood spouts from her, but Emil is not there with his grail. I get down on my knees.

"God grant her light soil," I say aloud.

THE KEEPER IS NOWHERE to be found. The girl has been taken away. The butchers open the doors now. They stand glistening, knives and rope in hand. They look at Sněhurka and come forward. I force myself to watch them, as one should watch the gutting of a deer you have shot. They cut her tendons. They fold her up, as though she were going back to the womb, not to a truck.

Emil

NIGHT FALLS AND MORE birds are shot from the sky. We let out a Rothschild calf now with a plaster cast on a foreleg. It hobbles into the yard. Sobotka pushes back his spectacles with lenses so thick his pupils are magnified to cartoon proportions, like the professor overlooking the Ohře. He shoots the calf in the head. I run forward through blood that is deeper now, that is over my ankles. I brush aside a hornet. I fill the jar. I signal to a butcher to bring me meat scissors. I take the scissors, the kind they use to separate joints, and I cut up the length of the cast. I examine the leg.

The bone has grown back together. I look at it for a long moment. Finally, I manage to frame it. If I can have one memory from this night, it should be this.

On a corridor at the back of the Národní Muzeum in Prague sits an artifact in a glass cabinet. It is a figurine of polished black stone, a depiction of a bald man metamorphosed into a beetle. The face is perfectly human, as are the arms, delicate fingers, and trimmed fingernails; he might be an Assyrian scribe. About the torso is a shell, from which grow insect legs staved with bristles and hooks, enclosing the yellow fluids and membrances of a beetle and wings, visible in gossamer through a scabby slit down the back. I stand here in blood. For a moment I do not see myself as a *vodník* waiting to catch a falling stewardess in a Venetian lagoon, but as a man metamorphosing into a beetle. I fly toward the light. I hit a window. I fall on my back. I cannot turn over again. I give myself out in lesser and lesser movements.

A STRANGE GIRL HAS APPEARED out of the witching night, unprotected and distraught. She has been detained for some hours in the trailer and is now brought for questioning. I instruct the StB officer not to send her away but instead to have her hold up the flashlight for Sobotka in place of a butcher. She is doing that now. She is shining a beam in the eyes of a reticulated bull. She blinds and stops the bull with that light. She trains the beam at the back of the head. Sobotka fires. The giraffe falls. The hunter is a miracle. He is drunk and cannot keep his rifle straight. It sinks in his hands.

From revulsion also, he says. He sets it down. He crosses himself. He drinks some more. He breathes deeply. He levels the barrel again, for a split second.

"Giraffe!" he calls.

He lets off another shot. The rifle kicks into his shoulder. He is a sharpshooter. The bullets hit where they are supposed to. They fire up through the wonder net, through the brain, lodging most often in the frontoparietal cavity. He knows before anyone else when he misses. He climbs higher on the fence, the girl holds him by the ankles, he fires again.

The giraffes keep crumbling like minarets and like the towers of Palermo. I run forward with my jars, making calculations of the cosmic collapse of veins as I go. I mathematically transform the deformation of arterial walls and the viscosity of flow into measures of time. I collect the blood. One fountain here, another, then a third.

The keeper speaks now only to call out the names and years of birth, which I mark on the jars.

"Božena! 1975," he calls. "Luděk! 1971."

Others are named:

Eliška!

Šohaj!

Honza!

I try not to look at their horns or neck markings. I still wish to remember them on a barge passing under the castle at Meissen. It is foul to me to splash blood over their hides, staining the mazed lines, which contain the circulatory system I have come to know, of a red flow unidirectional to the heart; not Communist red, but crimson of stars that give no light, black-red of vaulted aorta and proximal arteries, blue-red about the veins of the wrists and ankles, and tidal colors of the wonder net's channels, which absorb the flow, give out, and are then drawn back.

Tribal peoples made sandals of giraffe hide. It is sad to me that a piece of any creature pushed up in defiance of gravity should be fashioned into a shoe striking the dust on the ground. Giraffe hide is also burned in other tribal cultures and the smoke inhaled as a cure for hemophiliacs, as though breathing it would be enough to thicken thin skin into an antigravity suit.

MY CHEMICAL-WARFARE SUIT ITCHES. I cannot wear the hood up. I am blond still, like fictional Emil. I think of my namesake, of what became of him, of where his detectives are. I move slowly around the giraffes. I see how the legs are the length of the necks. This goes unnoticed when they are alive and upright. Even though they push the giraffe above all living things, the legs are forgotten. It must be that the memory of a giraffe begins with the neck and moves to the head, just as it does with people.

MAY DAY COMES, too late. At the end now, I have to ask a butcher to cut out a tongue. I order the burning of the giraffe keeper's papers along with his clothes and I personally expose the rolls of film the StB officer shot with his PhotoSniper. I keep the jars of blood for myself and the tongue also.

. . .

I STRIP. THEY SPRAY ME with disinfectant. My eyes sting. I am led, momentarily blind, into a tent. I gather myself. The girl is in this tent also. Her head is in her hands. I want to see her face, I want her to look at me.

"My hair is clean now," I say.

She says nothing. She does not look up. It is as if she were in a trance, or sleepwalking like a giraffe.

I SEE VOKURKA. He does not approach me. He does not recognize me. He moves between the StB officers and the senior Communists. He is not as innocent as his name. He has grown predatory, into one of those tarpon he spoke of, who have learned to come up for air in the mangrove swamps while smaller fish asphyxiate in stagnant waters.

I FIND ALOIS HUS ALONE, sitting on quicklime. He looks up at me desperately, then with recognition.

"Freymann," he says without surprise.

"Yes, Alois," I say.

"You were in there?"

"I had a scientific interest," I say awkwardly.

I am in my clothes now. I can put my hands in the pockets of my tweed trousers. I do so.

"Was the shooting done cleanly?" he asks.

"As cleanly as possible."

His hands and knees are muddy.

"I've been in a field," he says. "I've been on my knees all night. I've been listening to the shots."

"I'm sorry," I say.

"They didn't have to kill them," he says. "They could have done something else. It's political. They don't want animals running free."

There is silence, then he strikes up again.

"They could have dug a pit and filled it with solution," he says. "They could have walked the giraffes through the pit and ducked them under the solution, just for a moment."

"Like a baptism?" I say.

"Yes," he says, his eyes far away.

Amina

THEY HAVE SET UP a centrifugal fairground ride under the Gothic winged cow to celebrate May Day. You stand in a cage and it spins around. There are no doors, no belts. You spin around and around and gravity binds you in.

I cross the town square. I step over the sundial shadow of the plague column. Children with hooked paper noses go by me dressed in black. They carry broomsticks. One child chases the others, desperately, as though the space between them were a wasteland.

. . .

THERE WAS A TIME when witches were burned at the stake in
the town square and the corpses were thrown into the Labe
to float away, toward the sea. We are taught in our stories that
there were three sisters before there were witches. Kazi had
the gift of healing. Teta had the gift of finding what was lost.
Libuše had the gift of foreknowledge and ruled this land
before it was Czechoslovakia. She went down to flowing
water and saw the future in the pools. She sat cross-legged on
a carpeted platform under a linden tree. People came to her
and she dispensed justice to them. Women had authority
then; they were the shamans. When Libuše handed power
over to men, many women refused to be subjugated. They
rose up; they cut down hundreds of men in pitched battles.
They fought for seven years, and when the men finally took
power, many of the women fled to the forest. They were sat-
urnine. They kept themselves apart. They became witches.
They ruled the imagination of Czechoslovakia by night as the
priests did by day. They nurtured the memory of the three
sisters. They directed their spells against men and the animals
that profited men. They lived in caves and in dwellings of
green branches. They gathered wild herbs and seeds. They
tapped sap from the trees and scooped out from hives combs
of wild honey. Czechoslovakia came to be afraid of the
witches. They believed the witches spread disease among
their livestock. Every year on the witching night they took
lengths of cord, had them blessed by the priest, and tied them
around the throats of their cows and sheep. Only then did

they celebrate the end of winter and carouse through the night, into May Day. Čarodějnice is no longer about the protection of animals, which are units of production, and have no blessing in the Communist moment. No cord is tied around the neck of a cow tonight, save to bind it tight in the dark shed of a collective farm.

I RUN TOWARD THE ZOO. I take the secret path, behind the chapel of St. Michael. I come to the town swimming pool. It is very beautiful now. It is filled for summer and is ghostly blue from the lights within it. I keep out of sight. I creep from the pool up the slope. I slip in the mud. I get up to the path that runs by the zoo wall. I can smell the elephants on the other side. I can hear them thumping. Soldiers are patrolling the path. They are marching up and down with their machine guns. Against what enemy? I wait in the shadows for them to pass. I find a gap in the wall. I squeeze through.

I find myself in the zebra enclosure. A crowd of maneless zebras is around me. They eye me. They roll back their lips. They whinny. They run away. A firework breaks overhead, and another. They are shooting up from the sandy floor of the outdoor ice-hockey rink. They rise in burning phosphor and explode into spheres, like Christmas decorations I have dipped.

I see a secret policeman standing by the ostriches. He is wearing some kind of warfare suit and holding a gun. I run the other way, toward the floodlights arranged over the giraffe house. I know all these paths now.

More fireworks are bursting. I come to the sycamore tree. I kneel down beside it. Red fireworks go up in celebration of the Communist moment of 1975. My world turns pyrotechnical. I feel inconsequential, not just slight and aerated, but invisible, as though I am looking for my reflection in a tray of red spheres in the factory. I see the giraffe house bathed in red, a truck idling red by the yard, three red giraffes in the yard, red men wearing warfare suits carrying knives, saws, and cleavers. I see a man balanced on the fence with a rifle.

"Giraffe!" I hear him shout.

I see the giraffes fall in Christmas red and shatter on the ground, like a decoration. The firework gives out. There is only the weak glow of floodlights.

I run toward the giraffes. I am knocked to the ground by a secret policeman. I get up unsteadily. My hip is bruised. I am awake. I see everything around me in great detail, but I am not in another place; I have not awoken as operatic Amina, in the arms of my love.

I am taken and locked in a trailer, where I can see nothing but hear shots ringing out in quick succession after long silences.

I am taken now to an StB officer. I brush the quicklime from my dress.

"How did you get in here?" he asks.

"Through the zebras."

"What?"

"Through the cages."

"You're in serious trouble," he says.

The giraffe keeper arrives.

"Amina!" he says quietly. "You've come."

I push forward and embrace him. I have not seen him since the quarantine began.

"You're under arrest," the StB officer says.

The keeper steps in front of me.

"You'll have to arrest me first," he says.

"We need you," the StB man says.

"She's useful," the keeper says. "The giraffes know her."

We are silent. We stand off from one another. A young man, a scientist, comes forward. He takes the StB officer to one side. The keeper turns to me. "You can be a comfort to the giraffes," he says. "You can do that."

THE STB OFFICER HAS BEEN persuaded to let me stay. I must hold up a flashlight to the giraffes. I must still them in their eyes and then shine on a spot at the back of the head where the sharpshooter is meant to aim.

"If they see you in the last moment, that will be something," the keeper says, but oddly.

I place my hands to his cheeks. I look at him closely through his goggles. He is sleepwalking. He has walked inward from this moment, far away. There are some who, though asleep, behave as though they were awake.

THE SHARPSHOOTER IS KINDLY, but drunk.

"Shine it at the back of the ear," he says.

I aim the flashlight.

"Down. Across. That's it!"

"Wait," I say.

I run into the giraffe house. I go up the stairs to the loft. I take an armful of browse cut from the acacia trees overhanging the fountain of St. George. I bring it back to the fence. I sort the branches.

"Now," the sharpshooter says. "They're opening the doors."

I hold a branch up. A young male approaches. He leans toward the branch. I shine the light in his eyes. He stops. He pushes back his head, he stretches up. Tears roll down his cheeks.

"Giraffe!" the sharpshooter calls, then pulls the trigger.

The giraffe is hit. It falls.

I begin to cry. The sharpshooter climbs down from the fence. He sets down his rifle and holds me tight.

"Don't cry," he says. "Look at me."

He smells of drink. He pushes back his spectacles.

"What you are doing is a mercy," he says.

THE YARD IS FILLING with blood. The stench is stronger than the foulest cowshed. The giraffes do not lean. They do not notice me. The keeper and the scientist must light a fire under them to get them out of the giraffe house. Tails burn in the darkness.

All I can do is find their eyes and fill them with light.

I WATCH THE SCIENTIST move with precision through the blood. He puts jars to the springs of blood and fills and stoppers them. Butchers splash in behind him. I see one of the butchers holding up the head of a giraffe by the horns now, as though waiting for it to deflate.

FIRST LIGHT WASHES OVER the Svĕt. It is May Day.

"Go to the keeper," the sharpshooter says. "You've done your part. There are only a few left. I can see them without the flashlight."

I AM IN THE keeper's room. He is not here. The light is breaking through as it did on the morning of Christmas Eve, when everything was as cold and crystalline as Franz Josef Land. From in here I can hear and smell what is going on outside. I am too awake to step inward to fireflies, butterflies. There is shouting from the butchers: Another giraffe is being hauled up into a truck. I block out the sounds. It is a mess in here. I push back my hair and kneel on the floor and sort the keeper's papers and his studies of Czechoslovakian animal history.

"Don't bother with that."

It is the scientist. He is at the door.

"We'll have to burn everything," he says. "It's all contaminated."

"My dress?" I say bitterly.

"That will be burned too."

He is covered in blood. His hair also. He lifts up his goggles.

"There can be no record of the contagion," he says. "It will be exactly as if this night never happened."

I drop the papers. They scatter over the floor. There will be no more notes of polar bears or of the giraffe with a fractured pelvis who walked over the Julian Alps.

"What is the contagion?" I ask.

"You've seen the swellings on their flanks," he says.

"Most have no marks."

"The State cannot afford the risk," he says.

He takes off his surgical gloves, scrubs his hands, and snaps on a clean pair. He brushes back his hair. Strands are stuck together with blood.

"Did you read the stories of our early Slavs?" I ask.

"Yes," he says.

"There was a story of a boy captured after a battle."

"Why are you telling me this?"

"Your hair reminds me of that story."

He arranges his jars of blood neatly on trays. He labels the test tubes. He takes a syringe. He draws blood from a jar. He injects it into one of the test tubes. He seals it. He checks it. He places it in a metal case. "My hair?" he asks.

"A raiding party was captured. They were roped together and sentenced to be executed from the youngest to the oldest and richest. The boy was near the front of the line. He had blond hair, down his back. His friends called him Fine Hair. He was untied and pushed forward. He spoke up when his enemies were about to execute him. He told them they could do what they wanted with him, but they were not to get a drop of blood on his hair."

The scientist looks up from his test tubes and smiles now, a half-smile of this place, like the half-light cast by the floodlights.

"His enemies took his hair and had it wrapped around the forearm of a servant. 'Now die,' they said. The boy shrugged and knelt. He told the servant to hold his hair up tight when the ax fell. The ax came swinging. At the last moment, the boy jerked forward, dragging down the servant's forearm with his locks. The blade cut off the servant's hand. The boy's hair was covered in the servant's blood. He jumped up and berated his enemies for the mess they had made of his hair. They gathered around and beat their shields. They favored displays of courage. They were delighted with the boy. They gave him a sword and released him."

"Where do you work?" the scientist asks.

"The Christmas-decoration factory in the town."

"Why are you here? The keeper?"

I shake my head. "The giraffes. They awaken me."

He nods. He is about to say something more, but stops. There is another rifle shot. He takes three empty jars and runs out again.

I AM ESCORTED FROM the zoo in the daylight. I cannot look back. I can only look down. The army dogs are barking outside the walls, the wolves answering from inside. I am giddy. I imagine the gorillas calling out to me as I pass: *Viva! viva! viva! viva! Amina!*

All the paths are quicklime, marked with footsteps, and little bodies of shot birds.

"Keep moving," the secret policeman says.

So I do.

. . .

I AM IN A SHOWER. I lift my breasts. I scrub myself at their command. They hose me with disinfectant.

There is no operatic aria in here. I do not walk over a turning mill wheel to my lover. These men wear goggles and face masks. I see under their suits the red-star badge of the StB.

"You carry the contagion," one of the men says.

"You are a risk to national security," the other says.

"Once more," they say together.

So we begin again with the disinfection.

They open the flap of a tent. They sit me down here on a bench. I put my head in my hands. My hair falls down. I am naked under these overalls. I am shoeless as in my sleepwalking, but am perfectly awake to this May Day. I cannot dull myself. I hear a voice speaking to me.

"My hair is clean now," the scientist says.

I feel myself to be in that centrifugal ride. I go around and around. I cannot lift my arms up, much less lift off like John the Baptist toward an unimagined color. I am no longer aerated: The chlorine does not pass through me but burns my skin. The centrifugal ride has me. I am pinned to the cage. I am so heavy now, I cannot lift my head. I cannot reply.

Jiří

IT IS MAY DAY. The gore I have produced is there for all to
see. I wade through the yard. I climb the fence. Emil, if
that is his given name, is here by the last truck, exposing film
the StB officer took through the night: *It will be as if this night
never happened.*

I walk away in this suit slowly, deliberately. I seem to hear
zookeepers crying. A kangaroo hops up in its cage. I see other
beasts indistinctly. I cannot tell one cage of apes from another. I come to the zoo gates. Secret policemen and func-
tionaries come up to me.

I am slapped on the back.

I turn. It is Máslo.

"Well done, Sobotka!" he says excitedly.

I AM TAKEN INTO A disinfection unit. They take the Mauser and drop it in a vat of solution. They take the satchel, the thirty-three remaining cartridges, and the cigarettes.

"This is all for burning," they say.

I am stripped of the suit. My spectacles are taken and dipped in solution too. Goggles are placed on my face.

"Eyes shut. Tighter."

My hair is soaped and soaped again. They spray me with disinfectant. I am hosed as a horse is hosed. They take off the goggles and wash out my eyes and nose and now my ears and mouth.

I AM GIVEN BACK THE clothes I arrived in. I am led to an empty tent and made to wait here. It is a field-hospital tent. There are plastic windows stitched into it that let in a watery light.

The flap opens. A secret policeman brings in the girl who held up the flashlight for me. He sits her down across from me. She has been disinfected also. They have given her overalls to wear in place of her dress. She is bent over, her head in her hands. She does not look up. I cannot see whether she is weeping quietly or is asleep.

. . .

IT USED TO BE THAT farmers would take straw and rub it in the mouth of an infected cow and then take the straw and spread it in the mouths of the other cows, so the herd would share the sickness, be milked together, the milk dumped, and would together develop an immunity and recover. I do not know what the contagion is, or if it has been contained through destruction, just as you cut down trees to save a forest during a fire. Perhaps a swallow escaped into the night and infected the cowshed of a collective farm or a fox slipped out through the cages, like the girl slipped in. I know the May Day parade will proceed around the town square with red tractors and brigades of children whirring like clockwork to anthems. The cows will be milked across the ČSSR today, the milk poured out for children, and the surviving okapi will move about its cage in the zoo undisturbed, sneezing quicklime.

"REMEMBER," THEY SAY. "You were hunting black grouse."

"Yes," I say.

"You can go, comrade."

I AM GIVEN THE MAUSER. I do not have to sign for it. I have not signed my name to anything.

"The strap," I say. "I'll need the shoulder strap."

They find it and hand it to me.

. . .

A TALL MAN GRABS ME NOW. I look up. It is Alois Hus, the zoo director. While I have been shooting, he has been crying. I flinch. He might hit me, or embrace me.

"Comrade Sobotka," he says, embracing me. "Did any survive?" he asks.

"No."

He bites his lip.

"Alois, forgive me," I say. "It was a horrific night. I will have nightmares about it for the rest of my life."

"Twenty-three of those giraffes were pregnant. Did they tell you?"

"No."

"I'm happy it was you."

"Just a single shot each time," I say.

"This was the greatest migration," he says. "You must understand that they found us on the grasslands, at the edge of red hills. They came to us. You can't imagine."

It is true. I understand okapi and cannot imagine what it is to be a giraffe and to move in harsh light at such a height, with long steps. I do not tell him of the burning pages of *Red Truth* swishing through the witching night, or of how difficult it was to thread those heavy heads with my sparkler. I do not tell him how the felling of each giraffe was more violent to me than finding birds' nests and squirrels crushed in trees I have cut.

. . .

Soldiers are drifting off toward the May Day parade together with secret policemen. I attach the shoulder strap to the Mauser. The barrel drips onto the white-powdered path. I see Emil sliding a metal case onto the backseat of his official car, a Tatra 501. He is showered and smartly dressed. He gets into the front seat and is driven off behind the last truck, just departed, carrying the cow Sněhurka.

I do not take a lift home to my village at the end of the Svět when one is offered to me. I walk up the hill to the forest by the town swimming pool. It is a bright morning. I see Michael touching the pink roof of his chapel, lancing demons and hydras. I break into a run. I enter the trees like a deer from a field.

There is the pine-fresh smell. I am in my living gloom. I go across, deep into the forest, where an okapi might hide. The forest floor is a trampoline of fir roots under me. I pass the secret military base. Its siren will sound out the Communist moment at midday. Squirrels and birds will scatter. Deer will lift their heads. Missile silos will open, as a carp opens its mouth at the surface of the Svět. The siren will cease. The silos will close again. Some of the soldiers will leave the base through a gate in the electrified fence and celebrate May Day with a game of soccer in a clearing.

Tomáš

A Slaughterhouse Man

ČARODĚJNICE

APRIL 30, 1975

C OME OFF IT," I say, upset. "We've just finished our shift."

"Tomorrow is May Day," Jaro says.

We're a team, Jaro and I. He drives the truck, I cut the meat.

"There's a new television drama starting tonight," I say.

"There's a bonfire celebration," Jaro says. "It's witching night."

"No dice, boys," the boss says. "Finish your beers. This is the job you were warned about."

It's true—we have been warned. We spent a week getting

the metal paddles of the Destruktor in order. We were told to
prepare the machines for the heaviest kind of horses.

WE DRIVE BACK to the plant. There's an StB officer here. It
must be something different. I was thinking brewery horses,
or something. We're all here. Every driver, every butcher.

"Sharpen your knives and look alert, boys," the boss says.

"This is a matter of national security," the StB man says.

"You'll be properly compensated, if we keep our mouths
shut," the boss says.

WE'RE GIVEN INSTRUCTIONS. Take the Vamberk road, head
for the mountains, keep away from the industrial towns,
through a forest to a zoo. A zoo! Well that narrows it down.
Jaro and I take the three-ton Robur, the other boys are all in
seven-ton Škodas.

THE VB HAVE US lined up on a gravel road that runs along
one of those big fishponds. We've been waiting here for hours.
That's how it goes. You wait around to get at the animals, and
then they expect you to steal in and sweep them up in a minute,
and we're telling them, "No, pal. We're not garbagemen. We're
slaughterhouse men. We'll take our fucking time."

SOLDIERS COME BY THE TRUCKS calling for butchers.

"Just the butchers," they say.

So I go with the other butcher boys up to the zoo. I went to a zoo once when I was a kid, but I can't remember anything. It's a real army-and-secret-police powwow here. They're everywhere, these guys. Sure enough, when they get us through the gates, they have us put on some kind of nuclear-war suit, so we look like idiots to one another now. We march through the zoo in these suits with our butchers' aprons over the top and all the knives and cleavers hanging off our belts, and I'm thinking, What happens if I accidentally cut a hole in this suit—what happens to me then? I see a rhinoceros and one of the boys points out some small deer asleep on the ground. We go up the hill to the giraffe house. Jesus and Mary. Giraffes! It's all about giraffes. They give us another speech. The same thing as back in the plant. Only this time they say there is a plague, a contagion or something, not harmful to us, to people, but harmful to other animals. I guess that explains the powder all over the place.

THE KILLING BEGINS. We're not usually in on the kill. We usually pick up dead animals at the end of fields or on a riverbank and such. They're animals you never think much about, except at lunchtime, cows and sheep mostly, which are meant to die. This is something different. It turns your stomach. They run the giraffes out into the yard. There is a hunter balanced on the fence. There are fireworks coming up from some celebration and the hunter—he calls himself a hunter—shoots the giraffes by the light of the fireworks.

green
blue
yellow
red

The fireworks have run out now and it's me, some luck, holding up a flashlight at the fence. I'm supposed to shine it in the eyes of the giraffes, sort of stun them, and then at the back of the head to form some kind of target for the hunter. The yard is filling with blood. It's getting ripe. The giraffes are too scared to run out. So the keeper starts lighting their tails with bits of burning newspaper.

"See that, pal?" I say to the hunter. "That's love."

I BEGIN TO THINK of the flashlight as a weapon. I aim it. I don't like it at all. So I go over and complain to the StB man, the one photographing everything.

"Fuck off, then," the StB man says.

"Steady, comrade," I say.

He brings out a pretty girl in my place. Amazing. A tiny thing. She flew in here out of the night, through all these soldiers, like a bird or something. They say she's the keeper's girl. She's up on the fence now, aiming the flashlight. I don't feel guilty. I go over and complain straight to the hunter's face. He's reloading. He doesn't look up at me. He just takes another swig from his rum bottle.

"I can't watch you anymore, pal," I say. "I love nature and all that. I'm a hunter myself."

"I'm under orders, comrade," he says. "I don't like this."

"Well, if you ask me, it's a misuse of the hunting profession."

THERE IS THIS YOUNG scientist type, who kneels down over every one of the giraffes, as if he's giving them the last rites or something. He puts a jar to the bullet hole. The blood shoots up. You don't see that with animals at the end of fields. They're usually rotted and bloated. These giraffes spray blood right up to your waist. When the jars are full, the scientist closes them up with a rubber stopper, like a pickle jar, or one of those old beer bottles. Then the boys and I jump in. We do our stuff. We've got the hang of it already. It doesn't take long. Three or four animals. One body is like any other. You find the tendons, cut them, and fold it up. The thing is, these giraffes just keep coming. There must be fifty of them. That's a lot of meat. That's a hundred and fifty cows. Jesus and Mary, that's five hundred sheep.

WE GET SOME TEA and meat and bread rolls. I look up at the stars. I like to do that as much as the next guy. It's a clear night. The first warm night of the year. It's the witching night too. I see bonfires burning on the hills all around here. Workers are getting drunk there, having a good time, not cutting up giraffes in a crazy nuclear getup, at gunpoint, for twelve crowns and fifty heller an hour. I ask you.

. . .

WE'RE ALL TIRED. The blood sits in shallows now, like you get at the end of a meadow, by a river. I'm sitting on the fence, smoking. I'm watching the scientist trying to cut out the tongue of one of the giraffes. He's making a mess of it. He seems pretty upset. I jump down. I wade over.

"You're doing this all wrong, pal," I say to him.

"You do it, please," he says.

So I put my hand in there. I find the root. It's long—that's the thing. Much longer than any heifer's tongue.

"You always need to find the root, pal," I say.

I slip my knife down there. I slice it free. I roll the tongue up. He seals it in another of his jars.

THE LAST GIRAFFE IS a saddening sight. She almost kicked herself to death inside the giraffe house before the hunter got her. She was running around on broken legs. The hunter just stands there, drunk, crossing himself. We drag her all the way out and fold her and winch her up into the Robur with a calf and the bull I cut the tongue from. The secret policemen check us for leaks.

"All clear!" they shout.

"On no account should blood leak on the road," the StB man says through the window. "Negligence will be punished with prison terms."

Fuck you.

. . .

JARO DRIVES INTO THE DAWN.

"I'm getting some shut-eye," I say to him.

"Fair enough," he says.

WE'RE BACK IN THE hygiene or rendering plant. That's what they call it. We've got other names for it. What we do is render diseased and rotten meat into pellets of meal that are fed back to other animals or scattered over fields.

After a few years here, your fellow workers become your only friends. If Death were to open his robes, well, that's the stench of this place. You can't get rid of the smell. It's on your breath. You sweat it out in summer. You piss it out in winter. You shake hands with strangers and there is a moment of rejection. I always hold my hand there a little longer to see the reaction. Women hate the smell. I've had women retch on me. It's not only that. It's the whole place. It's at the end of a road. It's surrounded by rape fields on all sides, as far as you can see. It's like it's another place, an island on a yellow sea that exists out of time or something.

I OPEN THE DOOR TO the truck. That's the smell. Death opening his robes.

"We're being watched," Jaro says.

There's another StB man looking at us through binoculars from a distance. There's a few armed secret policemen patrolling closer to the truck. They'll gag if they get any nearer. Here comes the boss.

"Boys!" he says. "You know the score. Get them out. Cut them up. Into the machine."

"Yes, boss," we say.

"Then disinfection," he says.

"Off with these suits," Jaro says.

WE DROP THE TAILGATE of the Robur. We rope up the calf and drag it out onto the concrete cutting floor, then the giraffe bull with no tongue, and finally the cow with the white belly, who broke her legs running around inside.

We gaff them and hoist them up on metal chains. They hang before us now. I open up the calf and the bull. Jaro scoops out the innards. We kick and slide the gray pile together across the concrete into the sinkhole for the offal and waste. It's horrible, that sinkhole. White-blue and gray and glistening, deep as the Labe, but you wouldn't want to drown there. I swing the ax at the calf. I cleave the head and neck. I part the torso. Same for the bull now. I haven't touched the cow. There's something stopping me. I don't know.

"Hand me a knife," I say to Jaro. "No, not a gutting knife. Something sharper."

He hands one over. I look up to see if the StB man is watching. No.

"Keep watch," I say.

I get it. It's beauty that's been stopping me. I cut off a large piece of the hide, from the flank and the snow-white belly. I roll it up tight. I hide it among my knives. I'll tan it. I'll make it into a rug.

NOT A MOMENT TOO SOON. The scientist from the zoo is here. He's standing shoulder to shoulder with the StB man. He comes closer. Give him credit. He comes right in here in his nuclear-war suit. He holds his arm up to his mouth. I'm holding the ax. Jaro has the gaff. The scientist points to the cow, swinging here on this metal chain.

"Which one is that?" the scientist says.

"The last one," I say.

"The one that was shot all those times," Jaro says.

"Sněhurka," he says. "Some of her hide is missing. Why?"

He's sharp—give him that too.

"Look around you, pal," I say. "There's a lot missing here."

"We need a count of how many giraffes were pregnant," he says. "What about these?"

"That was a bull, that was a calf," Jaro says. "So, no."

"She was pregnant," the scientist says, touching the cow. "Check her."

So I slide a joint knife in.

"She's full all right, pal," I say.

His time is almost up. He's going to gag. You can see it.

"Comrades," he says.

He takes a step backward. He doesn't gag. He makes it back to the StB man and lowers his head and breathes heavily. That's right—that's the routine.

I SETTLE THE AX. I quarter the cow. I heave some part of foreleg up into the machine, which is called a Destruktor because that's what it does—it destroys. It's a truck-sized cylinder with four small doors. We have to cut all the animals into pieces small enough to get in there. So I cleave.

I gaff the cow's head now and push it inside the Destruktor. Jaro closes it up. We start the machine. Boiling water rushes in. The drum inside the cylinder starts turning over. We walk away. We're done. I tuck the giraffe hide under my arm.

OTHER BOYS COME TO clean up. The Destruktor will keep heating up. It'll keep turning. The metal blades will start churning. Those giraffes won't want to be liquidated. They're heavier than brewery horses. They'll bend the blades out of shape. The boys will have to stop the machine, let it cool, climb in there with hammers, chest-wading, and beat the blades back into shape. They'll start it up again. They'll turn the heat up. The drum will start turning over again. It'll get hotter and hotter and darker and darker. It's hell in the Destruktor. It's the kind of place where an angel would unsheathe his sword, where life is undone. Those giraffes will lose their spots in there. The hair will come off their tails where it wasn't singed off with the burning newspapers, their flesh will soften and peel from the bone. Their eyes, their lips, their little horns, their lungs, brains, veins and arteries, the ligaments holding their necks in place, the vertebrae themselves, their hooves, the little unborn one, will all melt. The drum will keep turning. They'll just be ligaments and bones. The ligaments will snap, the bones will break, and break again. They'll be a slop, slopping, a berry porridge. The drum will keep turning. All the liquids that made those giraffes will evaporate. They'll just be dry meal left, to feed to cattle.

Sub specie aeternitatis.

Emil

THERE WAS A JOURNEY in 1973 when Sněhurka stood behind me. I leaned back against her legs on a barge, and I looked back at her through a narrow window on a truck, when she opened her eyes to a beekeeper and to the beer offered up by villagers. I follow her now to the rendering plant. She lies in the truck ahead of me, like a fallen tower of the Qasr al-Qadim. I could not watch her death, or take a sample of her blood. I imagine it now, as I have imagined her birth and her captivity. She kicked out in the giraffe house until her legs were broken. She ran on broken legs. The crack of the rifle came to her like the sound of thunder. She was hit. Gravity snatched at her. She was hit again, and she fell. There was a coldness, a sinking. She felt no pain; she was aware only of memory slipping from her, as dreams slip from the waking. She died. She could see a zebra, and then only stripes of a zebra, and then only a space where the shape of the zebra was. She remembered she was single, then her thoughts became mingled.

Death is a confirmed habit into which we have fallen.

This was scribbled in my uncle's copy of *Great Expectations.* I would further underline *fallen*. I follow a convoy of trucks packed with the secretly liquidated beasts. I follow them through bursting spring, through leaded exhaust fumes, spluttering black on the inclines, under hedge maple and elder, by verges of hawthorn and poppies, gardens of red tulips and green-rising wheat fields, and by a camp where professional cyclists from the Tour of Czechoslovakia are sleeping under canopies, and windburned mechanics move about with cups of coffee, spinning wheels on upturned bikes.

THE RENDERING PLANT IS A whaling station of my imagination, a pier smeared crimson with fat jutting into cobalt Antarctic waters in which elephantine mermaids feed on krill and penguins, but beached somehow upon landlocked Czechoslovakia.

The smell is of giraffes being rendered and of rancid chicken feathers filling a warehouse to the ceiling waiting to be melted into a putty and fed to other chickens, just as the giraffes will be ground into dry meal and fed to cattle in the neighboring collective farms.

"The meal will be perfectly sterile, comrade," the head of the plant says. "No contagion can survive our machines."

He hands over several files of paperwork.

"It hasn't been an easy night," he says. "We'll need compensation. The giraffe bones have beaten the blades inside our Destruktor machine out of shape."

"I'll see what I can do," I say.

I tear the files in two and hand them back to him.

"Put these in with your chicken feathers," I say.

MY ARM IS TO MY mouth. My goggles are steamed up with deathly fluids. I almost slip into a hole swilling with pale blue bowels. The butcher who cut out the tongue is here on the cutting floor. He's swinging an ax. Sněhurka hangs, enormous, upside down on a metal chain, together with the remains of a Rothschild bull and calf. Her neck is broken; her tongue hangs out. Her eyes are open. A square of hide has been cut from her body.

"Some of her hide is missing," I say.

The butcher shrugs. "Lots of things missing here, pal," he says.

I ask him about the pregnancy—she must have been pregnant. He takes a narrow blade, like a screwdriver. He sinks it into her belly. Clear fluid comes out. He moves the blade around.

"She's full all right, pal," he says.

· · ·

THERE ARE POOLS AT THE back of the rendering plant in which the blood, the giraffe blood, is cleaned into a clear fluid. The fluid drains into a stream and flows with the stream by fields of rape, through oak groves, down into the River Orlice, into the Labe with its Czech-speaking *vodníks,* down to the port of Hamburg, into the Heligoland Bight, across the North Sea, skirting the English salt marshes where Pip tended Magwitch, drifting into the Atlantic, washing chemicals over tapering glass eels, sinking deep off Mauritania into the ocean conveyor, circulating north on the conveyor all the way to the Barents Sea, where fictional Emil perhaps drowned soundlessly in a U-boat, and ending in a floe of jade ice on which a polar bear waits patiently over a breathing hole, with cocked paw, for surfacing seals. Our souls resemble water, Goethe says. So too our bodies. There is a flow within us, rising and falling, unidirectional to the heart. There is a flow without also. We circulate. We are drawn up, we fall back down to earth again. It is all hemodynamics.

I PUT MY HAND ON the shoulder of the other StB man. I drop my head. I breathe deeply. I have nothing left to vomit.

I LEAVE MY IMAGINED whaling station. I strip off the chemical-warfare suit; again I have had to wear it. I throw away the goggles. I am perfunctorily showered.

"How far is the nearest village?" I say to the plant manager.

"Five kilometers."

"I'll walk. I need some air."

I take the metal case from the car. I handcuff it to my wrist. I send the car ahead. I will return to Prague later today. I will sit on the roof terrace on Baba Hill, not mentioning any of this to my family, not looking in the direction of the Prague Zoo.

I AM SURROUNDED BY fields of yellow rape. The witching moon has faded into a blue sky. This is the end of the road. It runs from here in a perfectly straight line to the village. It must have been laid down by the Nazis when they built the rendering plant in their campaign to sanitize their Protec-torate. There are blossoming fruit trees lining either side of the road. The stream runs beside it in a ditch, headed for somewhere beyond the Barents Sea. The nettles are thick along the stream. I part them. I crouch down, I teeter. I put a hand to the water and calculate the flow. Finger-length trout dart away from me.

I go on under blossoms—pink, magnolia, apple-white, and snow-white. I am not Pip. Fictional Emil is far away, is soundless. I see a flight of newly returned swallows dip-ping toward the rapeseed and rising again. The professional cyclists of the Tour of Czechoslovakia must be awake now and racing hard toward the black mills of Austerlitz, follow-ing the route crows took in the time of Napoleon and still take now. I see the village in the distance, a little downhill. I walk toward it, back into the Communist moment. The May Day parade will be smaller there this year—the dairy workers will be forbidden to march. The road under me has been sprinkled with chloramine. I leave my footsteps in it, some kind of vertical outline of myself. I tighten my grip on the metal case, in which are my forty-seven test tubes of giraffe blood and a single giraffe tongue floating in preservative. Music comes to me, forms. It is the last piece of our Czech-born Gustav Mahler's *Song of the Earth:* "Der Abschied," or "Farewell."

ALL THE PAPERS ARE SHREDDED, the films exposed, the giraffes burned, so: farewell. The song plays symphonically in the weightless deep of my brain. A poet waits for a friend in the twilight. It is spring there too. While he waits, he looks upon the beauty of the earth. There is birdsong. Owls swoop in long, free cadenzas, not tethered by any conductor. Dragonflies flit on the water, deer move in the forest. Perhaps it is a place like that fishpond by the zoo, which they call the Svět. The friend arrives, only to say farewell forever. The moment is darkening, exquisite, finally resolute. The last words belong to Mahler:

> *The dear earth blossoms and greens again in spring*
> *Everywhere and eternally the horizon shines blue*
> *eternally, eternally*

Steve

A Foreign Correspondent

Sнoot Hrabal on the balcony," I say to the photographer.

It's getting late. The light is going.

Hrabal zips up his tracksuit and shuffles out with the photographer. He was a butcher of some kind, in some state enterprise. Not a Communist, not ever, he says. He's been unemployed for years. He's thinking of voting Communist now—there's the story.

I follow them out. It's freezing. Hrabal lights a cigarette, a Camel. He's got emphysema, but he can't help himself. I get him to show me the view. There's a nice red light; there's already snow on the mountains. The industrial town sprawls out on all sides in other gray panel-built tower blocks and extinct chimneys.

"The air is clearer now since the foundries closed," Hrabal says. "You can see all the way across to the ski jump now."

It's true. I see bodies launching off a ramp, seemingly out across the town.

"What's new, Hrabal?" I say. "What's changed?"

He points out buildings: a new supermarket, a new indoor ice-hockey arena, a new Škoda car dealership.

"Make sure you get the mountains in the background," I say to the photographer. "And tell him not to smile. He's supposed to look aggrieved."

"There used to be trams running far out into the country-side," Hrabal says. "All gone."

I see a Czech Railways train, just one carriage, red—like one of those little Swiss trains—moving away into a forest.

"That's where we're going tomorrow, Steve," the inter-preter says, pointing to the forest. "The fishpond, remember? The carp harvest?"

I turn to the photographer.

"You've got those pictures already, haven't you?" I say.

"Sure," he says, shooting Hrabal with a fisheye. "Good shots for the weekend paper. Carp in copper light, a castle, the works."

HRABAL INSISTS ON MAKING US TEA.

"Quickly, then," I say to the interpreter. "I don't want to be here all night."

We sit in his living room. It is quite bare. There is only, on the floor, an animal skin, russet and snow-white in parts.

"A<small>SK HIM IF IT</small>'s a leopard," I say.

The interpreter calls Hrabal in from his kitchen. She asks the question.

He looks at the skin. He laughs.

"*Žirafa!*"

"It's a giraffe skin," the interpreter says.

"From Africa," I say.

"*Ne!*" the butcher answers, directly. "*Není africká. Je československá. Je to československá Žirafa!*"

"What's that?"

"He says, No, the giraffe was from Czechoslovakia. He says it was a Czechoslovakian giraffe."

Acknowledgments

Giraffe is a true story. The names and the order of events have been changed to protect living persons.

Those familiar with former Czechoslovakia will recognize Amina's town as a composite of Dvůr Králové, Kuks, and Třeboň. The secret laboratory is in the garrison town of Terezín, where thirty-three thousand Jews and hundreds of Czechoslovakian resistance fighters perished during the Second World War. The rendering plant sits a little way from the village of Žichlínek.

The Dvůr Králové Zoo is still awaiting an official acknowledgment and explanation of the liquidation of its forty-nine giraffes, forty-seven of them on the night of April 30, 1975. It was the largest captive herd in the world. Twenty-three of them are thought to have been pregnant.

Thanks to the zoo, to veterinarian Dr. S., who was much maligned in the matter, to the sharpshooting forester Mr. P., who still has nightmares about pulling the trigger, and to all the sleepwalkers by day and by night in the ČSSR 1973–75.

Thanks to Prof. H., for returning from retirement to his secret laboratory. To the Vánoční Ozdoby Factory in Dvůr Králové—may your Christmas decorations twinkle on. To the butchers and drivers of the Veterinární Asanacní Ústav in Žichlínek.

Thanks also to K., A., and M., for your translation and insights; you dug out the truth.

Or most of it: Prof. K., Prof. D., and Dr. T. may shed further light on whether the giraffes needed to be shot. Their records have disappeared; their memory is faulty. At least one giraffe tongue was sent to the university in Brno: It has not been found. Nor is there any trace of the jars of giraffe blood collected by a security-service operative on the night of the shooting.

KABUL AND PRAGUE, JML